Green Man Running

Georgina Hammick

Chatto & Windus
LONDON

First published by Chatto & Windus 2002

2 4 6 8 10 9 7 5 3 1

Copyright © Georgina Hammick, 2002

Georgina Hammick has asserted her right under the Copyright, Designs
and Patents Act 1988 to be identified as the author of this work

First published in Great Britain in 2002 by
Chatto & Windus
Random House, 20 Vauxhall Bridge Road,
London SW1V 2SA

Random House Australia (Pty) Limited
20 Alfred Street, Milsons Point, Sydney,
New South Wales 2061, Australia

Random House New Zealand Limited
18 Poland Road, Glenfield,
Auckland 10, New Zealand

Random House (Pty) Limited
Endulini, 5A Jubilee Road, Parktown 2193, South Africa

The Random House Group Limited Reg. No. 954009
www.randomhouse.co.uk

A CIP catalogue record for this book
is available from the British Library

ISBN 0 7011 6677 0

Papers used by Random House are natural,
recyclable products made from wood grown in sustainable forests;
the manufacturing processes conform to the environmental
regulations of the country of origin

Typeset by Deltatype Ltd, Birkenhead, Merseyside
Printed and bound in Great Britain by
Mackays of Chatham plc

With love to Mau, and thanks to Sidney and Dinah for
their support

Acknowledgments

Thanks to Sherif Amin who took time away from his own work to teach me about stained glass.

It's Only A Paper Moon, Words by E.Y. Harburg and Billy Rose, Music by Harold Arlen © 1933 Harms Inc, USA Warner/Chappell Music Ltd, London. Reproduced by permission of International Music Publications Ltd. All rights reserved.

In The Summertime Words & Music by Ray Dorset © 1970 Broadley Music International Limited & Associated Music. Universal Music Publishing Limited, 77 Fulham Palace Road, London W6 (50%) and Sony/ATV Music Publishing (UK) Limited, 10 Great Marlborough Street, London WIV (50%) used by permission of Music Sales Ltd. All rights reserved.

Hope is generally a wrong guide, though it is very good company by the way.

Halifax

Before

T HERE WERE three gates to the Top Pasture. Two of these gave on to adjoining grazing; the third, which opened on to a narrow, high-hedged lane, was only ever used when there were sheep on the grass. When cattle were on it the lane gate was kept shut and secured to the gatepost by a chain. This was because although the lane was the shortest, by far, route to his farmyard, bad experience had taught Michael Bucknell that to attempt to drive cumbersome animals, not fitted with brakes or gears or super-grip tyres and weighing half a ton apiece, down Breakneck Hump, was a mistake. In any case, to reach the farmyard, it was not just a matter of driving the stock downhill. At the bottom of Breakneck the lane veered sharply right and at once began an almost equally steep climb up a hill named Gray's Rise, a climb that cows and heifers and steers were unwilling to make. The road route from the Top Pasture to Bucknell's cattle sheds was acknowledged to be a roller-coaster ride, the people who appreciated it best being teenage boy bikers, madcap motor cyclists, and, in hard winters with the lane closed by snow, tobogganists.

When, one sunny October afternoon, someone unhooked the chain on the lane gate, managed to kick the gate open a few feet – but then, on account of the claggy turf and dung and thistles surrounding the gate, failed to shut it properly afterwards – it did not take long for a curious bullock to notice and to barge a way through to freedom. The rest of the herd followed.

Out in the lane, the cattle turned left. The angle of the gate dictated their course, though in all likelihood, since left equalled downhill, they would have turned left anyway. The leaders at once mounted the verge and began to graze or to relieve themselves, but were kept on the move by the bump and bore antics of the curly-headed, leaky-nosed, mud-caked bully boys in the rear.

Twenty yards further on the lane's leisurely descent ended on a bend, and the precipitous incline of Breakneck began. The unwary bullocks, moving together as one, plunged over the crest like a waterfall. Pell-mell. Helter-skelter. Faster and faster. Faster.

A mile away, approaching Gray's Rise from the opposite direction, behind him the distant mass of Brown Clee Hill, on his left, and closer, the quarried jags of Titterstone Clee, was Billy Martin in his Ford pickup. The pickup, last of a series of beaten-up vans and pickups and jalopies Billy had snatched from the breakers, and scrounged replacement parts for, and (once he'd got the camshafts, or big ends, or gearboxes into more or less working order) drove through the lanes like Jehu, had a load of logs on board. The load consisted of oak, apple, ash, and some make-weight birch that invariably found its way into the loads and that certain customers complained about. It burned like matchsticks, they argued; it sputtered and spat great sparks that could leap a fireguard and set the house on fire.

It seemed to Billy as he rattled westwards that the whole world was on fire that afternoon. For one thing there was this all-over hot and excited feeling he had that made the palms of his hands so slippery he was finding it hard to keep a grip on the steering wheel. For another, the sun was dropping by the minute and everything its rays touched on – corrugated barn roofs, brilliant verge grass (so bright and fresh and green after recent rain you could almost believe it was spring coming), hedgerow oaks, hawthorn leaves and berries, tags of hay and straw in the hedge that the bale trucks had left behind – was red-gold and aflame.

Billy was the second youngest of five brothers, the sons of Jack Martin, farm labourer, and his wife Linda, whose maiden name had been Carter. Jack and Linda had known each other since junior school and they got married in 1944 when he was eighteen and she sixteen. It was quite usual in those days for young people to marry in their teens; at least half the couples Jack and Linda knew tied the knot before they were twenty. They did this even when there was no baby on the way and no real reason to.

Before Linda nabbed him there had been girls galore after Jack. He was considered a catch, not because he had brilliant brains or ambitions – he had neither – but because he was tall and darkly sexy and according to some looked a lot like Gary Cooper. He had a dry wit too, and the laconic, deadpan, cynical-seeming remarks he came out with, which disconcerted those who didn't know him well, made Linda fall about laughing.

Linda wasn't a looker in the head-turning way Jack was.

She was only five feet tall and her head always seemed a shade too big, and her face a shade too broad, for her diminutive hands and feet. But she was slim in those days, and vivacious and warm-hearted, and her large blue eyes were unusually sparkly. By nature an easy-going person, she took life as it came — which was just as well as how it came was hard and sometimes cruel. For example, her firstborn, a girl, had a heart defect and lived for only two days. Then the second child, Malcolm, was partially deaf and developed epilepsy when he was three. And it must have been around this time that Jack tripped while felling an ash with a chain saw. The saw all but removed his arm and the healing of it — though the pain never left him — kept him off work and wages for the best part of a year.

Money was tight enough anyway in the Martin household and it got tighter as more babies came along. Linda was not a moaner. She didn't complain about Jack's forty-Woodbines-a-day smoking habit and the chunk it took out of the housekeeping. Nor about the tied cottage they shared with successive dogs and cats. This was the middle strip of a red-brick Victorian terrace of three two-bedroomed cottages — bang on the road but not on the bus route, two miles from a shop, six miles from the town. The only form of heating the cottages had was a chokey coal fire in the front room and an unreliable coke stove in the kitchen, and the slates that blew off the uninsulated roof stayed where they fell. There were no plumbed-in baths to the terrace, and no inside toilets either. Not, that is, until 1968, when Jack's employer and landlord, possibly under pressure from the council, had the roof felted and three lean-to bathrooms built on at the back. But he forgot to instruct the builders to put in a dampcourse, and so before long a green, black-spotted mould decorated the bathroom walls.

Life was better in summer. The children could be turned out into the vegetable patch, and on sunny days Linda sat on the step and rocked the pram and watched the older boys fighting and the nappies blowing, and the clouds flying and Jack's brown hens nodding their way through the cabbage stalks. As a child she had been walked by her mother to the fields at haymaking and harvest times and spent whole days there. The days of farmworker family picnics were long gone by then, but when Jack was cutting grass for hay or silage she and her little ones would park themselves under a hedge and turn their heads to follow one man and his machine, and the tall grass falling over itself in their wake.

It was 1970 now, and all but one of the Martin boys were grown men. The three eldest had left home. Malcolm and Kirk were married. Malcolm, who still suffered regular but unpredictable fits, was temporarily out of work. Kirk, a meatpacker in his wife's home town four counties away, had three kids of his own. Unmarried Lionel, Linda's favourite, worked as shepherd on a big estate near Leominster and had a centrally heated bungalow all to himself. The only two left to keep her and Jack company in the evenings and to share the back bedroom were twelve-year-old John, a gentle, pink-cheeked, cherub of a boy – and Billy.

Billy was known to his log customers as the Wood Boy, even though chopping and splitting and delivering logs for J & M Forestry was mainly an autumn and winter job and only one of several things he did. He was a general farmhand who liked variety and hired himself out on a casual basis to whomsoever needed, and paid, him most. Tractor-driving, muck-spreading, fruit and grain and potato harvesting, coppicing, sheep-dipping, lambing, calving, bale-stacking, hedge-laying, ditching, grave-digging – these were all tasks Billy could turn his hand to and, more crucially, stick at till the job was done. A tearaway in his boyhood, useless in class (though Miss Spindle, who taught the Juniors, would never hear a word against him then or afterwards), he had had to work doubly hard to earn his present reputation as a reliable, if short-term, grafter – especially since, in his early teens, he'd been up before the magistrates in Mill Street more than once for joyriding.

Billy was twenty now and hadn't been in trouble for three years at least, if his appearance suggested otherwise. He was the tallest in his family, six foot three, rawboned and cavernous, and the clothes he habitually wore – a dirt 'n'grease stiffened jacket that had once been Sunday best for his father, a sweat-dark T-shirt (or, in winter, rough-rib polo neck), a pair of diesel-stained jeans that had originally been a stone-washed blue – hung off his back, or flapped unprepossessingly against his legs. The rancid smell these garments gave off was unignorable indoors. Anyone standing at the regulars' bar in the Crown or in the cigarette queue in the shop had no need to turn his head to know that it was Billy Martin who had just blown in.

Then there was Billy's pallor that no amount of sun and wind managed to whip into the ruddy, pre-leather tan his brothers had; and his haphazard gait; and his stoop; and the diagonally chipped front tooth (he broke tobogganing down the Double Dingle on Whitcliffe Common) that showed up unmissably when he smiled and which gave him a gipsyish, if not actually criminal, air.

Billy was not unpopular, however. The three old men, all in their eighties, who passed their days on a bench outside the Crown liked Billy because he always found the time to stop and say *How'ya doin then?* and to wait for an answer, which not many youngsters could be bothered to do. Desmond Bucknell, ten-year-old son of farmer Michael Bucknell, liked Billy because whenever Billy was doing a job for his dad he'd allow Desmond to work alongside, talking to him as though they were mates and the same age. The majority of Billy's peers, the boys he'd bunked off school with, and fished with, and gone night-poaching with, had left to seek their fortunes in Bridgnorth or Worcester or as far afield as Birmingham; nevertheless the few who remained got on all right with him. Also, and surprisingly – for he fitted nobody's idea of a ladies' man – girls seemed to have a soft spot for Billy. His crinkly mane, parted in the middle Jesus-style, was in fashion that year, which might have had something to do with it. Or perhaps the attraction was not so much Billy as his lurcher dog, Yellow, a familiar sight in the back of the pickup where he acted as quivering lookout atop the log pile. Whatever the reason, when Billy played pool on Saturday nights there was very often a shy or sly sixteen-year-old hanging around the pool table, or making up to Yellow in a corner.

Today, instead of his usual outfit, Billy had on a clean white T-shirt with cap sleeves, a worn, but clean, pair of denim flares held up by a leather belt, and a tan suede jacket that had a v-shape of cowboy-style fringing across the chest and back. The clothes – jeans noticeably short in the leg – belonged to Billy's brother Lionel, and the reason

Billy had borrowed them was a girl he'd recently met at a Youth Club social in the town. The girl, Marianne (he did not ask her other name), told him she was certain to be elected Rose Queen next year – 'just you wait and see'. She said she worked in the shoe shop in Broad Street but was going to pack it in soon because she was sick of the sight of feet. This remark, or maybe it was the way she said it, made Billy hoot.

Marianne had wide green eyes and straight blonde hair that tipped up, and bounced, on her shoulders. She had a naughty look and laugh, and Billy was smitten, the first time such a thing had happened to him. At the end of the evening he asked her out for a drink, or for a Sunday stroll along the Bread Walk, if she'd prefer a bit of air, but she said she wouldn't go out with him unless he had a wash and smartened himself up.

To his astonishment, Billy heard himself tell Marianne he'd do that. He heard himself say he'd meet her at the Buttercross after work Friday. They'd go for a drink at the Globe – and he'd be so damn smart and clean she wouldn't recognize him.

Marianne rolled her eyes when Billy had finished. She said, The Globe? You're expecting *me* to go to the *Globe*? It's the Feathers I'm used to. It's cocktails in the Feathers or nothing, *if* you don't mind.

Billy wasn't offended at all. He could tell Marianne was having him on about the Feathers. He knew she'd never set foot in the place, no more than he had.

Billy had two other jobs to do before he could get himself to the Buttercross. After he'd delivered his wood load – to a middle-aged couple called Tilson, newcomers to the area, who'd recently moved into the Red Cottage,

Bitterley – and stacked the logs (if the Tilsons wanted them stacked and were prepared to pay), he had to take a Land Rover wheel, belonging to Mr Johns, one of the bosses at J & M Forestry, in to the garage for repair. Mr Johns said that if it turned out the damage could be fixed then and there Billy must wait and bring the wheel back with him.

Normally Billy wouldn't have minded hanging around for as long as it took, or longer, because the forecourt attendant was a mate of his; but he didn't want to be late for Marianne. Time was tight enough anyway: as well as the logs and the wheel he had to do some grocery shopping for his mother. As soon as he'd mentioned he was going into town she'd found a pencil stub and written him a list.

It was hot in the cab and Billy had the windows down to allow the through-draught to cool his face and neck. The pickup had no sun visor and the angry red ball was slap in front of the windscreen now; except when a hedgerow oak or a barn fleetingly eclipsed it, the dazzle was blinding. He kept scraping the hedge. He kept having to stamp on the brake and stick his head out of the window to check there wasn't a truck or a tree heading straight for him. At the same time he had the radio on and was singing along to Mungo Jerry and 'In the Summertime'. The song had reached number one in June and stayed there. Even now that summer was over it was still high in the charts and Billy was sick to death of it. A week ago he would have switched off or fiddled with the tuner, but today was different, the song itself different. Today the words might have been written for him:

When the weather's fine
You got women, you got women on yer mind . . .

Sing along with us, dee dee dee dee *dee* —

He was singing along with them, thumping the steering
wheel to the rhythm, sticking his head out of the window,
thinking about Marianne, thinking about her hair, trying
to picture her mouth, imagining how she would look, and
how he would feel when he first caught sight of her at the
Buttercross — as he passed the red sandstone wall at the
entrance to Bucknells Farm and rattled along the ridge
leading to Gray's.

At the start of the drop he put his boot on the brake but
did not change gear. In his book it was chicken to change
down for hills. He only ever changed down if he could see
something bigger than him coming up.

CARNAGE — the word the headline writer on the *Advertiser*
chose to describe what happened when pickup and
bullocks collided in the little well at the bottom of
Breakneck and Gray's. Seven prize-winning steers killed
outright. Eight more so badly injured — some by flying
logs — they had to be destroyed when the vet got there. A
pet dog, belonging to driver of the vehicle Mr Billy
Martin and thrown clear in the impact, struck and killed
on the verge by a Land Rover wheel.

Astonishingly, Billy was not killed — although the head
and chest and spinal injuries he received provoked the
general whisper that it might have been better if he had
been. Better for Billy and better for his mother Linda who
was going to have to look after him.

The report of the tragedy took up most of the front
page and spilled over on to page 3. On page 2, along

10

with a picture of the wrecked pickup, were articles dealing with issues arising from the accident. One, headed PICKUP HAD BALD TYRES, listed all the defects the unlicensed, uninsured pickup had and called for tighter MOT controls and more frequent police spot checks. The logs in this case were green, it was pointed out, which meant they were particularly heavy and injurious – but wasn't it high time that all wood loads were tarpaulined and roped by law?

Another paragraph, headed RAMBLERS BLAMED FOR OPEN GATE, centred on the danger posed to cattle and livestock by urban visitors who either did not know, or refused to observe, the countryside code.

A third feature, in heavier type than the rest which gave it a funereal look, was a verbal portrait of Billy pieced together with the help of people who'd known him all his life. The heading – NO ANGEL – BUT HIS HEART IS IN THE RIGHT PLACE – came from a telephone interview with Billy's one-time teacher Miss Spindle, retired now, who said that Billy was one of the few of her pupils who could be relied on to keep in touch. 'He'd always drop in for a cup of tea if he was passing.' She was disappointed, and surprised, she said, that Billy's vehicle had not been taxed or insured, but put it down to forgetfulness. 'I'm sure he meant to do it. He was a reformed character in most ways.' Billy's parents and brothers refused to be interviewed (Billy was in intensive care at this time and they had been warned he might not survive) but Linda's cousin Ted Carter, a poultry farmer over Market Drayton way who didn't keep up with that side of the family, spoke, he said, for all of them: 'It's a tragic waste. The lad was just beginning to make something of his life. We're just hoping he can come through this. We'll give him all the help we can. He's got everything to live for.'

No, said Desmond. No, I didn't. I never leave gates open. You know I don't.

I won't be angry with you, his father said. Not if you tell me now.

Well I didn't. It wasn't me, repeated Desmond.

His father was rolling a pencil around on his desk. He called it a desk, though what it was was an oblong of laminated chipboard supported either end by a metal filing cabinet. Abruptly, he left the pencil alone and began shuffling a stack of papers. He stood them upright, sorted them the way he wanted them, laid them down flat, squared them up. Then he picked up the pencil and began chewing the end of it.

I hope you're quite sure about this, his father said, taking the pencil out of his mouth and examining the bite marks he had made. If you're not sure, if you're not absolutely certain about it, now is the time to tell me. We all make mistakes, lad, he added after a pause. I do. We all do.

They were in the farm office, a cell-like room with metal windows set too high up to see out of or to clean, which led off the boot room (which led off the scullery, which led off the kitchen). The office smelled strongly of old tin ashtray, and also of rubber boots and oilskins. Behind Desmond's father, on the cream-gloss brick wall, were framed photographs, ages old, some of them, of prize-winning cattle and sheep and pigs. The men, in overalls or long aprons, who stood beside these animals, keeping a firm hand on the head-collar rope, were Desmond's father, or else his grandfather, or else his great-grandfather. Above them, a foot or so off centre of the wall, was a large electric clock. As Desmond looked at the clock, mentally shunting it to the left as he always did, the big hand, seemingly stopped, jumped five minutes all at one go. *Clunk.*

I didn't do it, Dad, really, Desmond said.

You see, it's important to have trust, for people to be able to trust each other, his father said, looking up suddenly, straight at Desmond. I need to trust you, you need to trust me. Otherwise –

I know that, Desmond said. But I didn't leave the gate open.

His father put the pencil down and began rolling it again. I know you were in the Top Pasture on Friday afternoon, he said slowly, because Don saw you on the hazel track when he was checking the troughs. The pump's playing up – but I dare say you know about that. You were nutting when he saw you, Don said. You had a stick and you were bashing the hazels to get the cobs down.

Well it was half-term, Desmond said, so – he stopped. I didn't do any damage to the bushes. I don't think I did. No, I'm sure I didn't.

I know it was half-term. I know that *now.* But I forgot it when the police came round. I had to tell them where everyone was and what they were doing Friday afternoon. I told them you weren't anywhere near the Top Pasture because I knew – I thought I knew – you were at school. Or on the bus coming home from school. No one can be certain, of course, exactly what time the lane gate was left open.

But I helped you with the milking, remember, Desmond said. I don't do that on school mornings.

As I say, I forgot about half-term, his father said. That's really what I'm trying to say to you – that we can all forget things. We can forget to shut a gate – and afterwards we can forget, we may be able to forget, that we forgot to shut it. Sometimes it takes something, or someone else, to jog our memory. Don't you find that?

Clunk. The minute hand on the clock jumped another five minutes.

I climb gates, you know, Desmond said. I hardly ever go through them. It's easier to climb over them. Saves a lot of time.

Don said you had a bucket with you – to put the cobs in. A black plastic feed bucket – is that right?

Yes.

Don't you want to sit down? his father said. There's a chair right beside you.

Oh, all right then. Desmond sat down.

His father pulled a packet of Embassys from his jacket pocket and after it a box of matches. He shook out a cigarette, put it in his mouth and struck a match. The match went out; he struck another. He began smoking the cigarette slowly, taking long, noisy inhalations of breath. How did you get to the Top Pasture, by the way? he asked eventually, directing a volley of smoke at the ceiling. Did you go via the Six Acre or did you go by road?

I went by road – I biked there. I biked to the bottom of Gray's – and I left my bike in the hedge, and then I walked up Breakneck. And then I climbed the gate.

See anyone? In the lane or anywhere?

No, said Desmond, after a pause.

I imagine you threw the bucket over before you climbed the gate? his father said. That would be the easiest

14

thing to do – chuck the bucket into the field first, and then climb over. Is that what you did?

Yes. I think so.

But coming back? his father said, stubbing out his cigarette in the tobacco tin lid he kept on his desk and used for an ashtray. The lid was emptied from time to time but never washed, so that a silt of hardened and sour-smelling black ash covered its surface. But coming back? he repeated. That wouldn't have been so easy, would it? I mean to say, the bucket was full then so you couldn't chuck it over else you'd have lost all the cobs you'd collected. It's not that easy climbing a gate – an old, mossy, slippery gate – carrying a bucket, is it? And those feed buckets are awkward enough when empty. I've been trying to put myself in your shoes, and I think I'd probably have decided it would be simpler to –

I managed it though, Desmond said. It can be done. I managed it all right.

Clunk.

You're shivering, lad, his father said. I don't think you've got enough clothes on. It is a bit fresh in here, mind. Switch on the fire if you want it.

I'm not cold, Desmond said. There were huge, shaggy cobwebs in the windows and on the ceiling, and he took a good look at them. There were spiders in those webs, very likely.

Well, we can't sit here all day, his father said. I've got work to do and I expect you have. He sat back and locked his hands behind his head, addressing his next remark to the ceiling: You like Billy Martin, don't you, D? You've always got on well with him?

Desmond nodded.

Billy's going to be in a wheelchair for the rest of his life

– did you know that? If he survives he'll be in a wheelchair.

Oh. Desmond said it so quietly it sounded more like a breath or a sigh.

He's almost certainly got brain damage. They don't seem to know the extent of it yet or what it'll mean. It may mean . . . he tailed off. Well, off you go then, D. His father got to his feet.

When Desmond was at the door his father said, The insurance assessors are coming this afternoon. There was a fair bit of money tied up in those steers, as you can imagine.

It was perhaps six months after this interview that Desmond changed his name. The name he chose was Dexter, after the Sussex and England batsman and Test Match Captain, E.R. Dexter, Cricketer of the Year, 1961. Desmond had never seen Ted Dexter play, he was too young to have seen him. But he had seen him in some old Test footage they'd shown on television. And there were photographs of Dexter – about to take delivery at the crease, hitting out, running – in a cricket annual he had. He liked the look of Ted Dexter, and the style of him. He liked his name.

Well, that's a pity I must say, Desmond's mother said when Desmond announced his decision and asked his parents to call him Dexter from now on. Desmond was my father's name, we named you after him. I know you never knew your grandfather Newell, he can't mean much to you, but I do think it's a pity. I don't like the name Dexter very much – do you, Michael? Not as a Christian name. It sounds American.

Oh, let the lad do what he wants, Michael Bucknell

16

said, helping himself to potatoes. I was never that keen on Desmond myself. It wasn't my choice. Anyway, it won't make much difference because we hardly ever call him Desmond, do we? We call him D.

They were at the big kitchen table, eating supper, only the three of them because the girls were out. Elizabeth, aged eighteen, had gone to the cinema with her boyfriend. Anna, thirteen, was having her weekly piano lesson in the town.

If I was going to call myself after a cricketer, after a batsman, it wouldn't be Ted Dexter I'd pick, Michael Bucknell said. No, I'd go for the best. I'd go for Donald Bradman. Bradman Bucknell – now that sounds impressive. I quite like the sound of that. He took a piece of gristle out of his mouth and put it on the edge of his plate. On the other hand, I quite like the idea of a farmer's son choosing to call himself after a breed of cattle. We kept a small dexter herd here at one time – did you know that, D? Tough little fellows, but not a patch on our Herefords. Pass the mustard, would you, lad?

I don't know what his teachers are going to say, Margaret Bucknell said. Desmond Bucknell's the name on all his school books. I think he'll find he has to be Desmond at school.

FIVE PAST eight in the morning, and already the house felt airless. A coppery gauze was mustering above the city. The good news is, it's going to be hot and sunny almost everywhere, the radio weather forecaster had just told listeners, before going on to remind them that high pressure equalled poor air quality. Asthmatics be warned, he said.

'As though asthmatics could escape the poor quality air,' Dexter grumbled to Moy. 'As though, by taking thought, you could add one cubit unto your stature. As though you could avoid low-flying aircraft simply by –'

'If you want any more toast, have mine,' Moy said.

Moy was Dexter's live-in girlfriend, whom he wanted to make his wife. She was slight and small, barely five foot three. She had grape-black eyes and a wide nose and a cap of naturally black and shiny hair. No visible white hairs yet, and no overall dusty look, as can happen to women in their early forties unless they take measures to disguise it. It was probably her dark eyes and hair that made some people who met Moy for the first time, and before she opened her mouth, assume she was thirty and French. Or if not French, Spanish or Italian. It was these youthful French or Spanish or Italian looks of Moy's, and also her smile (slow and unsure, but which, in an instant, could open into something startling and wholehearted), that had first attracted Dexter.

Dexter and Moy had been living together for just over a year. They had been sleeping together for a lot longer than that, although 'sleeping', partly true now that they spent their nights under the same roof, did not describe the months before Moy moved in, when bedtime for them had been one action-packed hour in the early afternoon. After the hour was up, Dexter had had to tear himself away from Moy and her Battersea flat, and race across London, south-west to east, to collect his two sons from their primary school.

Moy got up from the table and put her plate and mug in the sink. She switched off the radio, still talking to itself on the worktop. 'I've got to go in a minute,' she said.

'No no *no*.' Dexter seemed not to hear her, he was reading a letter from his ex-wife. He would never have opened the letter had he known who it was from, but his ex-wife, to fool him, had typed his name and address on a businesslike envelope. He'd ripped the envelope impatiently, hoping for a cheque – he was owed several cheques that morning – and found only a double-folded sheet of A4 which, unfolded, had revealed his ex-wife's backwards-bending script.

'No they can't, they bloody can't.' He reread the letter. It was short, hardly more than a note but, because of the way Hyacinth had spaced it, took up all one side of the paper. He held it out to Moy.

'Read this –' he flapped the sheet of paper at her – 'Read it.'

Moy had one foot on a chair while she tightened the lace of her left canvas boot. She took her time over the lace, then swapped feet. The tongue of her right boot had lost itself in the uppers, and she had to feel around, and tug, and retrieve the tongue before tackling the lace. When no other delaying action presented itself, she straightened up and took the sheet from Dexter.

She sniffed the letter and read it twice. She turned the page over to check there was nothing on the back, no spiteful afterthoughts, no planned and poisonous post-scripts, and put it down on the table.

'Well?'

She shrugged and spread her hand.

'Say something,' he said. 'You must say something.'

'I don't know what to say. It's mild compared with the stuff she sometimes writes. If it weren't written by your ex, if someone just stuck it under your nose and said what d'you make of this? you'd probably say it was okay. It isn't offensive –'

He could not believe this. He could not believe that Moy could be so obtuse or so naive. He said, 'How can you say that? It's colossally offensive.'

'Well, it's something that she wants them, isn't it? It's something that she cares. When –'

'She doesn't want them. She doesn't care. She doesn't give a stuff what they want. It's just a way of getting at me – and at you, I might say. Anyhow, Christmas isn't for months. It's a power game, Moy.'

Moy picked up the letter and read it again and replaced it on the table.

Dexter snatched it up.

'Look, Moy,' he said. 'Look, this letter *is* written by

someone I know, someone I know too bloody well, so how do you expect me to be objective?'

'Well,' she began. And stopped. She didn't want an argument; she had other things on her mind. Also, what could she say that he would find acceptable? She unhooked a crumpled linen jacket from the back door and put it on.

'I want to know that you support me,' Dexter said. 'I need to know you're on my side. Sometimes I think you're not. Sometimes I get the impression you don't really —'

'Don't push it.' She dug into her pockets, feeling around for change for the Tube. 'I'd stop there if I were you.'

'I didn't mean that. You know I didn't. Of course I know you're fond of my kids. Of course I know you support me. I'm just enraged by this letter. I don't know how to answer the bitch.'

'Don't answer' — counting the change in her hand. 'Don't answer till you've talked to Dig and Frankie. When they get home, ask them what they want to do about Christmas. Then you'll know what to write. I need another fifty p. Have you got fifty p?'

He sat down suddenly, and closed his eyes in the resigned or weary way of his that Moy had recently decided was feigned. Or if not feigned, too self-conscious and attention-seeking to be entirely genuine.

'Late,' she said, opening the door. 'Gotta cruise.'

He remained in his chair, his head thrown back, his eyes shut, his arms hanging limp, like a dead man's, outside the chair arms.

'You could wish me luck, Dexter.'

'What for? Oh God yes, the interview.' He sat up. 'But

21

you're not dressed for an interview! I mean, shouldn't you have ironed that jacket? Shouldn't you be wearing a dress or a suit?'

'Fuck off.'

'Well then, your black skirt and your white silk shirt – those look good. And your black high heels. I don't think those boots do you any –' Her stare unsettled him and he began again:

'It's just that I'm worried they might think – I mean, they're business types, aren't they, and they may well associate –'

'I'm hoping for a commission not a post in middle management. They know what I do. They'll expect me to look *workmanlike*.'

'But your jeans aren't even clean.' Moy's lack of personal vanity, or lack of interest in her appearance, or whatever you liked to call it, had once enchanted him. Not making the best of herself – okay, her hair was always clean – had seemed to denote a seriousness of mind and of purpose. Paradoxically, he had also found it sexy, and could remember reading a poem to her. A love poem by Herrick, the one that began: *A sweet disorder in the dress/ Kindles in clothes a wantonness.* She was just like the girl in that poem, he'd told her then.

You won't catch me in a crimson stomacher – whatever that may be, Moy had said. And she hadn't worn ribbons since she was about five.

The dry way she'd said it had not offended him at all. He could tell that she was pleased, even if she hadn't said so. It was just that she had no idea how to handle compliments.

'I washed these jeans last night,' she said now. 'If they're stained, well, tough. If the interview panel have a problem with cement stains, then tough. It's their problem, not mine.'

'I hope you're right there.'

'Fifty p?' She held out her hand.

He got up from his chair and went to the worktop. Beside the electric kettle was a cardboard NSPCC collecting box, misshapen and discoloured from being steamed twenty times a day, and he turned this upside down and sifted through the copper coins. 'There was a five-pound note in here last time I looked,' he grumbled, 'and where's all the silver gone? There were at least ten twenty p pieces last time I looked. Now there's nothing but – ah.' He picked out a pound coin and handed it to Moy.

'About the interview,' Moy said. 'They asked for personal background. They said, Do you have some personal background you could bring with you? What is personal background? Because I haven't a clue.'

'I expect they mean a CV,' Dexter said.

'They've got my CV. They've had it all along.'

'I don't know then. Unless they require a list of all the men you've slept with.'

'Bye then.' She hefted a bursting leather satchel to her shoulder and was out of the door.

Sorry now, he ran after her into the street and threw his arms round her backview. He told her he loved her. He wished her, Good luck, Babe. He told her to really wow 'em. 'Gi's a bell lunch time and tell us how it went. Promise?'

'Yeah-yeah-yeah-yeah-yeah,' said Moy, disentangling herself.

Alone in the house, Dexter got on with the housework.

He was energetic and organized at this, but that was partly – he would say – because he had had to be. In the early weeks after his wife had jumped ship (the early part of what, since Moy moved in, he now spoke of as his *interregnum*), keeping the place together, keeping his sons in clean T-shirts and jeans, keeping them well, and inventively, fed, had been the things that had kept him from falling apart. He knew that Moy admired his efficiency and perhaps envied it, though she did not say so. She was as disappointingly bad at giving compliments as she was at receiving them. He knew that she admired his tuneful singing voice and certain physical characteristics he had – resilient pecs, dark blue eyes, black eyebrows, wiry, plum-coloured hair, long muscular tongue (like a giraffe's, Moy said) that could reach, without effort, the base of his chin or the tip of his nose. He knew because she told other people, some of whom reported her comments back to him. He had complained to her once about her want of verbal generosity – she was generous with her body, on the whole – and she'd said, Oh dear. Oh dear, it was the way she'd been brought up. In her family no one ever did make personal remarks. Direct compliments were unheard of, to describe something as 'quite nice' was about as far as you could go. But to get back to his own attributes, she'd said, and her failure to mention them: wouldn't he consider it patronising, really, if she were to praise such self-evident strengths?

Moy's excuses were pathetic, he thought. His own parents hadn't been great givers or takers of compliments; neither had they been demonstrative, to each other or to their children – not to their son, anyway. A hair ruffle, from his mother, an awkward shoulder cuff, from his father, was what he remembered, though he had the idea

24

his sisters had fared rather better. But you didn't have to be a replica of your parents, did you? Whatever Philip Larkin said. You could make a conscious effort not to resemble them in certain ways. Unpraised and uncuddled yourself, you could decide, when your turn came, to do it differently. He'd done it differently for Dig and Frankie.

He ran the hot tap in the sink. He had what he called a game plan for the chores – as though some risk, or challenge, or large sum of money, were involved; as though there were a brilliant and dangerous opponent to overcome. But game plan, his son Dig had pointed out, was merely a fancy term for the order in which he did the cleaning, and the time limit he set himself. First the breakfast things, wash, dry, and put away on hooks and in cupboards. Next the kitchen table – a wipe over with a wet sponge cloth, followed by a rub down with a rough dry towel one. After that he zoomed through the house with the vacuum cleaner and its various nozzle attachments, its brontosaurus necks and heads and obscenely sucking mouths. It was a noisy operation because apart from one small blue rug in the living room and one slightly bigger red rug in his sons' bedroom the floors everywhere in the house were uncarpeted board. Sanded and bleached and sealed boards downstairs, battleship-grey painted upstairs, including the stairs themselves.

This morning, despite the airlessness and sticky heat, he worked fast and vigorously. It was not a large, or difficult, house to clean. There was no narrow dark hall to negotiate, and no poky front parlour as the rest of the terrace had. The previous owner of his house, an architect and the first middle-class Wasp to move into the street, had taken down walls and raised ceilings to make one airy and light and, given the Lilliputian proportions of the place, decent-sized living room, which contained the staircase and whose only door opened on to the street. At the back of the living room, two steps down, was the kitchen area, a scullery or washroom in former times. The upstairs consisted of a biggish bathroom at the back and − face the other way and climb three more stairs − a little landing which led to his kids' play station (as he called their bedroom) on the left, and the front bedroom, his and Moy's bedroom, straight ahead.

Forty minutes was his self-imposed time limit for cleaning the house, except on Fridays. On Fridays he allowed himself a full hour because Friday was the day he washed the kitchen and bathroom floors.

When the vacuum cleaner and its extremities were tethered under the stairs, Dexter got out a jiffy bag from the cupboard under the living room bookshelves and unloaded its contents on to the glass-topped table-desk that stood under the back window and faced the back yard. He returned to the shelves and took down from the reference shelf the tools of his trade: Judith Butcher's *Copy-editing*, Hart's *Rules*, *The Oxford Dictionary for Writers and Editors* (known in the business as *ODWE*), and a selection of grammars and dictionaries that were his particular favourites. Having squared these up, in two fastidious piles, on his desk, he went back to the bookshelves. From one shelf he removed *The Faber Book of Aphorisms*, and from another, after a bit of peering and taking down and opening and shutting and putting back, a 1938 Penguin edition of Apsley Cherry-Garrard's *The Worst Journey in the World*. The *Aphorisms*, edited by W.H. Auden and Louis Kronenberger (Faber paper covered edition, 1970), was a constant on his desk and he thought of it as a talisman; the other book varied from day to day. He might choose a thriller or a book of verse; more often, as this morning, he'd pick a real life saga of endeavour and suffering and endurance. When his work got hard or monotonous, when he felt himself to be suffering, he would open *The Heart of the Antarctic*, or *The Long Labrador Trail*, or *On Foot through the Patagonian Ice Fields*, and read a passage that put the words 'hard' and 'monotonous' and 'suffering' into acceptable context. Or he would weigh up the truth of an aphorism; or amuse himself by turning an aphorism on its head: *When a man is tired of life, he is tired of London*.

Dexter was a copy editor, though he hadn't always been one. There was a time when he'd been a senior fiction editor in a London publishing house, but that was when he was married to Hyacinth, before she left home and dumped their children on him. He had been a good editor, he knew, everybody had told him so – the *Wunderkind* of British publishing, according to some – and for a while after this disaster his company had allowed him to carry on editing from home.

However, not being in the office meant he'd been unable to contribute to the inter-departmental meetings publishers have; it meant he couldn't interact, at a moment's notice, with the design team and the publicity team and the sales/marketing team and the accountancy team. As sole carer of his children, he'd been unable to attend sales conferences and book fairs and bonding away-days and bagel-breakfast summits and out-of-town brain-storming weekends. He wasn't around to give idle juniors a kick, or take money-making authors and agents and literary editors out to lunch. After several months of being patient and understanding, his bosses had reluctantly let him go.

Why don't you get yourself a nanny for your kids, or an au pair? After Hyacinth had been gone a year, several well-meaning colleagues had begun asking him this question. They pointed out that leaving the workplace was one thing, getting back into it quite another. Surely, now that his children were both at school there was no real reason for him not to go back, and a.s.a.p.? Also, wouldn't it be good for Dig and Frankie to have an attractive young woman at home, someone who'd collect them from school and play with them and get them their tea? Wouldn't Dexter enjoy that too? If he could organize his working day so that he arrived in the office early and left it early, he could be back by six-thirty to give his kids quality time. And what about the money side of things? Without a decent salary – and he'd lost Hyacinth's salary, remember – how was he going to pay the mortgage?

Dexter had listened to these arguments – which were not new to him because he'd put them to himself – and dismissed them. Before Hyacinth left, there had been a nanny, a nursery-nurse-trained 26-year-old called Marilyn, and the first thing he'd done after it was clear Hyacinth was not coming back was to tell Marilyn she was not needed any more. Marilyn's training had included a mini-course in child psychology, and she'd told her employer he was wrong. She was needed, she said. Dig and Frankie needed her. They had suffered one irreplaceable loss and should not be made to suffer two. What the children needed now, Marilyn had insisted, was consistency, the sense that life was continuing in its familiar routines even though their mother was no longer there.

She pointed out that her employer had had next to no experience of child care and displayed little of the patience required for it.

But Dexter could not be swayed. What his children needed now – and they were his children, he had reminded Marilyn, not hers – was the hands-on parenting only he could provide.

Six months after Marilyn's departure, he had sold the big and airy flat in Notting Hill he'd shared with Hyacinth, and moved himself and his children to a small terraced house in Bethnal Green, in the borough of Tower Hamlets. Financial necessity dictated the move – he and his wife had always spent their salaries a lot faster than they'd earned them – and he needed to put distance between himself and the habits of his married life. In any case, a part of him had always fancied the idea of living in the East End.

So now he worked from home as a freelance copy editor, a job more usually done by women. Copy editing was his main, not especially well-paid, job, the one, because it had a creative side, he took pains over and could sometimes quite enjoy. His other regular job was fiction reader for a literary agency. For this, he had to read whatever manuscript the agency threw at him, and write a report on his findings. It was not enough to write, for example, 'This ms sucks' – he had to give reasons. He had to point out the structural defects. He had to explain why theme, plot, characters, dialogue, point-of-view, prose style, ideas – when there were any ideas – were clichéd or failed to convince in some way. Finally, if he decided a manuscript were publishable, it was part of his job to suggest how, and by whom – and what sort of readership the book would, most likely, appeal to.

Those were Dexter's regular jobs. He supplemented

them, whenever anyone asked him to, with journalism: book reviews, author interviews, author profiles, the occasional radio or TV arts programme. Getting this kind of work had been relatively easy when he first started working from home because of the useful connexions he'd made at the parties and receptions that go hand in hand with corporate life; and in the drinking clubs he had been a member of in those days; and because of the reputation he had earned as one of the sharpest young fiction editors in town. Most people in the trade seemed to believe that Dexter's domestic problems were a temporary blip, and that once they were sorted he would be back – someone as ambitious as he was bound to be back – and at the beginning, literary editors of newspapers and magazines and planners of radio and TV programmes had contacted him: Dexter, any chance you can do me a piece on Elmore Leonard/James Ellroy? 1,500 words by Tuesday. Not bad money, by the way.

But that was four years ago; Dexter had not gone back, and increasingly he was having to do the contacting himself: Peter? Hi. How are you? Great, *great*. No, Dexter. Dexter *Bucknell*. I was wondering whether – Increasingly, he was having to hustle and tout and plead.

Today Dexter was wearing his copy-editing hat. The typescript he was working on was a whodunnit, the fourth in a series. The third had won a Silver Dagger for its author although the third, in his view, was the feeblest of the three. To his mind, the amateur-sleuth protagonist of these serial thrillers, a feisty female taxi driver by the name of Buster Crim, had run out of diesel half-way through book one. It was not his, copy-editing, job to say so. By the time a typescript landed on his mat it had already found a publisher. His copy-editing job was to check facts where there were facts, to spot inconsistencies and anachronisms. To correct spelling mistakes, duff syntax and punctuation. To query stylistic infelicities and dud jokes. Not that funny? Delete? was the sort of, tactful, question he wrote in pencil in the margin.

Not all the authors Dexter copy edited seemed to appreciate the textual improvements, the cuts and additions, the inversions and suggestions, he made. Some bought an indiarubber and erased ninety-nine per cent of them. Some wrote STET in gigantic capitals at the top of every page. Others phoned their publisher in a fury. Episodes like these he only got to hear about if the publisher phoned or faxed or (before his computer crashed finally and for ever) e-mailed him: Dexter! Didn't I warn you X's prose can't be tampered with? He's threatening to take the book elsewhere – and he's the only bankable literary author we've got. You've really landed me in it.

It was desperately hot and humid in the kitchen, even with the back door and window wide open. Dexter pulled his T-shirt over his head and sniffed it; then towelled his neck and armpits with it. Displacement activity. He picked up his pencil and cautiously rolled one end in a pencil sharpener, item from the special-offer School Maths Set he had recently bought for his son Frankie. The lead broke almost immediately. He tried again. This time the sharpener gripped the pencil in a positive and satisfying way, and red-edged brown flounces curled out on to the table, but the second the blade made contact with the lead the lead snapped. (A metaphor for sex? For life? For his own sex life? thought Dexter, whose business it was to make those sorts of connexions.) He gave the sharpener one more chance. Then he reached for the vegetable knife he usually used.

'Would a guy with a number-one haircut – see p. 23 – carry a comb?' he wrote in the margin; and looked up, and caught sight of his ex-wife's letter, half out of its envelope, glaring at him from the saucepan shelf. 'Go away. Go *away*.' He said it aloud, to get rid of her, to get rid of the idea of her. But she refused to budge – it felt to him like refusal – and eventually he got to his feet, and fetched the letter, and sat down with it at the table. 'I will decode you,' he said, opening the paper and boldly flattening it out, 'I will defuse you, I will *demystify* you.' And he began to examine, as though they were new to him, the individual ink marks on the page: the extravagant capital letters and dashes, the furious underlinings, the pretentious Greek Es. The Os, curiously squashed to resemble semibreves, the Ts, upper and lower case, whose vertical had no connecting horizontal (merely a pointy hat, like a circumflex, floating somewhere above); the grandiose loops and swirls. A vulgar hand, he had some time ago decided – though he had loved it once. A devious hand. A *malevolent* hand. So much so that each time he glimpsed it, each time one of her smart bombs found its way to his letterbox, and got wedged there (some of her recent assaults had run to twenty pages or more), or slipped, or tottered, on to the mat, he suffered what the Health Pages warned were heart attack symptoms: tightness in the chest, nausea, cold sweats, dizziness.

More threatening to him even than her handwriting was Hyacinth's letter-writing mode and style. The aspect of it he disliked and feared most was her habit of putting a question mark in places where normal people would normally put a full stop, a dodge that transformed an otherwise straightforward statement – one he might have been able to deal with – into a calculating and insolent threat. A slippery threat that defied effective reply. A reverberative threat that at night kept him hurling himself about the bed and punishing the pillows – and Moy too, if she happened to be in the way.

For over a year after their divorce, which Hyacinth, having no grounds, had not contested, neither he nor the children had received a single, written or spoken, word from her. Then one day a birthday card, with a ten-pound note inside, had come for Dig. Not long afterwards, a postcard, from India, had arrived for Frankie. And after that, as he'd explained it to Moy, *le déluge*. He'd begun to put off tackling the bulkier envelopes, the ones Hyacinth had had to strap with sellotape to prevent them bursting apart in the post, for hours or even days. Burning them unread might have been the solution – he had burned two – but Moy had said no. The letters must be kept, Moy had said, they were evidence and might have to be produced in court. If Dexter ever needed to go to court again. Evidence of what? he'd said, stupidly and wearily. Of instability, she'd said. Of persecution. Also lies.

So he kept his ex-wife's letters, though he still couldn't bring himself to read the longest ones. They had to be read, Moy told him, would it help if she read them? She would read them for him if he liked, and tell him the gist of their contents. Or she would read them *to* him, if he preferred.

Moy had invented a ritual for these openings, which she did late in the evening, after the boys had gone to bed. After he had braced himself with booze. First, she would execute a formal and sedate dance, a pavane, she said it was, around the room, holding the envelope tightly to her breast. Then, upping the tempo, she'd move into a sort of strip-tease routine, proffering the envelope in a tantalizing way, and then hiding it behind her back; bending over (so that he was presented with her butt) and waggling the envelope suggestively between her legs. While this was going on, and while she – slowly, and with coy or challenging looks – opened the envelope and withdrew the letter (and put it back, and repeated this sequence), she'd hum and dum-de-dum the definitive strip-tease tune. When eventually she got round to reading out a paragraph, she read it with a straight face and in a silly voice. A sweetly sincere, or hysterical, or clenched-teeth-vicious, voice that she liked to imagine sounded like versions of Hyacinth's own. These voices had not sounded at all like Hyacinth, but they were funny, he thought, and he'd felt grateful to Moy for her defusing antics. Except when he'd been too pissed or depressed to appreciate it, Moy's performance had usually managed to make him smile.

These Hyacinth-debunking happenings were in the past though; only last week Moy had told him she didn't want to take part in them any more. They'd lost their point, she'd said; they'd become laboured and predictable, they weren't funny. Also, she was finding it increasingly difficult ridiculing a woman who, for all her vindictiveness, was nonetheless Dig and Frankie's *mother*. She suggested they try her other idea: she would open and read the bulkiest letters, and if and when Dexter was in a mood to listen she would paraphrase the important bits, if any. Then he could decide whether a reply was needed.

What were those very long letters of Hyacinth's about? He had asked Moy to tell him – not in any detail, just, you know, vaguely, the vague gist – and she'd said they were about a journey. Most of the letters were about Hyacinth's journey, well, two journeys. An actual, physical journey to India, and a mental and spiritual journey towards selfhood. Towards self-discovery and identity. The two journeys were linked in some way, Moy thought, and the need to make them had been Hyacinth's main reason for leaving home. At least that was what Moy understood, though she had not read the letters carefully and if Dexter wanted to know more would have to read them again.

Hyacinth – what a God-awful name, he thought now, staring at her signature. Hya*cinth*. *Hi ya*, Cinth. In Moy's opinion, a boy's name, exclusively. She had said as much the first time he'd taken her out: I thought Hyacinth was a boy's name, you know, like Narcissus. I think of it as a beautiful boy, a beautiful *youth*'s name.

He'd told her she was right, the Hyacinth of Greek myth had been a boy, a very beautiful boy. Several men had loved him, or at any rate fancied him, including Apollo, who'd killed him by mistake. Hyacinth had got in the way of Apollo's discus, he'd explained – and maybe he too should have gone in for a projectile-hurling sport. Darts, for example.

Moy hadn't laughed, he remembered. She had moved the conversation sideways to hyacinths-as-spring bulbs and flowers. She had mixed feelings about them, she'd said. They were handsome, obviously, but at the same time weird-looking. The flower heads were too heavy for their thin stalks – a busty woman with slender legs, was what they made her think of – and had to be supported by sticks and string. Then there was their scent. A delicious scent to begin with, but cloying, didn't he find? Funereal?

35

Like all lilies. And, like all lilies, when they started to go off . . .

However, she did have a good memory about hyacinths – good because it involved her mother, Moy had explained. And she'd told him a story about how, when she was seven and in Freedom Fields Hospital, Plymouth (where her family was living then), with a virus that developed into pneumonia, her mother had put a bowl of hyacinths by her bed. Over the five days she was in that side ward, she'd watched the buds breaking into tiny curly bells. She'd tried to catch them actually doing it – swelling, bursting – but she never could, the buds always opened behind her back. Even so, she'd been happy, once she began to feel human, lying there, eyes half closed, drifting, watching – and sniffing. They were that dark, intense blue, she told him, their smell so powerful it had come into her dreams. So she was sorry his ex was called Hyacinth; she hoped the name wasn't going to be ruined for her for ever.

Hyacinth isn't an exactly easy name to say, is it? I mean to call someone, all the time, all day long. Did you find it easy? Moy had asked. (This was later, this was one afternoon when they were drinking coffee, after making love in Moy's bed, in Moy's flat.) Or did you call her something else? Did she have a nickname?

I called her Cinthy, he'd said, I only called her Hyacinth when I was pissed off with her – which eventually was most of the time.

Examining Hyacinth's handwriting, he remembered this lie. He had never called his ex-wife 'Cinthy'; when he loved her, he had loved her name, as people do. The most beautiful name ever invented, he had thought then. If he hadn't called her Hyacinth all the time it was because most of the time he had called her darling. Or *my* darling. Or angel. Or babyface. But he couldn't tell Moy that. From the first he had led Moy to believe that he'd drifted into his marriage by mistake – 'as happens to young guys sometimes'. Love hadn't come into it, he had told Moy. 'It was just, you know, a sex thing. It was sex, period – for both of us.'

Dexter took his ex-wife's letter out of its envelope. 'Dear Desmond,' it began. He hadn't spotted the 'Desmond' at first reading, and he thought, The bitch. The entire *bitch*.

> Dear Desmond –
> My last three letters must have gone astray?
> About Xmas plans?? Bobby and I have recently acquired a weekend cottage in Berkshire, and we think it would be fun if Digby and Frank could spend their Xmas holidays with us there? I'll talk to them about this? When I've heard from *you*? As you're aware, I haven't had them for Christmas *once* since you and I parted, so it's only *fair* they come to me this year? Now that I'm happily settled with my man and can make a *proper* home for them??
> Yours,
> Hyacinth

'Dear Hyacinth,' Dexter wrote in pencil on the spiral-bound notepad he kept permanently by him, 'You cannot have Dig and Frankie this Christmas because they DON'T WANT TO COME TO YOU. They can't stand your husband and, it's clear from everything they've told me, he can't stand them. If you don't believe me, *ask* them. I'd remind you that it's due only to generosity on my part that you now have access to the children one weekend a month, and I warn you that if you continue with these ~~threats~~ demands I shall apply to the court to have your access stopped. P.S. We didn't part, as you put it – you left me. You left me and our children.'

Dealing with Hyacinth, trying to deal with her, was like handling sand or olive oil. Thinking about Hyacinth was as bad for the blood pressure as for the soul. He was not sure if he had a soul, or if anyone had, but there was always the fear. And soul-searching, as it is called, was an occupation that he, at forty-one, increasingly found himself drawn to.

High blood pressure he did have, inherited from his father who had died from a stroke. He got up and ran the cold tap in the sink. When the water ran icy cold, he bent down and stuck his face under it.

'Dear Hyacinth,' he began again, 'How nice of you to suggest D and F come to you this Xmas! It's a great idea of yours to invite them to your weekend cottage and I know they'll be pleased when I tell them (they're away at the moment, staying with my mother, and won't be back till Sunday). Unfortunately we've been asked by friends – no one you know! – to their Jamaican beach hut for the whole of Christmas and New Year, and naturally the boys are already looking forward to the trip. But as I say, it's nice of you to think of them.'

'Dear Hyacinth – I was astonished to get your letter. The answer is no.'

'Hyacinth – Fuck off.'

Feeling better, he made himself a third cup of coffee. Apart from the messy NSPCC collecting box, there was no clutter on the work surface, no old bills or postcards or corks or paperclips or broken ballpoints. Hyacinth's letters aside, he dealt with his mail as it arrived, replying to the stuff that required a reply, filing the stuff he needed to keep, tearing into small pieces, and binning, the rest. The detritus family kitchens tend to accumulate during the course of a day never survived the night because he junked any there was in the swing-bin last thing before he and Moy went to bed. After he'd set the table for breakfast. Even an evening of fairly serious drinking seldom prevented him from sticking to this routine. Some of his female acquaintances – the stay-at-home, or part-time working, mothers he'd got to know since he took on the sole parenting role – found his mess-free house spartan and unwelcoming, a judgment he'd learned when one of them made it her business to tell him so. Though to his face the mothers said things like, 'Dexter, your place is amazing – how do you keep it like this? You'd never guess two small boys lived here, I really envy you,' secretly, so his informant said, a lot of them felt threatened by his organisational powers and inventive ways with fish fingers. Behind his back, apparently, the expressions 'anally retentive' and 'anal personality' and 'right up his own arse' often cropped up in connexion with him. The names 'tosser' and 'wanker' were bandied about. And although it had been agreed, apparently, that he was an interesting-looking, even attractive, guy, and though – encountered at the school gates and in the newsagents' – he was never less than polite, it had also been agreed that there was something chilly about him. Something quarrelsome about his mouth and its expression.

It was Dexter's kids the mothers felt sorry for, his informant, whose name was Diane, had confided to him. How could those two kids stand it never being allowed to run wild or make a mess, as growing lads needed to? What sort of adults was that Dexter Bucknell turning them into?

39

Well, thanks a bunch for the compliments, he'd said when Diane had finished. You've really set me up for the day. He'd said it brightly, but in truth he'd been wounded by the things she said, so at odds with a vision he had, in which the name Dexter Bucknell was universally recognised as one and the same with probity and fidelity and integrity and rectitude. He did not believe the things Diane told him, they were not justified, but he was wounded by them; and later on − in the night, in the street, sitting his kids down to their tea − he would pick over her accusations, and argue with them. These days, when he found himself, at half-past three in the afternoon, standing next to Diane and her double buggy with its cargo of snot-faced lookalikes, he kept his focus on the mosaic patterns in the school brickwork, or on the snack-wrappered pavement, and did not speak.

At half-past eleven, when he had at last stacked Buster Crim ready for the jiffy bag and was gloomily examining the first chapter of what its publishers described as a 'comic cricket disaster novel' − 'we've got great hopes for *Inswinging Yorker*,' the attached note read, 'which we acquired on the basis of a two-page proposal. TV rights have already been sold and press coverage of its highly promotable young author − he's only just left middle school! − promises to be tremendous' − his doorbell rang. Window cleaner. *Shit*. The windows needed cleaning and he liked them clean, but although he was fond of Wally, and usually enjoyed Wally's brand of misogyny and hypochondria, he was in no mood for it today. If he stayed put, Wally would think he was out, and try someone else. The bell drilled again, and he remembered the courier, and the manuscript, Bad Boyz Publishing had warned him to expect. Cursing, he put down his pencil and made his way to the front door.

''lo Dex.'

Mandy? No, *Sandy*, lone mother from round the corner in Wellington Row, fag in fingers, peering at him through a newly orange fringe. He'd sat next to her and her ashtray last Tuesday, at the Single Parent Support Group coffee evening he'd been bullied into attending.

'Oh. Hallo.' Oh *shit*.

'How you doin then, Dex? Hot, in't it? You busy? Got a minute?'

'Well yes, I am busy. I'm working.' Shit. Out of the corner of his eye he could see Wally, with bike and buckets and ladder, heading his way along the kerb.

'We're all working, Dex, one way or t'other, aren't we?' Sandy reminded him.

Not you, he thought, surely not. The word on the street and in the pub was that Sandy supplemented her Income Support by entertaining male visitors, in the mornings, at home. But not in the school holidays surely?

'I really am very busy.' He was aware, suddenly, of Sandy's stare, travelling from his face to his naked chest, to his midriff, to his cotton boxers, which had an all-over pattern of Daffy Duck and did duty as shorts — 'Really am.'

'Okay then. Won't ask m'self in for a coffee.' But she stood her ground, and waited. For him to ask her. Eventually, when he didn't, she took a step closer — so that she was half in the doorway — and whispered — so that he could feel, and smell, her three-packs-a-day breath: 'Was merely wondrin if your Digby would like to come to my Jordan's birthday do. I'm taking half a dozen li'l monsters to the rink. Hi, Wally.'

'Hi Wally,' Dexter called over the top of Sandy's head. 'Fraid I haven't any cash on me today. Better give us a miss this time round.' His tone, he hoped, implied an order rather than a request, a there's-no-more-to-discuss finality Wally would not be able to argue with.

But Wally was already unstrapping a bucket from his bike. 'I don't have no objections to cheques. S'long as they're big ones. Help m'self to water, shall I?'

Dexter stepped aside to make way for Wally and his buckets, and Sandy saw her chance, and nipped after Wally into the living room.

In the kitchen, she made straight for the electric kettle. 'I'll do the honours, okay? Coffee, right? Coffee okay for you, Wally?'

'Tea. Two sugars.' Wally turned from the Belfast sink. He had a too-large head for his diminutive body, and on top of it a quantity of yellowish white fluff – like chick down, it occurred to Dexter, watching Wally put down a full bucket and pick up an empty one. The tap gushed and groaned and water spurted over Dexter's immaculate floor. 'Coffee's poison,' Wally informed them. 'Never touch the stuff. Rots the liver.'

Dexter stood by helplessly as Sandy flicked her ash into the sink and went through his cupboards. 'Tea bags, tea bags, where are yooo?' Finding them, she called out: 'Biscuit for you, Wally? Where d'you hide the bickies, Dex?'

The voice that came out of his mouth was not his normal voice, which was deep and, he had been told, sexy. 'Wally has his tea and biscuits *after* he's done the windows. That right, Wally?'

'Right,' Wally said. 'But I'll have a drink of Adam's ale first, if it's okay with you.'

On his way out of the kitchen, Wally stopped in front of Sandy, who was leaning back against the worktop, propped on her elbows. She was wearing a magenta sleeveless vest with a low neck that revealed an area of brown and wrinkled bosom; and tight, orange hipster jeans. 'You seem to know me,' Wally said. 'You know who I am, but I'm blowed if I know who you is.'

'Course you do, Wally.' And Sandy laughed. 'Everyone knows me. Bin around for years. Sandy,' Sandy said. 'Sandy Hitchcock. Wellington Row.'

'No,' Wally said. 'Never seen yer. Never cleaned yer winders, I'd know if I had.'

'Can' afford you, can I? Your services, that is. Any more'n you can afford mine.' And Sandy laughed again, in perhaps a meaningful way.

'What sort of services would yours be then? Commercial Street?' Wally didn't wait for a reply, but shuffled off to the front door. It was his habit to clean the two street windows first.

As soon as Wally was out of sight and hearing, Dexter turned to Sandy: 'Look, I don't want to be rude but this house is a smoke-free zone. And I really do have to get back to work now.'

'I've made you a coffee,' Sandy said. 'It's here, getting cold.'

'I've already had coffee.'

'Well just gimme time to drink mine.' She brought her mug to the table and sat down. 'Like your phoenix chairs – Ikea, I'll bet?'

'No.'

'Do sit down, Dex. You're making me feel uncomfortable.'

'Look, I've got a load of work on, and I can't do it while you're –'

'Never bin inside this house before. Not since the Jacksons lived here. It's int'restin, in't it, what different people do. Don't you find all this white paint cold in winter?' As she spoke she ran a gold-painted, and chipped, and curling, fingernail down a stack of typed pages.

'Don't touch those!'

'Deary me. Tutty tut-tuts. You know how to make a girl feel really welcome. Us single parents are s'posed to stick together, remember. We have to create our own support network, like the lady said.' She was peering at three typewritten words on an otherwise blank top page. 'Drop Dead, Beautiful – is that the title? Funny, only yesterday my boyfriend called me that. He said, D' y'know Sandy, you're drop-dead beautiful, you're drop-dead *gorgeous* – you really are. What a coincidence, eh?'

'It's not a description here, though,' he said coldly. 'There's a comma after "dead". Which makes it an injunction. It's an order, or a curse. Or a prayer. Of course the title, hardly original need I say, is a nod to Chandler's *Farewell, My Lovely*. As no doubt you understood.'

Sandy drained her mug and got to her feet. 'You never answered my question, Dex.'

'What question was that?'

'I asked if your Digby would like to come to my Jordan's birthday do.'

'Dig's away this week.' He unlatched the front door and stood aside for Sandy to go through.

'Yeah'know.' Sandy, moving sideways, contrived to brush against him. And, appallingly, he felt his body begin to respond. In those brief betraying seconds he knew for certain how she would taste down there – could in fact already taste her. A rank, disgusting, exciting, tongue-burning salt.

'Yeah'know,' she said again, as he ducked behind the door and out of her reach, 'but I'm talking about *nex'* week. Jordan seems to think your kids is due back Sunday.' A pause in the doorway. 'Stopping with their mother are they?'

The bitch. 'No,' he said. 'Look, I can't answer for my son, obviously, but I'll tell him he's invited.'

'Shame your kids aren't here for most of Fun Week, though, in't it? Shame they're gonna miss out on the clown event tonight in –'

'What?'

'*Fun* Week, Dex. Starts today – Wednesday through Wednesday. You must have had the programme. There's loads of stuff for the kiddies going on round here, an it's all fer free.'

'Oh? Oh yes.' He could vaguely remember something about Fun Week coming through his door a week or two back. He'd binned it probably. You can't keep all the rubbish that lands on London doormats twenty times a day.

He shut the front door on Sandy, but not fast enough to miss her parting shot as she flip-flopped away: 'If y'must wear your underpants in public, Dex, how's about sewin' up the fly?'

Wally had finished the windows, and drunk his tea, and left; and Dexter was getting to grips with *Inswinging Yorker*. He had had a quick flip through before starting to read, noted that each chapter had a heading: 'First Slip', 'Second Slip', 'Third Slip', 'Googly', etc. Not good news usually, that kind of thing. But at least it was a novel. At least it was not a real-death account. Real-death accounts were legion, everybody seemed to be doing them (writing them, publishing them); in the past few weeks he'd had to work on three, one of them detailing the diagnosis and decline and, not entirely painfree, end of a child. A six-year-old who, from descriptions of the boy's looks and behaviour, had reminded him of Dig at that age.

He rested his elbows on the table top, played with his hair, fiddled with his pencil, put his pencil into an itching ear, turned the pencil round, put it down *Come on now laddie, concentrate.*

There were two stages, as he saw it, of copy editing, passive and active, in that order, and this was the passive stage. The reading and thinking and deliberating stage. (The sleep-inducing stage, he found it could be.) What he did was read the manuscript – in this instance a computer print-out – straight through once, while making notes in his notebook. It was only when the passive stuff was accomplished that he could move on to the active stage – the diverting stage, the correcting, querying, pruning, stripping, reshaping, restyling stage. He had his own name for it: coppicing, although Moy had suggested that coppicing was an inadequate description for some of the things he did to manuscripts. She was wrong, though. Coppicing was the exactly right word. An uncoppiced thicket was a dead thicket, as his father had been keen to point out. It was coppicing, his father had endlessly explained, that let in light and air; that regenerated; that allowed the best and strongest shoots to grow and show.

He had done a fair amount of coppicing work when he'd been an editor, but not as much of it as now. Not exclusively and relentlessly, like now. What's the difference between an editor and a copy editor? Is there a difference? – a question a lot of people had asked when he changed jobs. And he had replied, darkly ironical, *I'll let you know*. Now that he really did know, now that he could quip, *Thirty thousand a year?* nobody asked him. Except Moy. Moy had, he thought she had, right at the beginning.

But money was not the only difference, of course not, and if he were to be asked that question now, and if he were to answer it even half-way seriously, he'd list some of the things that editors do. Commission new work, read work in progress, buy in work from abroad, buy work at auction (having defeated the competition), oversee work from its beginning right through to jacket design and typeface and publication. All these things he had once enjoyed and now missed, as he missed the emotions that had been an inseparable part of them: anticipation, hope, excitement, disappointment, frustration, despair. The highs and lows you could expect when dealing not just with books but with the flesh and blood people who wrote them.

(Moy had asked him once if he missed his authors, and he'd said yes. Yes of course he missed them. If he hadn't enjoyed dealing with them, if he hadn't got a kick out of persuading, dissuading, nannying, cajoling and fighting with them, he would never have been in that job. He'd explained to Moy that copy editors seldom got to speak to the authors they worked for, even on the phone. Or if some did, he did not. He'd told her he suspected that most of the authors he copy edited didn't even know his name. He was just something called *the copy editor*. A dirty word, probably. He minded this, he'd said.)

Despite all the differences between the peopled job he had once done and the solitary job he did now, he still thought of himself as an editor, a part of him believed it. There was something shameful about working at home – he often felt this – and it was a truth that the work a man does defines him. So he was an editor. An editor was what, and who, he was.

John walked down the steps of the pavillion, an excited grin on his strong-featured face. Opening the batting for England! It had always been his dream –

The telephone rang.

'I can't talk to you now, Elizabeth.' He had told his sister many times not to call him in the daytime. He had explained to her many times that, although working at home, he tried to keep office hours and office discipline. So no personal calls. There were enough interruptions to his day without those. Nothing he said to her made any difference.

'I need to talk to you,' Elizabeth said. 'When can I talk to you?'

'Ring me after six. It'll be cheaper for you, too.'

The telephone rang again. A voice said, 'Have you finished with *Dead in the Water* yet?'

'What? Oh. Nearly.' Though he hadn't started on it. Hadn't even approached the jiffy bag.

'Okay. But I must have it back by tomorrow, latest. Bike it round, will you.' Click.

John stood at the crease, his heart thumping, bat at the ready. Out there on the stand were Mum and Dad and –

The phone again. His bank manager. He thought and spoke of him as his bank manager, although in reality Mark was the underling whose lot it was to keep D. B. Bucknell's overdraft in check. He liked Mark; Mark was a good man, no question, sympathetic, so far as he was permitted to be, to the chancy finances of the freelance and self-employed. But Mark's sympathy, as he'd made it clear, depended on his being kept fully in the picture. He usually tried to keep Mark in the picture, it was in his interest to keep him there, but this month he'd failed. It wasn't that he'd forgotten his promise to Mark, he knew he had to phone him. It was that he wanted to be able to tell Mark some good news. He wanted to be able to tell Mark that he'd landed a regular slot in one of the Sundays, that some idiot features editor was going to pay him two grand a week for writing a thousand chummy words on nothing at all. He wanted to be able to tell Mark that the handbooks he'd dashed off (that he dreamed of dashing off) – *Day Trading Made Easy* and *The Tough-Love Guide to Lone Parenting: 'A Daddy's Tale'* – had been bought at auction for six figures. He wanted to be able to tell him that he'd bagged a million smackers apiece for solving the Riemann hypothesis and the Poincaré conjecture; better still, that he'd won the Lottery in rollover week. No, not tell him. What he would do was saunter into the bank and, without a word of greeting to the no-smile, no-speak cashier it was always his luck to get, drop the paying-in slip and the cheque for £25.4 million into the little well beneath her bulletproof glass partition. Then, when Miss Pinsett picked up her rubber stamp in anticipation and was running a supercilious eye over his two bits of paper – to check that the sums on each matched – he would watch her gasp, and utter a little cry, and slump fatally to the floor. *Farewell, My Ugly.*

'You're over your limit in both accounts,' said Mark, 'and I've been instructed to warn you –'

'I'm waiting for three big, well, biggish cheques. I am

chasing them. They should be here any day now. Then there's the stuff I'm working on at the moment, and –'

'How much are the cheques for? Exactly. I need to know.'

Dexter told him.

'That won't do it, Dexter. It'd cover your current account temporarily – but what about your standing orders? You've got, let's see (Mark went off the air for a minute while he consulted his screen), a hundred and fifty going out on the second of next month – that's your kids' computer – and then there's the life insurance and the mortgage on the twelfth, and on the fifteenth –'

'Okay, okay okay.'

'Dexter, we have to talk. I don't think we can do it on the phone. Can you come in and see me one day next week? Wednesday p.m. would be best for me.'

The train fare to Ludlow. The train journey – there and back in one day, seven hours' travelling time altogether unless he spent the night with his mother. And in between, confidential, so-called, chats with Mark, fourteen years his junior, in a mahogany-veneered pisshole.

'One thing I need to have explained – those two considerable sums paid to Majestic Wines on your business account, beginning of August –'

'Yeah, yeah, sure,' he said. 'I can explain those.'

'– but the chief reason I need to see you is because they're moving me on. I'm leaving the branch in October, and –'

'*What?*'

'It's promotion,' Mark said in a wounded voice.

'But what happens to me?'

'That's what we need to talk about. If we can get your overdraft down, that's to say cleared, before I leave –'

'But can't you take my account with you? To wherever you're going?'

Silence from Mark; followed by an embarrassed cough.

'Shit.' He'd been hoping to wangle a loan for a laptop.

'Can you make Wednesday? Three-thirty?'

He sighed deeply. He said that he supposed he could. That he supposed he'd have to.

'In the meantime I'm afraid you can't draw any cheques or use your cash card. Though we will honour your standing orders — that is, providing the amounts you're owed come in before the orders are due. I'm putting a letter to this effect in the post today.'

'Great.'

'I'm sorry about this, Dexter. I really am.'

'Not your fault.' Though he felt, in some way, that it was.

'If you'd kept me in the picture I might have been able to — look, is there anything you could sell? That would raise a bit of instant cash? Furniture, or —'

'I sold the furniture ages ago, you know that — we live in a minimalist paradise here. I sold the car, let me remind you. And the Picassos. And my mobile phone.' This was a lie: he had lost his mobile, left it in a pocket. Had it whipped.

'See you Wednesday,' Mark said, firm and grim.

'I think that's all. We've enjoyed meeting you, and hearing about your work. It was all very interesting.' The chairman of the interview panel sat back in his chair; and clasped and unclasped his long fingers; and nodded; and smiled a professional smile. His panel looked up from their notes and smiled likewise.

'Do I take my slides away now?' asked Moy.

'No, we'd like to hang on to them for the moment. We'll let you know when and where to collect them.' The chairman stood up and leaned across the table and offered Moy his hand. After she'd shaken it (after her hand had collided with his hand), she shook hands with the rest of the panel, who remained in their chairs.

'Your briefcase,' someone reminded Moy.

She hoisted her satchel and backed towards the door. The brass drop handle turned but the door remained shut.

'Try it anticlockwise,' someone else called.

Eventually, the same someone, a Lady Something, left her seat and came to Moy's aid. 'Like this.'

'Fucking hell,' said Moy, as the door closed behind her, to the three babe receptionists chatting behind the horseshoe desk in the hall.

When Mark had rung off, Dexter went upstairs to his bedroom – our bedroom, he had to remember to call it now that Moy slept there too, *our* bedroom. At the back of his sock drawer, under precision-folded layers, he found what he was looking for: a tiny ring box, made out of metal of some kind and covered with a skin of worn purple velvet. It sat between two bigger, leather-covered boxes, one of which contained his father's collar studs plus assorted coat buttons and TA uniform buttons; the other, once home to a variety of cufflinks, was empty save for a drawing pin and five rusted curtain hooks. Selling the cufflinks, which he'd done in March, had raised enough to pay the phone bill, but not enough to make conspicuous inroads into the winter-quarter gas and electricity demands.

Hyacinth had always had to help him with his cufflinks, he remembered; and suddenly he had a picture of himself, in his shirt tails, arms held impatiently out, while his ex-wife poked and pushed and pulled his oval, plain gold cufflinks – or his rectangular, monogrammed platinum cufflinks – through layers of unyielding cuff. *Stand still, for God's sake*, he could hear her say. *How do you expect me to do this if you won't stand still?*

The ring box lay in the palm of his hand. He feared opening it. On the other hand, if he were going to sell them, it might be sensible to check, before setting off for Hatton Garden or Camden Passage or Bond Street or Burlington Arcade, or wherever – he had not yet decided – was the most trustworthy place to go, that the rings were actually in there. That they hadn't been stolen or, as he could easily believe, spirited away. He sat down heavily on the end of the bed, and braced himself.

They were there. The diamond ring an unknown godmother had willed to him (with the instruction, 'For the girl you choose to make your wife'), comprising three square-cut diamonds set in gold, its dazzling half-moon rising out of the yellowed satin; and lying beside it, a gold wedding band. Simple, grave, eloquent, fateful. These were the rings that, on two very different occasions, he had placed on Hyacinth's unresisting finger. The ones that, fourteen years later, she had placed on their bedroom mantelpiece before leaving the flat in Oxford Gardens for ever. Along with a note which said, *I'm sorry*. Just those two words. She did not sign them.

He had been out, on duty, the evening she left him. First, at a book launch drinks party where, as the author's editor and host, he had had to make a speech; afterwards in the showy and overpriced restaurant to which he'd taken his author, his author's husband, her agent and her two best friends for dinner. Hard work, the husband and the two best friends, made harder by having to watch his drink intake: he couldn't afford to get trashed on duty. At some point during the dinner he excused himself and went to the payphone in the lobby and called Hyacinth. He wanted her to know what a hard time he was having. He was going to describe the outfit – beige and apricot, with a frilled eighties neckline – the younger of the best friends was wearing, and relay snippets of the wearisome conversations he'd been having to endure. He was hoping to make her laugh, and to make himself laugh. More than that, he wanted to hear her voice.

The nanny, Marilyn, answered the phone. He knew it was her but couldn't hear what she was saying. There were people in the lobby in the process of leaving the restaurant and there were others arriving, which meant the street door was constantly being opened. Added to the racket from the street and in the lobby was the racket from the kitchens. The big swing kitchen doors, faced with a grey rubbery plastic that made him think of hospital theatre doors, were only a yard or two from his left ear. He hunched his head on to his chest to try and block out these noises, and shouted at Marilyn to speak up. Hyacinth had already gone to bed, Marilyn shouted back. She'd come home around nine after a late meeting with a client, and had gone straight to bed. She had asked Marilyn to answer any calls because she was tired and needed to sleep. She was going to switch off the bell on her bedside extension.

Annoyed and disappointed, he hung up the receiver. Well, fuck you then. Fending off an ambush of giant palms, he made his way back to his table.

At home, around one, he was greeted by silence and darkness – only the hall light on, on dimmer. His kids' bedroom door and the nanny's bedroom door just ajar. The master bedroom door, unusually – for Hyacinth liked to listen out for Frankie who was going through a wakeful and needy patch – shut. He poured himself a whiskey nightcap and drank it in the kitchen. He undressed in the bathroom. (Only one bathroom was the disadvantage of a flat that in most other ways suited them well.) He was flossing his teeth, when his eye was caught by the assortment of floatable plastic – ducks and boats, a duck-shaped sponge, a wind-up whale, a wind-up submarine – that had got beached on the bottom of the bath. Marilyn hadn't tidied up the way they paid her to do. Holding them at arm's length, he shook, or squeezed, the waterlogged toys before dumping them in the big plastic tortoise-box where they belonged.

Then, in the dark, he felt his way to the bedroom.

How long should it take a normally observant, tired but not drunk, husband to realize that the marital bed is empty and the bedroom empty? That his wife is not in the bed, nor underneath the bed, nor anywhere in the room? Five seconds? He was not sure how long it took him, but could worry, if he allowed himself to, that it had taken a lot longer than that. Minutes rather than seconds. He had the idea that he'd crept under the duvet and was well into his pre-sleep routine of leg-stretching and feet-flexing and stomach-and-butt clenching before he became aware of any sensation of absence. Absence of human breathing and body warmth. Absence of smell – and Hyacinth's night-worker face-and-neck cream was pungent stuff. He could recall reaching a hand across the vastness of the emperor-size bed. And then, when his hand found no correspond-ing hand, met with no breast or hipbone but only a coldness of cotton sheet and pillow, sitting up. Grabbing his bedside lamp.

It was finding her rings, loose, on the mantelpiece, that had really hurt. A woman who loves jewellery does not easily surrender an old and beautiful diamond ring, one she has worn on her finger for fourteen years or so. (And indeed, she had taken the rest of her jewellery, the junk fashion stuff she'd bought for herself, the semiprecious necklaces and bracelets and brooches he had given her, to mark birthdays and Christmases, throughout their marriage.)

Leaving her rings behind was an insult, the most humiliating and, finally, injurious thing. An act not just of rejection, he had come to understand, but of disavowal, denial, annulment.

But to begin with, there had been her going to come to terms with, the seismic shock of it, the after-tremors, the domestic upheaval it had triggered. And there had been Dig's grief. He had imagined his younger son would be the one to suffer most, but it had soon become clear that Frankie could be consoled or distracted by almost anyone. Dig's desolation, which had manifested itself in, first, a nightly crying out for his mother, and then, when that did not bring her back, a punishing speechlessness (he would not even answer when spoken to), Dexter tried never to think about.

People had been kind to him at first, as people tend to be kind when a spouse takes off without warning. (They blame the bolter and rally round the abandoned one.) These sympathetic friends and acquaintances, most of whom were married and with children, had immediately concluded, as he himself had, that Hyacinth had not bolted alone. A third party must have been involved, they decided; irresistible love or sex must have been the catalyst. What else could account for it? Any minute now there would be news of another household similarly devastated, or of a second, abrupt and inexplicable, exit from Frocks, the upmarket fashion chain for which Hyacinth had been head buyer. When this did not happen, when nothing emerged to make sense of her flight, they had begun to ask themselves questions. What must it be would make a wife walk out, just like that, on her husband? What would cause a mother − a good and loving mother, so far as an outsider could tell − to renounce her children? Just what had gone on in that marriage bad enough to make her go? Something very bad, surely. Regular beatings from a drunk husband, perhaps. Or rape. (There had been a lot in the papers about marital rape at this time.) Or prolonged, and finally insupportable, verbal abuse.

At least that's what he feared they were thinking and asking. He had no proof that they were; no one said anything to him. He feared it because after a few weeks of rallying around, of bringing pre-cooked meals to the Oxford Gardens flat, of taking his kids off for the day on fun outings, of offering to do anything at all that might help ('You only have to ask, Dexter, and we'll be there!'), his support network began to fall away. Wives stopped dropping in, impromptu, 'just to check you're all okay', the phone no longer rang in the constant way it had. And when he called these friends himself − to ask a favour or suggest a meeting − he got excuses, or promises so vague as to be meaningless: 'We're very very busy at the moment, Dexter − you know how it is.' Or, 'Nice to hear from you. We must meet soon.' Or, 'Can't talk now, just dashing out. Catch up with you later.' For whatever reason, the married friends he had had then, that he'd thought he had, almost without exception were not friends now.

Sitting on the bed, he stared down at the rings, faced them down. Then snapped the box shut.

There were several routes, or rather variations on one essential route, from Jesus Green to Liverpool Street station, and Dexter, who had had to wait for the Bad Boyz courier to slam down his visor and rev and roar away before he could leave himself, chose what he considered the architecturally interesting and culturally diverse one. This was a variation that took him, usually at a jog and after a bit of weaving and criss-crossing, into Brick Lane – leather shops at this point, and bagel bars, three at the last count – and along the walkway under the iron railway bridge, and on past the old Truman Black Eagle brewery, newly reinvented as music hall and art gallery and internet café, and housing a variety of themed bars that he kept meaning to check out. Once beyond the brewery, the air in Brick Lane – TB centre of the universe, according to his friend Steve, though Dexter had not seen too much evidence of this – became heavily sweet and spicy, and at the same time thumpingly musical, due to the Bengali sweet shops and sari stalls, the music shops and curry houses and bar-cafés, that proliferated there. He had to leave Brick Lane after the best of these, to turn right into Fournier Street, where a jogger could find himself blocked by knots of students and sightseers standing back on the pavement to get a view of the Huguenot silk-weavers' houses or, at the very end of the street, of the Hawksmoor Christ Church – a building he was in two minds about. Struck by evening sunlight, its cleaned stone turned a seraphic gold, its spire in touch, you could believe, with a heavenly afterlife; more often the whole structure appeared to him earthbound and ominous, a giant tomb, on dark days, lying in wait.

Another hazard Dexter sometimes encountered, though this was not confined to Fournier Street, were the, after dark often, organized tours of 'The Ripper's White-chapel', 'The Back Passages of Spitalfields', 'The Kray Brothers' Mile End', 'The V2 Bomb Experience'. Tourist attractions, these – not something an East Ender would subscribe to, not anything he would ever do. His son Dig had begged to be taken on the Ripper tour, and he had said no.

Dexter loved the East End – home ground, he'd described it to Moy, surprisingly because he was not London bred and had lived in the area less than four years. He loved it with the encompassing zeal that perhaps only a foreigner, or an adherent of lowlife movies, can truly know, so that even the godforsaken bits, that most people would find desolating, gave him a buzz. Sometimes, needing a break from the confines of desk and terrace, he would pocket his notebook and camera and wander out into his home ground. Hopeless estates, treeless wasteland dumps, defunct gas towers rusting in poisoned ground, abandoned malls and drug-pushing streets of boarded-up warehouses and chained and padlocked shops, were the sights he looked for (and easily found, and photographed, and wrote notes about). North Hoxton, the poorer parts of Dalston, Bromley by Bow and the eastern fringes of Poplar, the East India Dock Road, were some of the areas that provided Dexter with the sights and sounds and smells that gave him this buzz. He would afterwards extol these places to Moy as authentic, the people who lived in them as real. Moy, homesick for a south-of-the-river London she had lived in for years before D.B. Bucknell came along (and which had its own housing, and drug, and racial problems for God's sake), would challenge him. How did he mean, *real*? Did he actually want to live on one of those authentic, sad estates? On the *Boundary Street* estate? Did his definition mean that she was not real? That he was not real?

The midday sun was burning down, and by the time he breasted the Christ Church he'd run out of jogging steam. Panting hard, he crossed Commercial Street at a walk. In front of him, loitering in the entrance to Spitalfields market, were two small boys. A black boy and a white boy, in identikit jeans and trainers, cropped heads bent over a shared crisp bag. They were taking turns to dip fingers into the bag, and watching them he felt he might burst into tears. It was sights like these that could make you believe, for a full second, that the world was okay. Or if not okay, heading in something like a sane direction. It pained him that although his kids had black and Asian friends, he had managed to make none for himself. Unless you counted Marcia, the Trinidadian hospital nurse who had looked after Frankie in the Royal London after he'd broken his leg, multiple fracture, a couple of years back, and who brought her own two kids to the house on a twice-yearly visit for Sunday lunch. And aside from his mate Bala, who owned the newsagent's.

He dodged his way on through the glass-covered market. Past the bookstores – without stopping to look – and the second-hand clothes stalls. Past the Cycle Surgery and the five-a-side football pitches and the row of old Citroën cars – out of a Jean-Paul Belmondo movie. He stopped and ducked into a doorway to avoid a troupe of pint-size clowns, chanting and skipping – with knees exaggeratedly high, like Morris dancers. Chanting, *Fun* Week, *Fun* Week, Fun *Wee-eek*.

He had a stitch now, in his groin, and his chest hurt. A stabbing pain, under the ribs, over the heart. He was leaner than he had once been, in the days of publishers' lunches, in the days when he'd thought nothing of jumping a taxi to ride two blocks – or even, God help him, round a corner – but not fit. Not what he would call *fit*. Despite his daily, almost daily, morning run – three times round the Green unless it was really chucking it down – and the fact that he biked or jogged or walked nearly everywhere these days, his once gym-built body did not feel, did not quite behave, as a fit body should.

A London-in-the-heat smell of drains, rising from the pavement grilles, assaulted him, and he moved out into the crowd.

'PHONE'S RINGING,' Frankie said. It was late afternoon,
or early evening, and he and Dig and Gran Margaret
were in Gran Margaret's garden, picking raspberries. This
was the first fine day after a week of rain, and a lot of the
biggest raspberries had a fuzzy coat on them. He put his
punnet down and cupped an ear towards the house. 'Yep.
Definitely.'

'It'll be that, er. Bird. That starling,' Gran Margaret said,
'imitating the phone bell. He often fools me. It has to be
him, Frankie, because you can't hear the phone from here.'

'I can,' Frankie said.

'I can't hear anything,' Dig said. 'Ow.' There were
nettles in among the raspberry canes, seasoned and vicious,
and one of them had found the gap between the sleeves of
his Arsenal shirt and the cotton gardening gloves Gran
Margaret had made them both wear. 'Owwwwww.'

'It is the phone,' Frankie said, 'I'm going to answer it.'
And off he bolted.

Dig sucked at his stung wrist. 'There's one born every
minute, you know,' he informed his grandmother.

After so much rain, the lawn resembled a sopping and

tangled hayfield, and Frankie, in rubber boots several sizes bigger than his feet, staggered and tripped as he ran. If the ringing stopped before he got there, something bad was going to happen. But he could hear it, louder, as he skidded across the concrete strip that edged the garden side of the house, and louder still as he booted open the swollen french windows.

'Hallo, hallo, hallo? Is that you, Ma? Is there anybody there? said the Traveller,' a man's voice said. His dad's voice.

'Hit's me,' puffed Frankie. 'Hit's, huh, huh, Frankie.'

'You're out of breath,' his dad said.

'H–huh huh.'

'Did I get you in from the garden?'

'We're, huh, huh, huh, picking raspberries.'

'Raspberries?' his dad said. 'Haven't the birds had them?'

'No, not all of them,' Frankie said. He was waiting to be told the reason for the call, to be told who it was his father wanted to speak to. Definitely not him. It was never him. 'D'you wanna speak to Dig?'

'Well, I was hoping to speak to your gran. But of course I'd like a word with Dig first, if he's around.'

'Dig's in the fruit cage. With Gran. Shall I ask her to phone you supper time?'

'Fruit cage, eh?' His dad laughed, probably because the net casing of the cage had been missing for years. You could see where the cage had been because the twelve rusted metal poles that had supported it were still there. 'Could you fetch her *now*?' his dad said. 'It's kind've urgent.'

'Okay then. She'll be surprised though. She thought you were a starling. I fed the pigs today,' he added. 'Gran's getting out of pigs, you know. Everyone who's got pigs round here's getting out of them. I like pigs. I'll miss those damn pigs.'

'Me too,' his dad said, 'I've always liked pigs.'

Frankie couldn't think of anything more to say.

'See you Sunday,' his dad said. 'I thought we might go to Heathrow one day next week and watch the airing planes taking off – whaddya think?'

Airing plane was the name Dig, but not Frankie, had come up with as a two-year-old, before he learnt to say aeroplane. The only person in the family who still used airing plane for aeroplane was their father.

'Cool,' said Frankie, who was uninterested in aeroplanes but who found his dad's disappointment difficult to bear. In any case, Dig had explained to him that Dad got a kick out of watching jets take off and land. When Dad was a publisher, and doing deals, Dig had told Frankie, he was always flying off to New York and Frankfurt and places, and now he flew nowhere.

'Make sure you pack everything,' his dad said. 'Make sure you don't leave anything behind.'

While he waited for his mother to come to the telephone, Dexter imagined himself into the room Frankie had just left. In his early boyhood it had been the dining room, in which Sunday meals, barring breakfast, had been eaten; and for a moment he saw it the way it had been then, when the spinach green self-stripe wallpaper and mismatch sage velvet curtains were comparatively new. The dining table, ringed by 1920s Jacobean chairs, had taken up most of the floor space in those days, leaving just enough room for the sideboard – 1950s 'contemporary' with, surprisingly, filigree drop handles.

Sunday lunch had been a formal business, the mood dictated, Dexter thought, by the room itself and by their church-going clothes, which, except at lambing and haymaking and other times of crisis, they kept on until the meal was over. What remained most vivid for him about those lunch times, though, was not the discomfort of his suit – too tight, as it always seemed, in the waistband and under the arms – or the *non sequiturs* that passed for conversation, but the spoonful of blood he and his sisters were given to drink on the days when they had beef. (Hereford beef, always, from the home herd.) The blood was not called blood, it was called meat juice, and his father doled it out from the sideboard when he'd finished carving. What his father had done was fill a serving spoon with the pink-brown liquid in the carving dish, and call them up from the table in turn – Elizabeth first, Anna next, him last. The meat juice glittered in the spoon, it was warm and salty-sweet, he liked the taste, found it easy to believe his father's promise, 'It'll make you big and strong.' But blood? It never occurred to him the stuff was blood. He must have been eight or nine, he thought, before logic, or his sisters, insisted on classifying the meat juice.

Another picture he had, that overlaid and confused the first: the convalescent home dayroom the dining room had turned into after his father's first stroke in '83. A place of occupational therapy gadgets and contraptions, where the gas fire and the rented, wide-screen TV had remained on all day. He could smell that dayroom now – a warm, nauseous mix of urine and cigarette smoke and burnt wool carpet. He could see his speechless father canted over in his wheelchair, cigarette between the fingers of his non-paralysed left hand, a long tail of ash just about to drop. (The burns in the carpet were still there, black and accusatory.) This room was now known as the TV room, and also, informally, the junk room because, since the brick lean-to on the north side of the house had fallen down two years ago, it had become a repository for most of the rubbish the lean-to had contained. The dining table, which no one had eaten off for years, was jammed against an end wall, its surface buried under box files, loose papers, bleached and ring-stained and long-outdated works on husbandry; plus an assortment of wooden or metal, or a combination of both, household items – such as screwdrivers, fire tongs and men's shoe trees. Along with these were things awaiting repair – and that had been waiting a long time by the look of them: table lamps, china jugs and cups and plates and saucers, lidless teapots, drawer handles, chair legs and struts – but where were the drawers and chairs they had once belonged to? – framed watercolours of Highland glens, that had fallen off the wall and that displayed smashed glass and snapped picture wire.

The floor was similarly obstructed. In his mind's eye, Dexter could see the no longer needed baby cot and highchair and buggies his children had once occupied; the old, rolled-up carpets with moth-infested felt underlay; the musty horse rugs; the feed buckets, still with traces of oat feed in them; the mildewed pony tack; the newspapers in bindertwine-tied stacks. Anyone wanting to watch TV had to climb over or round these hazards in order to reach the viewing seats: one collapsed sofa and two spine-chilling armchairs.

Obstacle race and assault course was how he'd described this shambles to Moy before she saw it for herself. 'Irish rot' was another term he'd used, though there was no Irish blood in the family. He had offered, on his infrequent visits, to clear out the TV-cum-junk room. He would clear it out, he'd told his mother recently, bin or burn the trash, put whatever was worth selling – in his view there was nothing – into a local auction; then, with the proceeds, decorate the room. (He'd nearly said 'fumigate', but stopped himself.) He would turn the former dining room into a games room for visiting grandchildren, he'd told his mother. What he proposed to put in there, he'd explained, was a second-hand ping-pong table, or billiard table if he could get hold of one; a dart board, a carpentry corner with decent workbench and tools, a –

His mother had said no. Leave well alone, his mother had said. There were a lot of things in that room – the baby equipment, the horse and pony tack – that might be needed again one day. (She was probably thinking of his sister, Anna, an orthopaedic nurse, in her forties, husband-less and childless, so far.) He should leave well alone.

If he wanted to do something useful, his mother had said, he could lend a hand on the farm. They could always do with an extra hand, especially at lambing. And if clearing out was what he was after, he could clear out the farmyard.

He had expected his sons to back him up over the games room idea, but Dig and Frankie had taken their grandmother's part. The reason they'd given was that the junk in the room made ideal islands when it came to playing Shipwrecks, and ships when it came to playing Pirates. They didn't play those games any more, being too old – Dig was too old – but felt some sort of loyalty to the time when they had played them. His kids were conserva-tive, Dexter had noticed, and liked what they knew. The first thing they did when they arrived at Gran Margaret's was to check out the places and objects that meant most to them – places and objects they would discuss and test each other on at night in their Bethnal Green beds. Some of these things held magic powers, apparently. The stained-glass window on the landing, depicting a knight in armour and on horseback, for example, and the painted wood parrot on a perch who swung from a cuphook on the TV room mantelpiece (and had been there, Dexter assured them, in its dining room days); and the box on wonky wheels that had ten red and nine green building bricks inside. One green brick had gone missing more than thirty years ago, when, during a fight between him and his elder sister, Elizabeth had launched the bricks, one by one, into the shrubbery. Elizabeth would have been about thirteen then. Too old, you'd have thought, and too disdainful, surely, to pick fights with a boy of five. He'd said as much recently, when he and Elizabeth were arguing on the phone, and she'd jumped on him at once: 'But you were a *pain*, D, an absolute little pain. You ruined everything.' A pause, before she'd added, 'And you still are a pain.' Oh, ha ha ha. Oddly, he could recall, when they weren't quarrelling, when she wasn't pinching him, admiring Elizabeth. An attractive girl, even he could see, rangy like their mother, as adept at throwing balls as bricks, good at catching, good at running, good at riding the ponies, Welsh mountain and Exmoor, that had been a daily part of their childhood on the farm. Brilliant at handstands and headstands. Better, at fourteen, than he would ever be at cricket, batting and bowling. A girl he'd been interested to watch, on summer evenings from his bedroom window, cartwheeling endlessly round the so-called lawn.

You wouldn't guess any of that, meeting her now. He didn't think you would. She wasn't attractive now. Years of suburban, committee-driven life must be partly to blame, he thought, along with her ageing Tory-Party-Conference clothes. Box pleats! And she wasn't fifty yet — why didn't she wear jeans? As his mother did, often; as Anna did.

At least he imagined Anna wore jeans. He hardly ever

saw Anna. Christmas would be the time – but she was usually on the ward at Christmas. (No hardship, she insisted, they had great times with the patients, she really enjoyed Christmas on the ward.) He did not know Anna, a small woman with a neat waist, big hips and thighs, a toothy, engaging smile – or anything about her personal life. If she had a personal life. There were only three years between them, so as children they must have done stuff together, but when he thought about that time and tried to summon her, he couldn't. A vague, benign presence, was all he got. A round white face, across the table at mealtimes. Someone who, when their parents were working late, remembered to feed the dogs.

There were noises now in Dexter's receiver. The french windows banging, the sound of someone tripping over something. A rolled-up carpet? He heard a muffled curse or maybe groan. Laboured breathing.

'Well,' said his mother at last, 'what's the, er, problem?'

'Problem?'

'You must have had a good reason for bringing me all the way from the fruit cage. Frankie said it was urgent.'

'I never said urgent. I said *convenient*. I said to fetch you *only* if it was convenient. I made a point of that.'

'How could it be. How could it be con, convenient? I was the other end of the garden.'

'Well, I'm sorry.' Fucking hell.

'What is it you want to talk to me about? Hang on a minute, I've got to sit down. Hang on.'

He could hear her receiver bang down on the little table, complicatedly carved and with a beaten brass top, that his Great-Great-Uncle Geoffrey Bucknell, the only member of his family to do really well for himself, had reputedly brought back after Empire-building decades in what had then been called Madras. And now a chair was being dragged up, one of two reproduction 'Hepple-whites', he guessed, chipped french polish and greased brocade. He considered replacing his own receiver and pretending later – if his mother should decide to ring him back – that they'd been cut off.

'So? Where were we?' his mother said.

'Nowhere.' It came out ruder than he had intended, and he said, 'I'm sorry about the pigs, Ma. Frankie told me. You must be sad about that.'

'Yes, it is a blow. We've seen it coming for months, but it is a blow. It's hard to imagine this place without pigs. We've always –'

'I know. Of course.' A pause. A sympathetic pause before a change of subject and of gear: 'Look, Ma, what I need to know is, can we come to you for Christmas?'

'What?'

'Thing is, I need to make plans. I really need to get it sorted. Before the boys get back on Sunday.'

This was the moment when he should explain his need to make urgent plans for a Christian festival that was still four months away. The point at which he should tell her about Hyacinth's letter and its threatening demands. But he would not do that. His mother had once been fond of Hyacinth, and he had a suspicion she still was. He feared that Hyacinth was still in touch with his mother. Sometimes, from odd remarks his mother came out with and from insinuations in Hyacinth's letters, he could believe that his mother and his ex-wife were not just in touch but in league.

'Did you hear what I said, Ma? I said I need to know if we can come to you for Christmas because if not I must make other plans.'

'I heard you,' his mother said. 'I'm just surprised you're

asking. Last year when I invited you you said Dig and Frankie preferred Christmas in Ba.' A long pause. 'In London. Anyway, I'm afraid it's not on because I'm going to Liz's this year. She asked me in January. She said, We've had a wonderful Christmas with you, so next time you're coming to us – is that a deal? And I said yes. Don says he'll see to the, to the animals, which is good of him. He's very lame now, you know. We're two lame old things together.'

'I see.' He had forgotten about his sister. 'I see. But how would it be if Liz's lot come to you again – and if we come as well? It'd be fun for the cousins to be together, don't you – ?'

'No,' his mother said.

'Why not? Why wouldn't it be? You've got room for all of us.'

'No.'

'If you'd let me clear out the TV room, I could turn it into a temporary dormitory, with mattresses and camp beds. All the kids could sleep in there. They'd enjoy that, they'd have a –'

His mother laughed, in a disbelieving and ridiculing way. 'Are you off your head? Do you really imagine that Iona and er, and er. And K, K, *Kat, Katta* – who are sixteen and fourteen, remember – would want to share um. To share a *bedroom* with two small boys? They wouldn't share with their younger sisters, you know, unless in an emergency.'

'Katta? Who is Katta?'

'Did I say Katta?'

'Kitty is what you were after.'

'Kitty. Oh. Oh yes.'

Somewhere in his mother's house a dog began to bark.

71

She had two old, white-faced black mongrels who slept their lives away on coke-blackened beanbags by the stove, smelly creatures who, in Dexter's judgment, unfailingly chose human mealtimes to release their solid-fuel gases.

'But apart from all that, you and whatsisname. Jerry. You and Jerry don't get on,' his mother was saying.

Jerry Wright, an insurance broker in Eastbourne, was married to Dexter's sister Elizabeth, and the father – Dexter often wondered how – of Iona and Kitty and Louise and Alice, four intelligent and likeable girls. On all the occasions he had met Jerry, Jerry had been wearing the same, Worthing Golf Club, tie. You won't believe this, but he even wore it on his wedding day, he had once told Moy, who at that time hadn't met Dexter's elder sister and brother-in-law. Another black mark against his brother-in-law that he had shared with Moy: Jerry's habit of referring to writers as 'scribbling johnnies'. How many of your scribbling johnnies actually make you money? was a question Jerry had been fond of asking in the days when Dexter had had a desk and an office and a secretary and a salary.

'Jerry and I get on all right.'

'Since when?'

'Oh forget it. I've got to go now, Ma. I'm busy. I've wasted enough time and money already on this call.'

'Don't you get shirty with me,' his mother said. 'I was busy too when you rang. I was busy with *your* children. Which reminds me – the, um the, um, the *Mullinses* aren't planning to leave for London until four on Sunday, so don't expect the boys till eight at the earliest. No, what am I thinking of? Nine or ten. David insists on delivering them to your door, which is kind of him, you know, because it's miles out of their way.'

The Mullinses were farming neighbours, and old friends, of his parents. David Mullins had been his father's closest friend – and rival. He could see the two of them, side by side on the rails at the cattle market, keenly taking note of each other's successes and failures. (Sometimes, when one of them managed a better price – for a Suffolk ram, say – than the other, they would not speak for days.) On Sunday the Mullinses were driving to London to visit their married daughter in Peckham, and had offered to give the Bucknell grandchildren a lift.

'Did you take that in?' his mother was saying. 'What's the matter with you, D? I know there is something the matter.'

Her question, the unaccustomed gentleness of it, got to him. Unmanned him. And suddenly he felt a need to unburden himself. To trust himself and his woes to the special unquestioning empathy mothers are said to feel for their male children. He would confess that he was in debt and unable to see a way out. He would explain that although he loved his kids – 'to bits', in Hyacinth-speak – he no longer enjoyed the role of single parent, of hands-on mummy-daddio. If he ever had, truly, enjoyed it. The decision he'd made, when Hyacinth did her bunk, to work from home and look after Dig and Frankie on his own had been the wrong decision, he would admit to his mother now, motivated by pique and a desire to show Hyacinth up. Point-scoring had been the mainspring, he would admit, not selflessness. Not a bona fide conviction that the arrangement would be the happiest one for Dig and Frankie.

I dread the boys' return, he would tell his mother now. If you want to know the truth, I dread the noise and the disruption and the mess.

73

I want my old job back, he would sob into the receiver. I want the hands-off fatherhood I used to know. I want to be able to come home after a money-making day, kiss the wife, pour myself a whiskey, climb the stairs and read a bedtime story or the riot act. Whichever is required.

And then there was Moy. This was the moment to get off his chest that he was no longer sure of his feelings for Moy, or of her feelings for him; that since she'd moved in things had not been good between them. The house was too small, he would explain, for two adults and two children. There was no study for him, no proper playroom for the boys, no privacy for anyone who might require privacy. And the bedroom was too small. What had been just about big enough for himself and his clothes was not big enough now it had to accommodate Moy and Moy's clothes and Moy's hideous armchair.

And then there was Moy's brother Joe.

And while he was about this *cri de coeur*, why not confide other, less specific, more wide-ranging, ills he suffered from? Information overload, data smog, carbon monoxide poisoning. Loneliness, boredom, disappointment, guilt. Guilt that his contribution to suffering humanity and a suffering world amounted to paying double the asking price for *The Big Issue* and to emptying his pockets of small change into every collecting tin that blocked his path. (Whereas a different decision at A Levels might have ensured a laboratory and fieldwork life in oncology, say, or neuroscience, or marine biology, or cloud physics.) Guilt that, through a lucky accident of birth, he was not a native inhabitant of a country where famine and disease and genocide were the everyday norm. That it was not his lot to raise his kids in Easterhouse, Glasgow; in Kensington, Liverpool; or anywhere in Salford.

74

My life is shit. The world is in shit. Help me, Mummy.
Save me, please. As though he were an eighteen-year-old,
bleeding to death on the battlefields of the Somme.
Spreadeagled in a ditch, the soft tissue of his torso ripped
open to —

'Are you there, D? What is going on?'

One ceases to be a child when one realizes that telling one's
troubles does not make it any better — Pavese.

'D?'

'No. I mean yes. I mean thank you. It's very kind of the
Mullinses.'

'Is it your book? Is your book not going well?'

'What book?' he heard himself scream. 'Which particular book do you have in mind?'

'The book you're um. The book you're writing.'

'What is this? I'm not writing a book. Who said I was
writing a book?'

'Of course you are,' his mother said. 'Last time we
talked you. You er. You told me you were working on a
thriller.'

'Wor-king on. Not writing. Working on someone
else's thriller. It's my job, you know. It's *what-I-do-for-a-*
living.'

'Ah,' his mother said.

'Mus' go. Moy will be home any minute, and I
haven't —'

'How is Moy?' his mother asked. 'Is Moy the matter? Is
it something to do with Moy?'

'No, Moy's fine.' He took a deep breath and with it an
imaginative leap. He said, 'Ma, don't tell the boys yet
because I want to tell them myself — but I've got some
very good news. Moy and I are getting married.'

75

'You said you'd phone me,' he reminded Moy when she got home that evening. 'You promised to let me know how it went.'

'Didn't feel like it. Anyway, you could have phoned me – I was in the studio from midday. I thought you might. Are you going to open that?' She threw her jacket on a chair. 'I fucked up, so there was nothing to tell.'

'Bet you didn't.' He said it breezily, easing the cork from the bottle between his knees.

'Yes, I think I did. I mean I'm certain I did. You weren't there.' She peered at him. 'You okay? You pissed already?'

'Well, you were a lot later than usual, I was getting anxious. But yes, I'm okay –' handing her a wineglass, smiling. 'I am if you are.'

'Could we have that down a minute? Quite a bit down? It's deafening. It's meant to be light and sensit—'

Goodbye Vega Wind Quintet playing Malcolm Arnold and Gustav Holst and Franz Danzi and Antoine Reicha and Paul Patterson. Playing, at the moment he snuffed them, in mid-blow as it were, Arnold's 'Three Shanties', was it, or Patterson's *Comedy for Five Winds*. Not his bag anyway, the hornpipe. He'd put the tape on to please Moy who owned it and for whom (because her mother had been keen on Arnold? Because her great-great-granddaddy had sailed before the mast?) this music held some arcane significance. The music he would have liked to hear, that would have suited his melancholy, was the adagio from Mahler's tenth, or Gorecki's *Symphony of Sorrowful Songs*. Or, more harrowing still, Janáček's piano sequences *In the Mists* and *On the Overgrown Path* – the final three pieces of the *Path* series so unshowily anguished; so lucidly pictorial; so lyrically beautiful; so truthfully hesitant (with their attempted, hopeful, puts and stops); so angry (with their unforeseen outbursts of despair), they could not be shared with Moy or with anyone. What he had done – in his interregnum, before she moved in – was wait till the boys were in bed and asleep, pour himself a big drink, pull down the blinds, put on the disc, switch off the lights, close his eyes. The overgrown path he then saw, so clearly it might have been a memory of his own, wound through a dense birch forest. A Czech birch forest that, for reasons, he supposed, to do with his passion for Tolstoy and Chekhov, he nevertheless understood as Russian. There was water – a spring, a crystal stream, a waterfall – close to the path, that he could hear but not see; and, until Janáček's eponymous Barn Owl banished them, there were birds and birdsong. There was a clearing sometimes. In it he would see a woodman's hut, and gone-to-seed willowherb growing round stacks of birch logs whose papery bark and bloody, rough-sawn ends he could touch and smell.

Listening alone had allowed him the freedom, when the music came to an end, to sit on in his chair for as long as he wanted. Drinking and grieving in silence, in the dark.

But Upbeat Romantic was how this evening was supposed to go. Had got to be. No gloomy or discordant stuff allowed, which meant no Lightning Hopkins and 'Bad Luck and Trouble'. So he'd put Lightning back in the cupboard, and with him other inappropriate choices he'd made: Tom Waits's 'Kentucky Avenue' and 'Heart Attack and Vine', the 'Blue in Green' track from the Miles Davis *Kind of Blue* album (said to be a great seduction piece, but he had never found it so), Lena Horne singing 'Stormy Weather', the Sinatra version of 'Here's that Rainy Day'. Instead, he'd picked from the CD shelves a couple of albums of feelgood love songs to play through supper, and finally, at 6.45 (Moy usually home by seven), slotted the wind quintets into the tape deck and turned the volume high. As he'd tweaked the roses he'd bought on his way home into some sort of, unscented, life, checked the oven, wound the clock, checked his watch, dusted a few surfaces, he'd imagined Moy's reaction as she walked through the door. *Oh babe, how lovely – just what I needed.* Or, *What an angel you are to put that on.* Or, *How typically thoughtful of you to play that, Dexter darling.*

Moy had been late though. By the time she arrived he had had to endure two whole sides of cheery piping and fluting plus a further ten minutes of side A.

'You didn't have to turn it off,' Moy said, 'I only said down. I only asked you to turn it down.' She placed her wineglass on the table, shook her head sadly, ran her hands through her brilliant hair. Dejection seemed to make her smaller than usual, tiny in fact, a child. 'Give me a hug.'

Abandoning his drink, he moved in and wrapped his arms round her little torso, buried his face in her neck, breathed in the smell of her skin. *Ah, that's better.* Moy's skin smelled of sweet nothing. It tasted delicious too and was one of the marvels about her, one of the ways in which she differed so wonderfully from Hyacinth, who had looked good – that's to say glamorous, sexy – and who had smelled and tasted bad. A sour taste and smell, like old cabbage leaves or cheese, that had nothing to do with not washing (she would spend hours in the bath), but was perhaps chemical or hormonal and, to be fair to the woman, not something she could help.

Rhythmically, like a cat, he began to lick Moy's sweet-smelling, sweet-tasting neck. Contentment washed over him, and hot on its heels, desire. Holding her tight, he bent his knees to the point where his groin was more or less on a level with her groin and began to rub himself against her. It wasn't a hug she needed, oh no. Or that he needed. A hug wouldn't sort it for either of them. What might, what would, was a shag, an invigorating fuck, here and now, on their feet. While the knee-trembler was not his favourite arrangement (the discrepancy in their heights made it a tricky one for him, made it not just a knee but a back and thigh and calf-trembling business), it had its place and time. And if he really concentrated he could blot out images of his ex-wife, whose preferred position for sexual congress this had been. Who, in the early years of their marriage, had thought nothing of tipping him out of a warm bed at four in the morning in order to pin him against the wardrobe. Who, strolling home from a late movie, had dragged him into unlit alleys and unbuttoned him in shop doorways. Who on visits to his parents' farm had never failed to steer in the direction of an accommo-dating tree. Doing it on the hoof had been a common-place then and eventually – for him at any rate – a big yawn. Now, with Moy and with rarity value, the KT had regained some of the hasty, furtive excitement he'd discovered as a student in the graffitied corridors of his hall of residence. It had taken back for itself some of that remembered heart-stopping urgency and danger.

Excited now, kiss-licking her neck, his knees gymnasti-cally bent, he began to back her towards the door jamb, but it was unavoidably clear – from the little body braced determinedly against him, from the small hard head fighting to get free of his chest – that Moy was saying no. And soon there were sounds to confirm it, mumblings of No and Not now, murmurings (more kindly? more hopeful?) of Later. Later, Dexter. Later, darling. Later, sweetheart. Later. Latching on to this promise he let her go, straightened up, rearranged his thoughts and his clothes, stepped back.

Later, he consoled himself, reaching for his drink.

'I need a shower,' said Moy. 'I'm hot. I'm done in.' And she freed her T-shirt from the belt of her jeans, flapped the creased end of it away from her abdomen, sniffed at herself. 'I stink to high heaven. Cor. Phewee.'

Her excuses were so laughable, the one about her sweatiness so untrue, he found himself grinning a whole-hearted grin. And when Moy smiled sheepishly back, some sort of miracle occurred. *I love her* – he knew it suddenly. I love that woman. I love that little Moy.

We are lucky: the next revelation. We have each other. We have Dig and Frankie. We have a roof over our heads, a good roof, an excellent roof. We have everything we need to be happy. We are so fucking *lucky*.

If only he could remember this!

Tenderly, gratefully, he kissed the top of Moy's head. 'Poor baby,' he said, removing a hair from his mouth, taking her hand, 'come and sit down. You can have your shower in a minute. Have a big drink first. Tell me about the interview.'

'They kept me over half an hour. I was told they'd probably give me twenty minutes max. What is this? Is it corked? It's disgusting.'

'That has to be a good sign.' He took her wineglass and sipped. Then he tasted his own. 'It's okay.' He smiled reassuringly. 'There's nothing wrong with it. You liked it last time.'

'I don't think it is a good sign. I got the feeling they kept me so long because – oh I don't know. But you can

sense these things, can't you? They weren't rude or
anything. The chairman said he liked my stuff. But.'

'I'm sure you're wrong, darling. You were recommended to them, remember. And they're busy guys. They
wouldn't have given you one minute longer than they −'

'Dexter, why do you always have to argue with me?'
She laid her head on the table. 'Why do you always know
best? It's exhausting.'

> *Without your love*
> *It's a honky tonk parade −*

Later on in the evening, after Moy had had her shower,
after the supper of peppers stuffed with courgettes and
griddled tuna, followed by compote of blueberries with
port and *crème fraiche*, most of whose ingredients he'd
bought in the market on his way home and taken trouble
preparing, but which they'd toyed with in silence because
Moy said it was too hot to eat and to talk (and impossible
anyway to compete with Ella Fitzgerald), he pulled a tiny
parcel from his trouser pocket and placed it in her lap.

They were lying back on the sofa by this time, their legs
stretched out before them, gasping for air even though the
back door and all three downstairs windows were wide
open.

'What's this?' Moy was alarmed − the parcel's tiny size
was alarming − but she hoped she was mistaken. 'It's not
my birthday till next month.'

'Open it,' said Dexter, with a bright nervous smile. 'Go
on.'

'Later. The movie's about to start.' And she fumbled in
the cushions for the remote control.

'No, wait. Don't switch on yet, we must have seen it at

least three times. I want you to open your present. Please open it now.'

'You can see I'm not in the right mood for presents. I'm too wound up. I keep thinking of things I should have said and didn't say. And I know I didn't really sell myself – or my work. What pisses me off is that I was determined to get it right before I went in there. But when I did get in there – fuck.'

'Poor Moy.' He began stroking her arm with the tips of his fingers. 'Poor old lady.'

Moy was forty-two. A whole year and two months older than Dexter. 'Old lady' was the jokey, affectionate term he'd come up with when she first confessed her age. She hadn't minded old lady at the time because it was so obviously untrue: throughout her life she had looked younger than her age and younger than most friends of her age. (What had been a disadvantage at sixteen was a bonus at forty-two.) But Dexter, who had a tired look around the eyes and a rash of little craters on his cheeks and who, most people who knew them both were agreed, looked older than she did, five years older at least, had hung on to the old lady joke, coming out with it, it seemed to Moy, just when she was in need of comfort and reassurance.

'It was hell,' Moy said. 'No one took any notice of me for at least ten minutes. They had my cartoons spread out on the table and were pushing them around. Then they passed my slides along. They held them up to the light and whispered about them. And all this time I was just standing there – in that socking great ballroom. Boardroom. Nightmare. There was one guy on the board who hates stained glass and told me so. He said, I must tell you I don't think stained glass has any place in secular architecture – I like to see *out* of windows – but I've been outvoted by my colleagues. It's your job to tell me why I'm wrong. It's your job to *sell* me stained glass. Then he sat back and folded his arms and waited. Can you imagine.'

'Poor Moy. Poor you. Poor darling.' His fingers were still travelling her arm, stroking and pressing. Squeezing.

'Don't.' She removed her arm and reached for the glass of wine at her feet. 'Another thing — I don't think they cared for my boots; they got some pretty hard stares, some quite nasty stares.'

'I'm sure you're wrong. I'm sure they didn't even notice what you were wearing.' Having been proved right about the boots, he could afford to be magnanimous.

'So what I need now is a bit of escapism. Not presents. I want to watch the film. You wanted to watch it, remember. You asked me to remind you it was on.'

'Moy —' He tried not to sound desperate. He picked up the tiny parcel from her lap and placed it in her hand. 'Please open this.'

'But say I don't like it, whatever it is. I'm not too keen on surprises.'

'You will like it.'

'But say I don't.'

'I know you will.'

'Well then, you open it for me. Hurry up though.' She looked at her watch. 'You've got three minutes.'

Shit. He began to untie the skinny white ribbon he'd tied, in a perfect curly bow, that afternoon. When the ribbon was off he coiled it round his finger and placed the coil on the table, where it uncoiled itself slowly, like something about to strike. He handed the parcel back to Moy.

'Nah. You do it.'

He opened out the wrapping paper. As he did so he had a vision of an earlier, confident and enthusiastic, self choosing the paper (which was heavy and white, with a silvery sheen; and glamorous, and expensive. And hell to wrap so small a parcel in). He despised the sap who had gone to such lengths. The girl on the counter in Paper 'n' Pins had flirted with him, and because of this, because he had found her pretty in an obvious, blonde and blue-eyed way, he'd shown her what it was he needed the wrapping paper for. Wow, the girl had said, looking at the ring, and then, under her navy-blue eyelashes, at him, Wow – lucky wo-man, or what? He could hear her now, call out as he made for the door, If for any reason your girlfriend doesn't fancy it, if she's off the wall or something, bring it straight back here – okay? And he could hear her laughter, sexy and conspiratorial, that had followed him out into the street.

'Must I?' The present, now in the shape of a domed leather box, was back in Moy's lap. There was no escape, and she pressed the pin-head catch.

'Dexter. Hey. *Hey.* This must have cost a fortune.'

He looked up at the ceiling. There was a crack in the right-hand corner, a wide one, he hadn't noticed before, where the ceiling met the wall. A subsidence crack? He shook his head.

'But it's *rubies* and *diamonds.*'

'No, no, I assure you. Garnets and paste.'

She took the ring from its cream velvet nest and scrutinized it under the Anglepoise. 'You are an old liar, Dex.'

He said nothing. He folded his arms tightly across his chest, as though to protect himself from blows. He frowned and shut his eyes. And immediately another image arrived: of the girl who had sat opposite to him on the Tube journey home. A black girl, so formidably beautiful he'd imagined everybody in the carriage, male and female, child and pensioner, must be staring at her too (but when he checked out the other passengers, astonishingly, nobody was). This girl, or maybe woman, he could not guess her age, was wearing what he thought of as the summer uniform of city girls – except that in her case the white T-shirt was a dazzling, detergent-commercial white, the black jeans not some washed-out shade of sludge but a dust-free velvet black. And the girl-woman had breasts, sizeable without being grotesque, the springy kind you could cup and weigh and squeeze and push about (and they would always spring back), the kind that never failed to excite him. Staring at them, he'd thought momentarily of Moy, who had no bosom to speak of. Her beestings, as she herself dismissed them, had been the one disappointment of his sex life, though he'd tried not to let it show. I love your little breasts, he made a point of telling her, in the hope that if he repeated it often enough it would become true. So far it had not become true, and sometimes he wondered if it was possible truly to desire someone so far removed from one's physical ideal.

The girl on the Tube had looked up once and caught his stare, and – without registering embarrassment, or annoyance, or interest – stared briefly back at him before returning to her book. He'd tried, by shifting position, to see what book – it was suddenly desperately important to know – but she'd held the paperback flatly open on her knee. I love you, he'd told her silently, watching her graceful fingers turning a page. Not I want you, his usual unspoken declaration to the strangers he fancied on buses and trains and in the street, but – as you might when very drunk – I LOVE YOU, I ADORE YOU, I WORSHIP YOU. When, without consulting him, this goddess had got up at Edgware Road and, slipping her book into her bag, walked out of his life for ever, he'd felt resentment, followed by pain.

Moy put the ring back in its box, and the box on the two-seater between Dexter and herself. She said, 'No, I'm sorry. No, I can't accept this. I don't want us to get married. It's nothing against you. I don't want to be married to anyone. Not even Kevin Spacey – joke. But you know that. You've always known that.'

He opened his eyes on the centre of the ceiling. A blank white space. A safe white zone.

'There's something else,' Moy said. 'Anyone you married would automatically become a stepmother. On their wedding day. They couldn't avoid it. And you know how I feel about –'

'I never mentioned marriage. Who mentioned marriage? Not me.' Shit.

She removed the lid from the box and held the box up on a level with his chin. 'This is an *engagement* ring.'

He kept his focus on the white space above his head. He opened his mouth wide, and shut it again.

'Well, what else could it be?' She was losing patience now. 'I mean, look at it.'

'I have looked at it, for fuck's sake. I chose it. I bought it.'

She was about to ask why, when the answer suddenly came to her. Of course. Of course. Of *course*. She said, 'You bought that ring because of Hyacinth's letter, didn't you? You're afraid that now she's got a husband and a huge flat and a cottage and everything that opens and shuts she'll try to get Dig and Frankie back. You're frightened she'll get custody. You've worked out that your only chance of keeping the kids is to get married yourself.'

'You're a bitch, Hyacinth, d'you know that? A class A bitch.' He struggled to lever himself out of the sofa, but she pushed him back.

'Moy,' Moy said. 'My name is Moy. And we've got to talk about this. We really have.'

'I suppose it wouldn't occur to you that someone might just be passing a jeweller's window and see something pretty and want to give it to his girlfriend? But it does happen, you know. It's not unheard of. If you're interested in the truth of what happened, I saw the ring and I thought, Moy doesn't own any jewellery to speak of, she'd love that – and I went in and – don't stare at me, Moy.'

His story was not an out and out lie. He'd been standing around in the unshowy By Appointment Old Bond Street jeweller's he'd decided was the right place to take Hyacinth's ring (they'd be unlikely to rip him off in there), waiting for their stones expert, gemologist, what have you, to emerge from his sanctum and deliver his verdict when his eye had been caught by a glitter of red in a display tray under the glass counter. A Victorian, or Edwardian, diamond and ruby ring, pretty, not flashy, the rubies, it occurred to him, the deep jewel red of stained glass. The sales assistant had unlocked the cabinet and put the tray on the counter so that he could have a closer look; and when Dexter had, when he'd examined the price tag (£500), and handled the ring and let it rest for a moment in the palm of his hand, a desire to place it on Moy's finger had overwhelmed him, dislodging the need to pay off his overdraft. So, when the gemologist returned, and pro-nounced Hyacinth's ring worth around the £1,000

mark (not more sir, I'm afraid, because of these two flaws
– would you care to examine them?) he'd done a deal. He
would take the ruby ring on appro, to see if Moy liked it,
leaving the Hyacinth ring behind as collateral.

The deal hadn't ended there though, with an exchange
of receipts. They'd asked to see his driving licence, or
some other proof of identity. 'Unfortunately sir, just
occasionally people try to sell us stolen goods.' They'd
taken down his bank account details and employment
details and the names and addresses and telephone
numbers of two blue chip referees.

He'd put himself through this humiliating business just
for Moy. In order to please Moy.

He made a sudden, angry dive for the box, but Moy
closed her hand over it. 'Give it to me. Give it back.'

'Hang on,' she said, 'you haven't told me where you
got the money.'

Only yesterday Dexter had complained that he hadn't
any idea how he was going to raise his share of the
mortgage for September. Bailiffs had been mentioned.
High drama had been acted out.

'Where did you get it? Did you sell your body? Or did
you steal the ring?'

'Not funny, Moy.' He put his head in his hands. 'How I
paid for it's not your business. It's not your fucking
business. Anyway, what's it matter? You don't like my
present and I'm going to take the bloody thing back.'

It is my business, Moy thought. It is my problem. But
she was beginning to feel guilty now. Dexter could do
this, he had the power. He could set something up
without consulting her, he could spend money he hadn't
got on a surprise something – a gadget for the kitchen, a
case of 'bargain' good-vintage claret, tickets for a play she

had no desire to see – and if she wasn't immediately ecstatic, if she hesitated, or voiced doubts or, worse, said something positively negative about whatever it was, she was made to feel in the wrong. She was made to feel a spoilsport, a monster, an ungrateful class A bitch.

'It's not that I don't like it,' she said carefully, 'it's not that I don't *like* it, it's just that I know you can't afford it. It's very pretty. Victorian, I imagine? Or Edwardian? Original setting anyway. It's very –' she hunted for the right adjective, the one that was truthful and would not offend him – 'charming.'

'Oh sod off,' he said, moving at speed.

'Hey,' Moy shouted above the telephone, which had just begun to warble, 'don't go. Come and talk to me. Come back here.'

'You answer it,' he yelled from the pavement. And was gone.

On the fifth ring, just before the answer machine cut in, Moy picked up the receiver and said, Yes? in an aggressive and discouraging way.

'Hello?' said Dexter's mother after a pause, 'is that Moy?'

God Almighty. 'Yes it is,' said Moy, less aggressive now, but not encouraging, 'but I'm afraid Dexter's out. I'm afraid I don't know when he'll be back.'

'That's all right,' said Dexter's mother, 'that's all right, I've already spoken to him today. He told me your news, and I just wanted to say how. How d–um d–d delighted I am. I wanted to say congratulations –'

'I haven't got the bloody job yet,' she said under her breath. She was furious with Dexter. He had no business to tell his mother about the interview.

'– or do I mean c-c-com. Dash it. Com something. Commiserations?' Dexter's mother said. 'Commiserations are probably nearer what I mean. It's my son who should be congratulated – he's a very lucky man. Perhaps I shouldn't say this, but you know he was a bit of a mess before he met you. Of course it can't have been much fun looking after two small boys on his own, with no one, no wife, to share things with. Not much fun for the children, either, I dare say. They talk about you a lot, Moy; they're clearly extremely fend fend *fond* of you. Especially Frankie, I think. Only this morning he said "We're going to see *Moy* on Sunday." He – are you all right, Moy? What's that strange noise?'

Moy was aware of having made some sort of gargling or coughing or choking noise. 'It's the television. Hang on, I'll turn it down.'

'Ah,' Dexter's mother said.

Moy couldn't turn the television down because it wasn't on. Instead, she filled her wineglass with whiskey and drank it straight off. She ran through to the kitchen and found her jacket and the cigarettes in its pocket. It was over a year since she'd stopped smoking, but this morning, arriving early for the interview, she'd decided she couldn't manage without one fag at least. With twenty minutes to spare, she'd bought a pack of Camel Lights and sat in the, empty at that hour, Garfunkels coffee place in the Strand and smoked two. After the interview she'd stood in a crowded bar in Holborn and smoked three.

I will kill him for this, she decided as she lit her cigarette. 'Okay, I'm here,' she told Dexter's mother.

'I wouldn't want to um.' A pause. 'Under*estimate* the difficulties of being a stepmum,' Dexter's mother said, 'it's a huge undertaking. But you've got such an advantage, May, *Moy*, having won those two boys' hearts already.'

Moy took long pulls of her cigarette. There was no ashtray to hand, and she had to lean backwards to flick ash into her wineglass.

'You really have, you know,' said Dexter's mother.

'Are you still there?' she asked, because Moy still hadn't said anything.

'Yep.'

'Of course I can't help hoping that once you've both got used to being married and being a family D will decide the time has come to take over the farm – I confess I'm finding it a bit of a struggle. And Donald isn't getting any younger – he'll be sixty-nine in October. We're both getting too. Dash it. What is it? *rickety* for this job. I would sell up, you know, I will have to sell up in the next year or two if D really isn't interested. Do you think he is?'

Dexter had said nothing to Moy about taking over the farm. There'd been no mention of the possibility or likelihood of his taking over his mother's farm.

'I don't know,' Moy said, 'he doesn't talk about it to me.'

'Do you think you could make something of – ? I can't pretend it's an easy life, but . . . I think I remember you telling me you liked the place?'

'Well, yes.' She was unsure whether by 'place' Dexter's mother meant the house or the land or the assortment of animals on the land. Or all of it. She had liked the house – mid-Victorian, gabled, built of unmellowable red brick – on the two visits, the first in January, the second in September, she'd made there with Dexter and Dig and Frankie. She had liked it in the way you can afford to like, and feel romantic about, dilapidated and comfortless houses (that bathroom!) you visit for a short time and whose reclamation and upkeep are no responsibility of yours. It had been fun – almost like a game – hunting for enough buckets and saucepans and mixing bowls to contain the downpour that had gushed through the roof, in a dozen places, during the autumn visit. In their different ways, the bony January landscape and the choked September garden had struck her as beautiful. She had never owned a garden, had always wanted one. Had been very envious of that one.

'Perhaps you could try and discuss it with him?' Dexter's mother was saying. 'He changes the subject whenever I try. But I need to know. If I could be sure D was going to take over the, er, farm, soon, I'll hang on. Otherwise, I'll have to sell.'

'All right, then,' Moy said, 'I'll talk to him.'

'To get back to your wad, wed, *wedding* plans,' Dexter's mother said. 'What sort of wedding is it going to be? You're welcome to have it here, you know. And have you decided on a date? D was in a hurry when he rang and I didn't have a chance to –'

'No. No, we haven't. In fact –'

'Something else I wanted to ask him, and can now ask you – is it a, um, secret? Or am I allowed to tell people? You know, our neighbours here, people who've known D all his life, and care about him? And do his sisters know? He asked me not to tell the boys. I imagine you'll want to tell them yourselves.'

'Please don't tell them.' She dropped what was left of the cigarette into her wineglass, where it fizzled and died. 'Please don't tell Dig and Frankie – or anyone. It is a secret. No one knows. My father doesn't know.'

'Ah,' Dexter's mother said.

THE PUB was usually full by ten o'clock but the hot evening had driven most of the drinkers outside, where they stood in little gangs on the pavement and in the street. After so many days of rain and wind, the still heat had generated a carnival atmosphere, and beyond the open pub doors a lot of shouting and shrieking and laughing was going on. Some singing, also. *Do-wah-diddy diddy dum diddy do. (I Can't Get No) Satisfaction* – as though the crowd out there, most of whom must have been born in the eighties, were sixties babes, stuck in a sixties time warp. Dexter, standing at the bar, eyeing himself in the panel of frost-patterned mirror glass that ran along the back of the bar, could hear these noises. In the glass, he could see his head, his neck, his shoulders, and the top half of his black T-shirted chest. If he raised them, he could see his arms, and his elbows, and his hands. He knew they had to be his arms (and elbows and hands), and that the man in the glass had to be himself; but the physical distance that separated them, coupled with the backdrop of saloon the mirror man had that he might well not have, made the mirror man seem a stranger. The mirror man was smaller, and smaller-boned, than he was. He had narrower shoulders, but – a trick of the crude bar lighting, no doubt – a bigger and broader nose.

Another difference about the mirror man: he looked a lot lonelier than Dexter, who had chosen to drink alone, felt himself to be. He looked real *lonesome* – one of those bleak barflies, who'd long ago lost the battle with hooch, in a Hopper painting. He had the defeated air – take away Frankie's hat and mac and the dancing couples in the background – of Frank Sinatra, staring into his whiskey glass on the LP sleeve of *No One Cares*, an album that Dexter's father had owned, and that Dexter now owned.

There was no one else up his end of the bar. Apart from the customers queuing for refills and, once they'd achieved them, pushing their way out again, there were only five people in the place: Ken the barman, Yvonne his pug-faced assistant, and three solo drinkers, one of whom, a guy named Steve, Dexter knew. Knew not as a friend but as a drinking companion. Knew a lot about – job, wife, grown-up kids, political persuasion, sporting interests, taste in beer and holiday resorts and movies and TV, as Steve knew a lot about him – but not his phone number. The confessional stuff he and Steve sometimes went in for when they'd had a few did not quite constitute friendship, Dexter recognised. They'd never checked out each other's domestic arrangements, for one thing. (Steve lived in a maisonette, somewhere off the Bethnal Green Road.) For another, Dexter, so far as he was aware, had never set eyes on Steve's wife, though he knew her name, Helen, and that she managed a branch of Dorothy Perkins. Also that she had fantastic tits and was good in the sack. I'm lucky there, at least, Steve had told him once, I got no complaints in that department.

Another thing about the relationship that made it seem less, or other, than friendship: he and Steve had never met, by design, outside the pub. On the one occasion they had bumped into each other – literally, forcing their supermarket trolleys in the Weetabix direction – Dexter, while saying Hi there, and How *are* you? had had to rack his brains to place Steve (who was not where he should have been, wherever that was) and to remember his name.

He liked what he knew of Steve, who was a big, broad, bald, easygoing man of fifty or so, and he respected him – a surprise because they'd got off to a dodgy start. Early on in their first exchanges Steve had accused Dexter of being a yuppy. Not in a rude or scornful way, but cheerfully and matter-of-factly. Well, you would think that, Steve had said about whatever comment it was Dexter had made, that he could no longer recall, that's what a yuppy *would* think.

He had been offended by Steve's remark. He'd told Steve he was wrong there, there was nothing upwardly mobile about *him*. If Steve must know, it was downhill all the way. He'd pointed out that not only did he not drive a Beamer or an Alpha or a Jeep, he didn't own any wheels at all. Except pushbike wheels. Some yuppy, he'd said. Steve had stood his ground, however: You're youngish, you're urban, you're professional, course you're a yuppy. He'd gone on to suggest that Dexter's voice was the real giveaway. You don' talk like the rest of us round here, now do you?

Dexter was aware that he had a slight, slightly nasal, drawl. In his early twenties, partly to disguise his Shropshire origins, he'd cultivated a West Coast American accent, logical extension of the Mean Streets fantasy life he was living at that time. The accent had modified through the years, so that when he first met Steve he'd sounded, he hoped, a bit like Martin Amis – a bit like Martin Amis with a head cold or sinus trouble – though in fact his drawl was often mistaken for an Irish accent. When this happened he usually played along and played the Irish up. To Steve he'd said, Now why would I be talkin' like you? – I'm a Mick. Don't you recognize a Mick when you're hearin' one? Steve had smiled and pointed to Dexter's feet, gloved in black calf loafers with a chrome snaffle decoration. Dose shoes now, Steve had said, in stage Irish that even to Dexter sounded a lot more authentic than his own effort – dey're yuppy shoes for sure. Don' you go tellin' me they didn't cost a bob or two.

The loafers had cost Dexter a bob or two; he'd bought them when he was earning a heavy-duty salary. He kept them polished, but they were falling apart. He'd taken off his right shoe and shown Steve the hole in the sole that went through to his sock, and the split stitching in the uppers. Steve had grinned broadly at this evidence of penury. He'd said, yeah, but there's a safety net under people like you. Your sort never have to fall very far. Then he'd said, Don' mind me mate, I'm only taking the piss. What you drinkin'? Guinness? After that they'd introduced themselves. After that they'd had something approaching a decent conversation.

He could see Steve's huge bulk perched on one of the cowboy-saloon-style stools – wood seats with spine-injuring curved back rests, fancily carved – that had recently replaced the old plush 'n' grease ones, at the other end of the bar. He had his back to Dexter, and Dexter hoped he hadn't spotted him. He didn't feel like talking. He wanted to get hammered on his own.

'Another?' he mouthed at Yvonne, who was frantically drying glasses. He slid his empty mug towards her.

'What was it?' Yvonne snapped.

'John Smith.'

Steve must have heard this, or intuited it. He turned round. He raised his beer mug and called out Cheers, Dex.

'Cheers,' he said flatly. *Don't come near me.* But Steve had climbed down from his cowboy stool, and was on his way.

'That bad?' Steve said, leaning heavily on the bar.

'Yeah.' He lowered his head and took a slurp from his overfull beer mug.

'Work, women or what?'

'Yeah.'

'Cigarette?'

He shook his head, and Steve lit one for himself. Steve said, 'Your ex playing you up?'

Steve knew all about his ex. He knew all sorts of intimate and true, and exaggerated, and wildly untrue, and slanderous, things about Hyacinth that Dexter had confided during the two years they'd downed pints together.

'Something like that.'

'Wanna talk about it?'

'Nah. Don't think so. No point.'

They drank in silence. Eventually, he said, 'I'm not much company, sorry.'

'Wan' me t' go?'

'Up to you.' It sounded ungracious, so he said 'No. But let's talk about something else.'

'What you drinkin'?'

Dexter told him.

97

'Same again – or a short? Jameson's?'

'Better not.' Though a triple Irish, preferably Green Spot or Bushmills, was what he felt he could do with. The pub didn't stock Green Spot, only Jameson's, but even that was more expensive than Bell's or Grouse. Because it had to cross the water to get here? Because Ireland – Ulster and Eire – had devised a specially punitive export tax on their booze? He'd quizzed landlords and retailers and supermarket supervisors, but no one seemed to know.

'Vonny!' Steve called to Yvonne's harassed back view. 'We're dyin' of thirst down here.'

'All set for Fun Week then?' he asked Dexter, when he at last got Yvonne's attention.

'Oh sure. You bet.'

'Read any good books lately?' – Steve's next question. He usually asked Dexter this at some point, and usually Dexter didn't mind it. It was Steve's, unironical and unsatirical, way of asking about his job, and sometimes he was able to answer, Well yes I have, and tell Steve what the good book was, and a bit about the plot. Steve was a thriller man, exclusively, and whenever Dexter had a freebee proof or review copy of a thriller he thought Steve might enjoy, he brought it to the pub on a Friday, Friday being the one day of the week Steve was almost certain to be there. Then the next time they found themselves together at the bar, Steve would give a detailed critique of the book and mark it out of ten. Or he'd hand it back and say, 'Couldn't get along with the fucker, couldn't get along with it at all.' He and Steve had had some good and bad and impassioned arguments about the books, and the authors, Dexter recommended.

Today, when Steve asked his usual question, he merely

made a throat-cutting gesture with the forefinger of his right hand.

Their beers came. While they drank, they discussed the impending fifth Test Match, and England's, probable, first innings collapse. Listening to, or watching cricket was one of the few bonuses about working from home Dexter would admit to. When a Test was being played he geared his day to it, placing the radio close to his ear and keeping the TV on – that's to say, vision on, sound off – in the living room, so that he could dash through and watch when something exciting was happening – or sounded as though it were about to happen. When watching, he kept the TV sound down and the radio sound up, as cricket fans tended to, on account of the radio commentary, even post-Jonners, being so superior to the screen version. Another enjoyable thing, he found, about the radio commentary was the 'Leg Bye' (his name for it) chitchat, about hats and cakes and skies and pigeons, that Henry Blofeld went in for. When Blowers said, Oh dear, I suppose I'd better tell you the score, otherwise you'll all be ringing in to complain, Dexter felt embraced. He felt included in a cosy blood-brotherhood of cricket fanatics and aficionados.

'. . . they'll be daft if they select *him*,' Steve said. 'Bet you anything you like they will, though.'

'Who? What?' he said stupidly. He hadn't been listening. He'd been worrying about the rejected engagement ring. Every time he'd rootled around in his combats' thigh pocket for beer money, his fingers had come up against the smooth leather of the ring box. He must take it back to the jeweller's tomorrow, before he lost it. What exactly had he agreed with the assistant? He couldn't remember. He was aware, suddenly, of having drunk at least three pints too many, and gripped the bar rail to steady himself. He shook his head fast and vigorously. Time to interrupt Steve's monologue, he decided; time to contribute something scintillating to the cricket debate: 'I've got a soft spot for Mike Atherton, y'know, Steve,' he said, putting a hand on Steve's enormous arm, then gripping the arm tight. 'I've got a really really soft spot for that guy, d'you know that?'

Steve removed Dexter's hand. 'Time you went home?' he said.

'Can't go home.' He was feeling sick now. He rested his head on the counter, and felt worse. Mixed in with the nausea were other feelings, jostling for position: shame and rage and self-pity. Despair. 'Moy's at home,' he confided to the beer-puddled counter, 'Moy doesn't want me home. Moy — hey —'

Steve had put a hand under his chin, and was trying to lift his head upright. 'C'm on, Dex, c'mon now, c'mon.'

'D'you know what that bitch is up to?' He shouted into Steve's face. 'She's trying to take my kids away. She's got the court on her side, she —'

'*Moy* is?'

'My ex is. My *ex*. Hyacinth is.'

'She hasn't a hope, old son. She abandoned them. No court's ever goin' to —'

'That's all you know. But I know what I know. I know how clever she is. *I* know —' His impassioned forearm struck his empty beer mug, sending it spinning, without bouncing, clear over the back of the bar, where it landed in the tray of cleanish glasses Yvonne had just finished drying.

Dexter and Steve were sitting on a bench in the triangular

miniature park, officially named Jesus Green, that a triangle of streets shared and which, on its west side, faced Dexter's terrace. The Green was dotted with young sycamore and mountain ash trees and fenced with iron railings through which you entered by one of five small iron gates. People walked their dogs here, as early as six a.m., before they went to work, although dogs were not allowed on the Green. The bench Dexter and Steve were sitting on, and others like it, were taken up, on summer mornings and afternoons, by solitary old men and drunks of both sexes, and by youngish mothers who, while occupied with talk, contrived to keep one hand on their parked buggies and one eye on their roaming toddlers. After tea the junior school kids – boys mostly because the mothers round here seldom allowed their daughters to play out unattended – took over the Green. Football and cricket, although ball games were forbidden at any time of day, took over. Shouts and screams and yells took over. Not until it was almost dark did the feral teenagers steal out; and gloom around under the trees; and smoke; and crack beer cans. (And leave the beer cans where they fell, or were hurled. Where Dexter, after his early morning run, on a before-breakfast litter patrol with a black plastic sack, would find and dispose of them.) But it was one-thirty in the morning, and as far as they could see – as far as the street lights, two of which weren't working, allowed them to see – Dexter and Steve had the Green to themselves.

'You're lucky to have all this grass right outside your front door,' Steve said. 'Handy for the kids.'

'Yeah, 'know.' The handy grass had been a big factor in his decision to buy his house. He'd told Steve this ages ago, when Steve asked him what made him move to a part of London that he himself was desperate to get away from. We've got a communal mini park-cum-garden opposite our street, he'd told Steve, explaining that the only reason it existed was because so many streets had been pulled down. The demolition happened in the early seventies, he'd explained. They'd intended to destroy all the terraces, including his own, and to put up high-rises in their place, but had run out of cash and enthusiasm. He'd said he had mixed feelings about the Green, which was there more by accident than design. The accident had turned out to be a bonus for the whole neighbourhood, of course; it was a good place to look at and to walk in, but against that you had to weigh up the criminal destruction of street after street of essentially sound, unusually handsome, historically important, Burdett-Coutts terraces. Of communities also. Of *lives*. So he had mixed feelings. Sometimes, when he was kicking a ball around with his kids, he felt guilty, or maybe angry, he'd told Steve. He couldn't forget he was kicking a ball in someone's front room. What should have been someone's front room.

Steve hadn't been too impressed by these anxieties. He'd pointed out that cities the world over were constantly changing and evolving – they had to, didn't they, in order to meet the needs of each new generation. Of course the East End was a special case, having lost so much of its identity in the Blitz, but really it didn't matter what part of London you was stood in, you was always going to be surrounded by the ghosts of earlier Londons. The London that went up in the Great Fire, for instance. He didn't think Dexter had any cause to worry himself about the streets round him that had gone missing. The Green was a fact, it was there, and the kids had somewhere to play – why spit on your luck?

'You got an amenity here a lot of people would give their eye teeth for,' Steve said now. 'I know I would. Want one of these?' He offered Dexter his cigarette packet. He always did this – offered the packet before taking a cigarette himself – although he must have known by now that Dexter didn't smoke. He seemed to believe that Dexter really wanted a cigarette, and was denying himself, and would give in sooner or later if he kept pressing.

'Eye teeth,' Dexter said, '*eye teeth*. I can see that eye teeth are valuable to their owner, it would obviously be a huge *sacrifice* to give your eye teeth up – I suppose that's the point. That must be the point. But eye teeth haven't exactly got bargaining power, have they? I mean, say you pulled yours out now, had them pulled, rather, and handed them over to me, what the fuck would I –'

Steve ignored this, as, Dexter had noticed, he tended to ignore all his drinking partner's half-cut excursions into the surreal or the abstract or the cussedly literalist. 'I can't think why you don't get outta London altogether,' he said. 'I would if I was you. If I had a farm of my own to go to.'

'It isn't a *farm*. I've told you. It's a run-down smallholding. It's only my mother calls it the *Farm*.' For a moment he saw his birthright in its August mien: the sour fields of docks and thistles and venomous ragwort; the scruffy sheep; the crumbling and abandoned cow sheds and pig sties; the burst bags of fertiliser that, along with coils of crusty chicken wire and barbed wire and tyres and the wheels and spikes of long-defunct machinery, decorated the cracked concrete of the yard; the stinking, green fur-coated, slurry pit. He'd described these sights and smells to Steve. He'd explained the boredom of the winters in that place, the cold frugality that, all those years

103

ago, had made him work hard at his A Levels to escape his future there.

He had not told Steve – what he reserved, and painted up, for another type of audience altogether – about the benefits of that life. How the landscape could look in pale sunshine and under hard frost. How big and soft the night skies were in June (and how sweetly smelling, of hay, the night air). How, on days of blustery wind and sun, he could stand for hours on Brown Clee Hill watching the shadows of clouds chasing the sun over the jigsaw fields below. Also, the sweaty satisfaction he'd felt as a lad, helping his father in the lambing shed. Or mending fences, or mixing feeds. Or coppicing in the Lower Copse. Man's work, he'd thought when he was eight or nine. Real, hard, man's work, the only kind worth doing.

He had not told Steve how, on his most recent visit to the place, he'd found himself walking the entire three hundred acres. (For it was a farm; not the smallholding he had described to Steve.) On an impulse, he'd whistled up the dogs, pulled on his father's old cap, left his mother and Moy and his kids in the kitchen, and gone out into the rain. Trudging uphill along the mud track that bordered the Six Acre (pasture for as long as anyone remembered but now, let to a conglomerate, under plough), noting that the hedgerow sorbuses he'd helped his mother plant to mark the Silver Jubilee were now considerable trees, he'd said aloud what he normally chose to deny even to himself: This land is mine. This land my father and my grandfather and my great-grandfather farmed belongs to me. At the top of the slope he'd turned and looked back, rain streaming down his face like tears, and said it again. Not with pride, he'd believed then. Not with the pride of ownership, but with a feeling of yes, well, okay, *duty* and *responsibility* and *family history*.

'You'd hate it, Steve.' He said it with such passion he nearly fell off the bench. 'You'd hate that hillbilly, hayseedy, backwoodsy life. You'd be bored witless. And broke.'

'Okay, okay,' Steve said.

'The only thing my mother manages to make any profit from is the clay pigeon shoot she runs. And the farm shop – but of course she has to pay someone to run it. All the rest is debt.'

'Okay, okay. Change of subject then. Who was that woman gave you the come-on in the bar? I see her in the pub time to time.'

'Woman?' He couldn't remember any woman. Noticing one, being accosted by one. 'I don't remember any woman.'

Steve painted a picture of Sandy Hitchcock, graphically and unpleasantly recognizable.

'Oh her. Was she there? Fuck.' Sandy Hitchcock had a comic walk-on part in the situation tragedy of his life, he explained to Steve. He didn't know her. He couldn't say he knew her. One of her kids was a mucker of one of his kids, was all.

Steve dropped his cigarette butt on to the circular tarmac path that formed the centrepiece of the Green, and flattened it with a toe. 'She seemed to know you pretty well.'

'Oh yeah? Tell me what she said then.'

'She said she didn't think much of the gear you was wearing, she liked you better in yer knickers.'

'Quite witty for her.' He felt he ought to explain, he owed it to Steve to explain, he owed it to himself to

105

explain, what the knickers reference was about, but he couldn't be fagged. He was tired, and as soon as he admitted it to himself began to yawn.

'If you're okay now, I'll be going,' Steve said. 'God knows what Helen's going to say. Half an hour max, was what I told her. Just a coupla pints, an' I'll be back. You won' even have time to miss me, I said.'

'Shit.' Now that he was more or less himself, he remembered, or thought he did, that Steve had walked him several blocks to sober him up; and a sore left upper arm and elbow – where Steve had gripped him, presumably – seemed to confirm this. Deep breaths, he thought he remembered. Being made to stop and take them. He had a picture of himself tripping and staggering, and of Steve catching him, each time, just before his legs gave way. And he seemed to recall an argument with Steve when Steve had insisted, after an hour or so of walking, or marching, or staggering the streets, on seeing him home. On seeing him to, and through, his front door. But when they reached his front door he had refused to go in. He'd said he couldn't face Moy, who was a night owl and probably still up. (There had been no lights on in the house to corroborate this fiction.) Don't go yet, he'd begged Steve. Let's go and sit on a bench. They were grown men, he'd reminded Steve, they were adults, it was a fine night – who said they had to go home? Who the fuck said they had to?

And kind Steve had hesitated, and been lost.

'She's not going to believe my mobile's packed it in,' Steve said. 'She's never goin' to believe I tried to phone her. She'll say, You a BT engineer and can't get your phone sorted? Tell me another.'

'I'm really sorry,' he said as Steve got to his feet. 'I hope I haven't landed you in it. You're a star.'

'Hope you get it sorted with Moy. Hope she changes her mind. If that's what you want. You going in now?'

He said he was going in. But not quite yet. In a bit.

'See ya, then,' Steve said, over his shoulder, walking away.

THE FIRST time Moy set eyes on Dexter she had been standing in his front doorway, and now, whenever he looked like taking too much control of her life, she worried that her lover's home ground had been an unnatural and possibly inauspicious place for their first meeting. He had opened his own front door, and let her into his house, she would remember then. He had graciously allowed her to inhabit his space for half an hour or so. His assuming of power so early on – even though hardly his fault or plan – was bad news, surely, if not a bad omen.

Neutral territory – such as trains, or boats, or planes, or cafés, or art galleries, or churchyards, or pubs or clubs or supermarkets, or other people's living rooms – was where two people who were destined to share their lives ought first to exchange significant looks and words, Moy believed.

She had not known that Dexter Bucknell existed until a few hours before she rang his doorbell. If she hadn't phoned a married friend, Leila Davis, after work to ask if

Leila was on for a movie, she would not have met Dexter that evening and maybe not at all.

About the movie Leila had said yes, in theory she was on, there wasn't a problem about babysitting because Robert was at home. But it would have to be a late movie because she was tied up till nine.

How tied up? Tied up how? Moy had wanted to know.

With a *creative writing* course, Leila had said with heavy and jokey emphasis. She was half-way through a ten-week course of two-hour sessions – Wednesday evenings, seven till nine. Don't ask her why, Leila said, because really she wasn't sure. She saw the advert and thought, Well, it'll get me away from the nappies for a few hours. I might turn out to be a genius. Why not give it a go?

Was the course any good? Moy asked, did Leila enjoy it? Had she written anything she was pleased with? How many students were in the class? What sort of students? Was Leila going to be rich and famous?

Leila said she was going to be very rich and very famous but not, she thought, through creative writing. She said that to that end a course in creative book-keeping might be more useful. She said that most of the class, which was not called a class but a workshop, were loonies or a hundred years old. There were fourteen students alto-gether, or there were supposed to be, but not everyone turned up every week. One girl called Ruth something, the only student who could loosely be termed a girl, the only one she felt she had anything in common with and who'd shared the sofa with her the first evening, had not returned for more. This had surprised her, Leila told Moy, because they'd had to pay for the course in advance, and also because Ruth had seemed keen, the one person in the room who really wanted to hear what the tutor had to say.

But perhaps Ruth had been faking interest; perhaps she was incredibly rich and could afford to enrol for courses and then not go to them. Perhaps she did that sort of thing all the time. There was only one man in their group, a white-bearded know-all with moist red lips – he *always* turned up; the rest, as she'd said, were old women. Oh, apart from a silent youth of about sixteen – she'd forgotten about him.

Moy had imagined Leila's creative writing course to be a borough council thing, a Further Education thing, that took place in a Dickensian hall or a sixties glass 'n' concrete flat-roof, but when she asked, Leila said, No, it wasn't like that. The course was private. It was run by an ex-publisher called Dexter Bucknell from his own living room in Bethnal Green. The living room was not exactly large, Leila said, and there was a shortage of chairs. For the initial session, which everyone had tipped up to, three people had had to make do with cushions on the uncarpeted floor. Old Whitebeard had complained about the lack of chairs. If the seating arrangements weren't adequate the following week, Old Whitebeard had said, if they weren't entirely satisfactory, Bucknell would have to give their money back. It was a disgrace also that they were expected to write on their knees; he had not unnaturally assumed that tables would be provided. Another thing: Bucknell had no business allowing his small children to interrupt the workshop in mid-session – it was not what they were paying for. (Leila explained to Moy at this point that early on in the evening, while their creative writing tutor was giving a run-through of how he envisaged the course working – and warning them what a hard taskmaster he was going to be – a small boy had shouted down the stairs that there was no loo paper in the

110

bathroom. Fits of giggles, plus a good deal of bumping and banging on the living room ceiling, had followed. Twice, their tutor had had to abandon his spiel and dash up the stairs to read the riot act.)

Moy said that Leila had plenty to write about, at least. She certainly wasn't going to be short of material. *Tales of Old Whitebeard* was a book she really looked forward to. 'Old Whitebeard and the Bog Roll' was a story she simply couldn't wait to read.

Leila said she doubted she'd ever get to finish a story because everything she wrote between sessions was taken apart in the workshops. Not just by the tutor either – everyone was allowed a go. Also, at least half of what DB gave them to do for homework consisted of reading, not writing. At the end of the first workshop, he'd handed them a reading list and said, Get on with that. Work your way through that – in the order I've given you. We're going to spend the last twenty minutes of every session discussing the books on this list. The library should have them. If not, they're all in paperback. Leila said she thought Old Whitebeard was going to have a heart attack when DB produced his reading list. He had three completed novels in manuscript, he informed the class, and had expected a professional appraisal, plus advice about publication. That's what he'd paid for. He had not paid for reading lessons which –

Moy had used the wall phone in her studio to make this call, and there was no chair within reach. She needed to sit down. She said, Sorry to interrupt, but perhaps they ought to try for a movie another evening? It sounded to her as though Leila would not be fit for much after her creative writing class. Anyway, what cinema could they get to in time when Leila couldn't leave Bethnal Green till nine?

111

And it would be well after nine, wouldn't it, by the time Leila actually got away?

Leila said, okay, they'd scrap the movie, there was nothing on she was desperate to see. But if Moy could bear to get herself all the way to Bethnal Green, why didn't they go out to supper together instead? There must be *somewhere* round there where they could eat. She'd ask her lovely tutor if he knew of anywhere.

Was her tutor lovely? Moy wanted to know, after she'd agreed to go all the way to Bethnal Green. Was he lovely to look at?

No, not at all, Leila said. She didn't think so. He was weird-looking. He was a bit odd too, a bit abrupt, a bit lofty and superior, she wasn't sure if she liked him. But Moy could make up her own mind about that when she met him. Had she got a pencil? Because the walk from Liverpool Street was quite tricky. Bethnal Green Tube station might be marginally nearer, Moy might prefer to go to Bethnal Green, but she couldn't tell her the route from there because she'd never tried it. Either way, Moy was going to have a bit of a hike.

'Try and get there by quarter to nine,' Leila said, 'then you'll be able to sit in on the last quarter of an hour of our workshop. I'd like to know what you make of it.'

Despite Leila's directions, Moy got lost trying to find Dexter Bucknell's street. She'd left Clapham Junction earlier than she thought strictly necessary to allow time for hold-ups, but it turned out to be not early enough. Somewhere between Tower Hill and Aldgate East the swaying and smelly train had groaned and stopped; and not moved again for ten minutes. (A youngish guy in her carriage had left his seat at this point to pace menacingly up and down before kick-boxing the carriage doors.) Then on the walk from Liverpool Street she took a wrong turning out of Brick Lane and, when she'd resolved that one, another out of Columbia Road. Then several more wrong turnings. All the little, mazed, streets at the back of Columbia Road looked exactly the same. When she eventually pressed Dexter Bucknell's doorbell, it was twenty to ten.

'You haven't told me yet what you thought of him,' Leila said. They were sitting at one of ten big, round tables in the Vietnamese café Dexter Bucknell had recommended. The café wasn't licensed, but Dexter had told them there was an offie across the road, on the corner of Kingsland Road and Shoreditch High Street, and they could get a bottle there. (Which they had.) He said the café was a bit like a school canteen inside, but that shouldn't put them off, the food was excellent. And cheap. He said he wished he could go with them, he'd really like to, but he couldn't leave his kids alone in the house.

'I'm not sure what to make of him,' Moy said. 'He's not quite how I imagined. Of course, I can't tell what he's like as a person, but I didn't find him weird-looking. I thought he was quite attractive.'

This was an understatement: she had thought Dexter – his pallor, his dramatic eyebrows, his sideways and secretive look – very attractive. Not only that, he had seemed familiar in some way; she felt she must have met him somewhere.

'I just can't get over that poor Ruth girl,' Leila said. 'I'm sorry to go on about it but I can't get it out of my head. Did I tell you I sat next to her on the first evening? On that two-seater thing you sat on. Can I have a taste of that? It looks rather good. It looks nicer than mine.'

113

'Yes, you did tell me.' Moy pushed her plate within Leila's reach. 'And you told me –'

'Delicious, no?' Leila said. She waved her fork at Moy. 'Really, really good.' She put her fork down. 'No, as I say, I keep getting pictures of Ruth. I keep seeing her little ears and her earrings. She had that almost grey ash-blonde hair, and it was piled up on top of her head – like this? – in that casual-chic way. Though if I wore my hair like that it would be a mess – I just can't do scruffy. And I keep seeing her wrists – they were tiny – and her long, thin fingers – I always wish I had fingers like that. You couldn't help noticing them, she kept fiddling with her notebook – opening it, and shutting it again. I even envied her profile, for God's sake. It just shows you should never envy anyone anything, doesn't it? Because you just don't know.' And Leila took a long and thoughtful swallow of wine.

'I think you should try not to think about it any more,' Moy said. 'I think –'

Leila said, Okay, she knew she was being a bore, she would stop in a minute, but there were things she needed to tell Moy first, if Moy didn't mind. For instance, had she told Moy about the introductory business they'd had to go through on the first evening? No? Well, DB had made them coffee – it took ages, he hadn't got a big enough pot – and then they'd had to introduce themselves in turn and say something about themselves – give a sort of potted autobiography. Hideous, as Moy could imagine. They had to say how long they'd been writing, and if they hadn't written anything why they wanted to start. They had to say who their favourite writers were. 'I couldn't think of anyone, not at the time. Do you think we should go and get another bottle? What do you feel?'

'Well, I've got to work in the morning,' Moy said. 'I really should be at work by eight at the latest because –'

'Okay. I'll make do with water – better for Zuleika, anyway. She's mostly on the bottle now but has a late-night top-up from me. Where was I? Oh yes. While Ruth and I were waiting our turn she whispered to me that she wrote stories all the time, she had notebooks full of them. She said she was sure they were no good, but she was going to leave them with the tutor for him to have a look at, she wanted some proper criticism. But when she introduced herself she didn't even mention her stories. All she said was, My name's Ruth whatever, I'm a mother and I live near Victoria Park. Nothing else at all. When we got up to go she put the notebook in her carrier bag. I said, Aren't you going to let him see your stuff? You said you were going to. Anyway, that's why we're here, that's what he's *for*. And she smiled and said, No.'

'That's sad,' Moy said. 'I mean it's all sad. It's awful. Awful for her children.'

Leila had been talking about Ruth the whole time they'd been sitting in the café. Aside from ordering their food – fish balls to start with for Leila, tofu satay for Moy, with, to follow, stewed tilapia with a ginger and onion side salad (Moy) and something called Shaking Beef (Leila) – and apart from Leila's one question to Moy about what she'd made of Dexter Bucknell, Ruth, and Ruth's suicide, had been the sole topic of conversation so far. Leila had learnt the news about Ruth from the tutor, after the other students had left, in the three-quarters of an hour they were alone together waiting for Moy to arrive. He'd had a letter from Ruth's husband that morning, he told Leila. The reason Ruth hadn't come to the creative writing classes was because she was dead. Because she had committed suicide. It had happened five weeks ago. There'd been no warning. She hadn't seemed depressed beforehand, although she had had bouts of depression in the past. Ruth's husband felt he should write and explain her absence because Ruth would have wanted him to. She was a courteous person and wouldn't have wanted Mr Bucknell to think she wasn't interested in his class and couldn't be bothered to turn up. The truth was, she'd been very interested in the class. She'd bought all the paperbacks on the reading list Mr Bucknell had given her and had already started on the Chekhov stories. Two of these, 'Ariadne' and 'The House with an Attic', they'd read aloud to each other in bed.

After describing the letter, Leila told Moy, Dexter had given it to Leila to read. He'd said he probably shouldn't do this, but he needed to share it with someone. He'd rather Leila didn't tell the other students about the letter, though; he'd prefer it if no one else knew that Ruth had topped herself. He said he couldn't bear the idea of Norman Willson-Jones (Old Whitebeard, Leila explained) knowing anything.

'The letter was extraordinary – it was full of spelling mistakes, it was barely literate,' Leila said. 'It didn't mention suicide, it said *took her own life*.' She said she found the letter, especially the *took her own life* and the spelling mistakes, painful. She wasn't sure why, but it was the spelling mistakes and the all-over-the-place handwriting that really got to her and made Ruth's death feel real.

Moy was very sorry about Ruth – what had happened was tragic – but she thought they'd talked about her long enough. And she thought Leila was making a bit of a meal of the death of someone she'd met only once. She hardly ever saw Leila now that Leila was married and had a toddler and a baby to look after. Having to talk about Ruth all evening, having to talk about *death*, was a waste of their time together.

She had another reason for wanting to change the conversation – or rather to push it sideways – Dexter Bucknell. All the time she'd been listening to Leila, nodding and giving her friend sympathetic or shocked looks, she'd been aware of his submerged presence – in her mind, or her consciousness, or whatever part of the brain it was that dealt with emotion and perception and memory. An exciting, waiting-to-be-explored, presence that felt more like an absence. While Leila had been describing Ruth's hands and ears and hairdo, Moy had been trying to describe Dexter Bucknell to herself. To draw him, to colour him, to give him believable shape. She had been trying to recreate his drawl, and to hear in her head the things he'd said. The exact words, was what she was after, and the precise intonations. Then, using the most unmissable items as reference points – wall hanging, clock, fireplace, blow-up of old black and white photograph of a farmhouse (above the fireplace?), floor-to-ceiling bookshelves in the alcoves either side of it – she had tried to reassemble his living room. Not too difficult a task, she'd imagined earlier, perched side by side with Leila on Dexter Bucknell's uncomfortable two-seater sofa, sipping a glass of cold red wine, the moment when she'd decided to commit Dexter, his room, and everything in it, to memory. Not too difficult a task, with a room as minimally furnished as his. (Moy hadn't seen all the impermanent and distracting chairs Dexter had put out for his students; by the time she arrived at the house they were back in the kitchen and in the two bedrooms, and one bathroom, where they belonged. Leila, apparently, had helped Dexter put the chairs away.)

But in the café, when she tried to retrieve the things she'd seen, and to place them, she found it not so easy. She was aware of gaps. She had a sense of unfocused shapes and of possibly invented colours. Had the wall hanging really been essentially red, as she now saw it, or purple? The wooden toy box with a Rocket-type steam engine painted on its lid – where was that housed, exactly? Under the window? How many glazing bars did the window have? Four? Or two? It was like that children's memory game, she thought later, the one where you're shown a tray of thirty objects and, when the tray is covered over or removed, have to write the objects down. Easy peasy, the seven-year-old Moy had decided, grabbing a pencil. Easy *peasy*. Only to find, when the objects were uncovered again, that she'd remembered fewer than half. (Even more surprising – several of the things she did have on her list were not ones on the tray.)

'Edward the Confessor.' She said it aloud, by mistake. She had suddenly realized who Dexter reminded her of. The stained-glass Edward in Canterbury cathedral. His mouth; his delicacy; his pallor. His uncertain, or haunted, look.

'Come again?' said Leila.

A waiter, removing their empty plates, asked if they wanted a sweet.

Moy said she was full, but why didn't Leila have something?

The waiter told Leila the lychees in lemon syrup were very very nice; he liked them, he often ate them.

'Robert says I'm getting fat,' Leila said, spooning in her lychees. 'He says if I get any fatter he'll leave.' She didn't sound distressed about this. She sounded happy – as people who are loved and who know they are in no danger of being abandoned can afford to sound. And she sounded smug, as slim women always do sound when they complain about being fat.

'Are you still seeing Richard? You haven't mentioned him,' Leila said.

'No.' Moy wasn't still seeing Richard, whom she'd been attached to, and then semi-detached from, for nearly two years. It had been her decision to end it but a part of her minded because a part of her still missed him – or missed the habit of him. *You're so wise*, he used to say to her, *you're so wise, my babykin. My beautiful wise darling.* When one evening she'd said to Richard, after yet another tedious misunderstanding, Look, I really think there's not much point in going on with this, do you? he'd left without argument and had not come back. He hadn't phoned, or written, either – as she'd expected and half hoped he would. He always had before. She didn't want to talk about Richard, or to think about him. She wanted to talk about Dexter Bucknell. But how to introduce his name in a sufficiently casual and spontaneous way? How to bring him in and not sound, to Leila's sharp ears, a lot too interested?

'Is there anyone else then?'

'Not specially, no.' Though there was no one at all. No one specially, no one not specially either.

Over their coffee she asked about Leila's children, in particular Aaron, Moy's godson, aged two.

Moy must come and see him soon, Leila said, he was changing so fast she would hardly recognize him. He could make whole sentences now. The sentences were very repetitive – he was fond of saying the same thing

119

fifteen times over, which drove her crazy – even so this new skill was very exciting.

Moy's work came up next. Leila wanted to know if she was managing to get enough, and if she was earning enough to get by, and Moy said, Yes, just about. Though it meant doing a lot of garish stuff she didn't enjoy, such as parrots and peacocks and galleons in full sail, for people's front doors and windows.

Eventually, tentatively, Leila enquired after Moy's brother, Joe. Was he okay?

Moy's brother Joe was schizophrenic. He had been diagnosed at eighteen and was now forty-four. Throughout this time he had had periods in hospital, some of these for a month or more, although recently – because of NHS cuts? Or a change of policy in the treatment of mental patients? Or because the drugs they gave schizophrenics these days were more effective? Moy wasn't sure – his stays on the ward had been brief, usually under a week. When well enough to manage on his own, Joe lived in a housing-association flat in Tooting. A miserable and smelly flat because, even when he was reasonably well, Joe seldom did manage in the way the health authorities and social services seemed to believe he should. Personal hygiene was something he had never got the hang of – the bath was mostly used as storage space. Cooking and cleaning were difficult for him, and washing-up a skill he had never fully acquired. The washing machine, microwave and vacuum cleaner, aids to his managing, had had some malevolence programmed into their workings so that they repeatedly and dramatically broke down. There was a demon in the flat, too, who endlessly hid, or stole, vital equipment: door keys, wallet, cash card, Disability Payment book, travel pass, cigarettes, cans of beer. Also, and more injuriously, his medication. Joe would turn the flat upside down to find these items, which might take days, and afterwards not be able to put the flat right side up again. Often, when Moy arrived, the place looked as though burglars had just visited, and sometimes Joe would say they had, and that he knew who they were. He had phoned the police, he would tell Moy; he'd named names, he'd offered evidence – but the police had refused to come.

'He's okay at the moment, touch wood,' Moy said. 'At least I think he is. I haven't heard from him for a fortnight.' Not hearing from him was usually a good sign, she explained. It usually meant he was stable and coping. Usually, but not always. Sometimes not hearing meant that Joe had forgotten to take his pills, or had decided not to take them. And as a result had gone haywire, and been sectioned – and no one had thought to let her know.

'I ought to check up on him every week,' Moy said. 'I know I ought to, but I put it off. I ought to see him more, he's only a bus ride away, but I can't face it.'

'I don't blame you,' Leila said. 'I don't think anyone would blame you. I don't know how you manage as it is. I'm sure I couldn't.'

All this time, Dexter Bucknell remained below the surface. It was Leila who brought him up, as they were getting ready to leave. She said, 'By the way, I thought you were a bit rough on my poor tutor when we left, I thought you were really quite rough on him. A bit mean, don't you think, when you'd drunk his wine.'

'Oh?' Moy was fighting with the sleeve of her coat. She kept putting her arm into a hole in the lining, and getting nowhere, and having to take her arm out and start again. 'In what way?'

'You know, when he asked if you'd like to join his workshop. He wasn't serious, you realize. It was just something to say. He didn't mean it.'

'What did I say then? Remind me.' Moy knew exactly what she'd said, and what Dexter Bucknell had said, but she wanted to be reminded. He'd said, as he opened the door for them to leave, Why don't you join our workshop? It's not too awful, I think – ask Leila. I'm sure we could fit you in. And she had replied, I spend my days being creative. I'm quite creative enough already, thank you very much.

Leila reminded Moy of this remark.

'That wasn't rough,' Moy said. 'You can't call that rough. Anyway, he didn't think it was, clearly; he laughed, if you remember. Shit, we're the last to leave.'

They were making their way through the suddenly deserted café, threading their way round abandoned chairs and tables. All around them were almost-drained glasses and full ashtrays and trampled napkins.

Their waiter was already at the door. He opened it wide for them. 'Good-night ladies, thank you, good-night.'

'Good-night *sweet* ladies, doesn't he mean,' Leila whispered to Moy.

Ten days after their supper outing, Moy had a telephone call from Leila. Dexter Bucknell had asked her for Moy's phone number, Leila said. She wasn't prepared to give it to him without Moy's say-so. 'I said I'd find out from you and let him know next week.'

'Well?' said Leila. 'How d'you feel about it? Do you want me to give it to him?'

Her voice had an edge to it, Moy thought. A little edge of impatience or annoyance. Or jealousy, even? Dexter

Bucknell was not Leila's property, of course; Leila loved Robert and could have no real, emotional or sexual, interest in Dexter. Even so, he was someone she saw once a week and had established some sort of rapport with. He was, together with his creative writing workshop, Leila's current *thing*. Some people don't like it when a friend looks like appropriating what they think of as their thing. It had happened to Moy a few times, and she hadn't liked it.

'I don't know anything about the guy,' she said carefully. 'I mean, I know he's got two kids, you told me about them. But has he got a wife or a partner? Is he a serial killer? You never said.'

'He did have a wife. As far as I can gather they're separated or divorced. I don't know what else goes on in his life. How could I? I don't know any more about him than you do.'

'I don't suppose it can do any harm to give him my phone number. The flat number, I mean. I hate being interrupted when I'm working.' She was smiling as she told this lie. She hoped Leila couldn't hear the smile, but feared the way her words came, out of a suddenly wide-stretched mouth, must be a give-away.

Moy had to wait another four weeks for Dexter's call, during which time she went through the various sorts of hell people waiting for a telephone call have to endure. She tried staying in all evening, and when that failed to draw him, being out. Keeping busy, the cool option, would not only limit her time for hoping and moping at home, it might act as a spur to him. Not might, *would*. (All at once, superstition was playing a big part in her life.) Eight of these keeping-busy evenings she spent at the cinema, sitting through films she wouldn't normally be bothered to leave home, and her TV set, to see. She invited herself to friends for supper and babysat, twice, for a neighbour. She took her brother, plus two mad acquaintances he'd asked along for the ride, out for a curry. (The management, when Joe and Gareth and Callum launched into a thunderous rugby singsong, asked them to leave.) And one night she went clubbing with Daria, the painter who rented the studio space on the floor above Moy's own, a girl ten years younger than herself, who still did the drugs-and-clubbing scene. Whatever she did to fill her evenings made no difference: the answerphone's red eye might be winking when she got home, but none of its messages was from him.

She could have phoned him, of course; he was in the phone book. She would have telephoned Dexter if a part of her hadn't felt sure he would get in touch eventually. If she hadn't been certain his call was worth waiting for.

He rang one Thursday at eight in the morning, as she was leaving for work. It didn't occur to her that it could be him at that hour. It was Joe, most likely. Her brother phoned when he felt the urge, which was sometimes at four in the morning. She did not feel like listening to Joe's relentless and uninterruptable monologue, which he'd been known to keep going for an hour or more.

But it might not be Joe. It might be a friend – Janet from art-school days, who'd written to say wasn't it high time they met up? – or a call to do with work. She put down her bag and listened while the answer machine went through its tricks. Then, on an impulse, just before the long tone, she picked up the receiver.

'Hallo?' a voice said.

She knew at once it was Dexter. 'Hallo.'

'Ha*llo.*'

'Hallo.'

'It's Dexter Bucknell,' the voice in her receiver said. 'Am I saying hallo to Moy Colley? Is that Moy Colley saying hallo to me?'

Moy said it was.

He'd wanted to call her before, Dexter said. He'd wanted to call her hundreds of times, but thought it best to wait till his creative writing course was finished.

Thought it best. Why? Who for? What did the course have to do with anything?

Dexter must have interpreted her silence as a question, for he immediately answered it: 'Because you and Leila are friends. I didn't want there to be any cross-linkage, if you get me.'

Moy said she wasn't sure if she did.

'Well I knew when I did call it would be to ask if I could see you,' Dexter said. 'And I was afraid you might tell Leila about it – about my call, about our meeting – that is, if you agreed to come out with me. Leila knew I had your phone number – I had to ask her for it because your number's not listed – and I thought she might quiz you to see if I'd been in touch. And then ask more questions. That would be quite natural of course, it's the sort of thing friends do, but I didn't like the idea. I didn't like the idea of – shit, I'm not explaining this at all well. What am I trying to say? What I'm trying to say is, I thought any conversations or meetings you and I might have ought to be, well, private. Not overheard, so to speak, by someone I was seeing professionally who also happens to be a close friend of yours.'

Not that close. Not really, now Leila had babies. 'I

haven't spoken to Leila for weeks,' she said. 'She hasn't quizzed me about you at all.'

Silence. Then Dexter said, 'The course ended yesterday. So. So – is there any chance of seeing you?'

What an extraordinary speech. (She decided this later, on her way to work.) What complicated anxieties. It occurred to her that if anyone else had voiced them she might not have believed him. She would probably have read the anxieties as blandishments, part of a trumped-up excuse for not phoning sooner. Or seen them as evidence of paranoia, or of some, controlling and calculating, personality disorder, and hung up. But she believed Dexter. When he said he wanted their calls and meetings to be private, she was touched by what seemed to her proof of a laudable attentiveness and seriousness. His lack of restraint in explaining his motives, she thought brave – a strength more than a weakness. Here, for the first time in her life, was someone who had no interest in double-dealing or even in less artful games playing, and did not mind saying so. Mixing it, muddying the waters – such jiggery-pokery, as her mother would have termed it, was not for him. I fancy this man, she thought. I could fall in love with him.

He wouldn't be the first person she had fallen for. She'd been through that illness fleetingly with Richard and, before Richard, with a host and variety of boys and men. It wasn't the fevered nights and transported days, the loss of appetite and concentration, the alternating lassitude and fits of consumptive energy, that she objected to, nor the way that the world around you appeared translated into a strangely harmonious place. Those early symptoms might be disturbing, but they were also exhilarating; they made you feel alive. And they never lasted long; often not long enough.

What she minded was the next stage, the stage where, if the relationship were to mean anything, you had to rid yourself of the fantasy you'd fallen for and come to terms with the man. As he had to come to terms with you. His personal history, his family, his friends, his politics, his drinking habits, his food fads (I'm sorry – pushing the plate away – I'm allergic to garlic/bread/potatoes), his taste, if any, in clothes and books and art and music; what made him laugh; what made him angry; what turned him on, and off, in bed, were all part of this steep and rocky learning curve. Shocks and disappointments, more than blissful epiphanies, were what you could expect, in Moy's experience. Several of her friends' true love romances, and most of her own, had not survived this stage. And no wonder.

There was an alternative, though, to that kind of shock and disappointment and bust-up, Leila had once suggested to Moy. This was to go along with your lover wherever he led, even if it meant bending yourself out of shape. You were doing something similar already, Leila said, in the first stages of love – adapting and adopting, conceding and accommodating, giving and taking. So bending yourself out of shape was only to take a natural desire to please one step further. It involved telling lies of course – pretending that you had always been a labour voter, say, or that Beethoven was your favourite composer, or that you were having serious thoughts about joining the Roman Catholic Church – but if you loved someone enough to tell him what he wanted to hear, and if you stuck with it and worked at it, the lies would, very likely, become truths.

127

In time they would. It had happened to her, with the lies she had told Robert early on. A marriage of true minds was what they had now, as a result of all the shape-bending lies Leila had told Robert.

Some of the stuff Leila had said was true, Moy had thought. The bit about adapting and adopting and taking was true. Moy had taken, and retained, something from nearly every relationship she'd ever had. Little practical things, such as tips on the quickest way of unblocking a sink, and how to keep a cyclamen alive beyond Christmas; big things like musical knowledge and an interest in Walter Gropius and Bauhaus functionalism. The things you retained from a relationship did become your own. The tomato sauce a married lover of hers, Bruno Weismann, had been good at making, was Moy's sauce now, used for spaghetti and rice and to cheer up broccoli. That sort of taking was normal and natural, and amounted to learning. She imagined that her ex-lovers, some of them, had taken things from her and made them their own.

But to – knowingly, purposely – bend yourself out of shape for someone? She had found that shocking. That is, when she'd checked with Leila that her recital had not been a joke. (Leila could tell them deadpan when she wanted to.) She asked Leila what would happen if a person who'd bent herself way out of shape to please her partner suddenly felt the urge to bend back again? To retract all those lies she'd been keeping going through the years. To do it explosively, over dinner, perhaps, with others present, when the assembled company were drinking their soup? Anyway, Moy had told Leila, a desire to please was not necessarily enough to keep someone in the home, let alone guarantee a marriage of true minds. Moy's mother had spent half her life trying to please her father, and had not pleased him. (He had taken off, eventually, with a much younger woman.) In her mother's case the shape-bending, if it was that, had amounted to a total surrender of self, appalling to witness, a 'my man, right or wrong' philosophy that, although she loved her mother and had tried to protect her, had succeeded in putting Moy off the whole idea of marriage. She told Leila about the group of songs her mother had been used to sing, either because she believed in the message of these songs, or because she needed to believe in it. A group of stand-by-your-man songs, written by men and sung by women in musical shows: 'Can't Help Loving That Man' from *Showboat*, 'So Long as He Needs Me' from *Oliver!*, 'What's the Use of Wond'rin?' from *Carousel*, 'Something Wonderful' from *The King and I* – songs that painted men as monsters or inadequates and women as dupes. No, not dupes, it was worse than that, Moy had told Leila. These women knew full well what kind of bully, or philanderer, or idler, or criminal they'd got themselves tied up with, but went along with it – with *him* – anyhow.

But the tunes were good, weren't they? Leila had said. The tunes of all those songs were terrific, 'What's the Use of Wond'rin?' was one of her own favourites. Had it occurred to Moy that her mother had sung those songs simply because of their terrific tunes?

Moy was thirty-nine when she fell in love with Dexter, and she hoped this second, hazardous, stage, when you might inadvertently start bending yourself out of shape, which some called courtship and which her mother had called walking out, could be avoided. She wanted to make a grand leap over it and land in a serene place where the

129

state of being in love had already given way to the one of loving and being loved, and where nothing had to be explained because everything – everything that mattered – was innately understood.

'Dexter Bucknell? Who he?'

In the gap between her first meeting with Dexter and his first phone call, Moy found herself mentioning his name to almost everyone she came in contact with. Saying the magic name out loud and, as sometimes happened, having it repeated back to her with a question mark, was not only a thrill, it was a way of summoning him, of keeping him in her life, of making a man who daily became less substantial feel solid and real. At least that's how she explained her behaviour to herself later. (For she never planned or contrived her conjurings of Dexter; they just came out.) How odd, that's exactly what *Dexter Bucknell* was saying to me only last week! she heard herself lie to her upstairs neighbours Travis and Paul, when they chatted on the steps after the three of them had dragged their refuse sacks on to the pavement. *Dexter Bucknell* has a glass table very like that one, she announced to the boyish salesman in the Lifestyles department of Arding and Hobbs as he wrapped the replacement coffee mugs she'd bought for her brother Joe, who'd complained that all his had been stolen. Oh, you must live only a stone's throw from *Dexter Bucknell*, she told a woman who'd wandered into the studio-shop to ask if Moy knew of any stained-glass classes in her own area, which was Shoreditch.

None of the people she dropped his name to knew Dexter, or if they did they did not say so. Perhaps – for she never qualified him in any way – they imagined that Dexter Bucknell was newly famous: a media personality, perhaps, whose chat show/house-makeover/garden 'n' cook programme they hadn't caught up with yet, and that they ought to have heard of him. Perhaps they thought Moy was showing off.

It was only after Dexter's call, and after she'd been out with him twice, that she came across someone who did know Dexter. She was in her studio one morning, wire-brushing the joints of a bathroom panel. (The design was of dolphins and waves, a variation on the fishes and bubbles and winding weed she was usually asked to do for bathrooms.) She had more or less finished the brushing, and was about to get started with the tallow wax and the soldering iron, when the lights went. A fuse, was it? – the soldering iron, though temperature-controlled, required a hundred watts and was plugged, illegally, into an extension lead – or a power cut? She went upstairs to Daria's studio to find out; and found the place in semi-darkness, and Daria perched on her work table among the litter of empty white-spirit bottles and squashed tubes of paint, chatting to a woman in a suit and expensive-looking shoes. The woman had a glass of wine in her hand, and Moy guessed her to be a buyer. Or a potential buyer.

Daria said, Hi. She told Moy to help herself to a drink – if she could find something to drink out of. She said the power cut was just great, wasn't it? They knew how to pick their moments. She dropped her cigarette on to the floor and stubbed it out with a toe.

Moy said she didn't want to intrude, Daria was obviously busy, she'd only come to check if the power cut was peculiar to her or a more general thing.

'Oh, you're English,' Daria's visitor said to Moy. 'I thought you must be French. You look French.'

131

Moy said she was sorry about that, about not being French.

'I was about to practise my schoolgirl French on you. I love Daria's work, don't you? It's terrifically good, *n'est-ce pas?*'

Moy said yes, which was not true. She was never moved by Daria's busy canvases. She was seldom shocked, or transported, by her lurid palette and glutinous sweeps and swirls. Slick and meretricious, was her opinion of most of Daria's work.

'Did you go to the self-portrait show?' the woman asked. 'Tremendously impressive, we thought.'

'Yes,' Moy said. Daria's latest show, entitled *Making an Exhibition of Myself*, had not been an exclusively painting show. All manner of materials and objects had been brought into play. Moy had thought some of these pieces – the weirder ones – worked a lot better than the canvases.

'We have three Seeleys already, and I've bought – I hope I've just bought, if Daria's prepared to sell – that one over there. The big pink-purple one. It's wonderful. But you can't see it properly in this light. I wish you'd paint some smaller pictures,' she said to Daria, 'we're running out of wall space. Jamie says if we're to go on collecting you we'll have to move house.

'Jamie is my significant other, as the saying goes,' the woman explained to Moy.

'Moy's an artist too – stained glass,' Daria said. She put a little, satirical, emphasis on 'artist' that some might not have detected, but Moy did.

'Oh?' The woman took a paper handkerchief from her bag and blew her nose. ''Fraid I know nothing about stained glass. I'm a complete ignoramus on that one.' She shut the bag with a click. The bag was black and shiny and had hooped leather handles that stood stiffly upright, as though they had been wired.

The lights came on. And immediately went off. And came on again; and, after a few seconds of flickering and dimming, stayed on.

The woman, who Moy now thought of as Daria's patron, cheered.

'I must go.' She had left the soldering iron plugged in. 'Nice to meet you,' she said, for something to say.

'Nice to meet *you*.'

'Moy, you haven't told me how it went with Dexter,' Daria called out as Moy made for the door. 'Fun time? Did you score?'

She had her back to them, fortunately, so they couldn't see her expression, and did not reply.

'The only Dexter I know, that I used to know – well, see occasionally – is a chap called Dexter *Bucknell*,' Daria's patron said. 'A publisher – as then was. A ladies' man, too, as I recall.'

'That's him,' Daria said. 'That's him, isn't it, Moy?'

Moy, at the door, stopped and turned her head.

'I haven't seen Dexter for ages, our paths don't cross any more,' Daria's patron said, 'but I rather gather he's looking for a wife. So my spies tell me.'

Moy said, Oh?

'So unless you're looking for a husband, perhaps you should watch out. Beware Dexter Bucknell – he's looking for a wife!'

Merry laughter followed Moy into the corridor.

When she saw Daria a week later, Daria told her that the woman Moy had met in her studio, whose name, Daria said, was Helena Smythe, had not bought the pink-purple painting after all. She'd got out her cheque book after Moy had left, she'd asked Daria if she had something to write with and then, when she'd written the date on a cheque, she'd put the pen down. She said she realized she probably ought to let her husband see the painting before she went firm – just in case there was another painting of Daria's he liked better than the pink-purple one. 'After all, he has to live with it too!' she'd explained, snapping her cheque book away in her bag.

Helena Smythe had brought her husband Jamie – 'a commodity broker, stinking rich' – round that evening, Daria told Moy, and he hadn't liked the pink-purple painting. He didn't, in his words, feel *strongly enough* about it. He'd looked at all the other canvases Daria had lined up against the walls, but hadn't felt strongly enough about any of them. 'I think we'll wait for your next show,' he'd told Daria. 'I think we'll hold our horses till then.'

Helena hadn't argued with her husband or tried to persuade him to buy, Daria said. While Jamie, dressed in a dinner jacket because, as Helena had explained to her, they were on their way to a dinner at the Fishmongers' Hall, was looking at Daria's work, examining it up close or standing thoughtfully back, a forefinger pressed to his chin, Helena had wandered the studio in her finery, staring into space and humming a tuneless tune.

Moy said they were shits, it was really shitty behaviour. She said that sort of thing was always happening to her. 'The rich ones are the worst, I find. It's invariably the rich ones who make grand promises and then don't deliver.'

Daria said, Yeah, okay, but it wasn't as simple as that, was it. The rich were the ones who could afford to buy and therefore the ones who often did buy. She reminded Moy that the Smythes had already bought three pieces of her work. Anyway, there was nothing wrong with being rich or having aspirations. She wanted to be rich. When she was rich she'd commission Moy to do a vast stained-glass something for her Manhattan duplex.

But she had minded the waste of her time, Daria admitted. Time when she could have been painting. And she had resented the two bottles of wine she'd had to buy – good wine, 'because people who're rich and successful need to think that you are too, or that you're going to be. They won't buy from you if they think you're not going to make it. Even if they like your work they won't buy if they suspect you're not a good investment. They can smell a loser a mile off.'

Moy had expected Daria to mention Dexter at some point in these exchanges, which took place in the little dark hall and at the bottom of the stairs behind Moy's studio-shop. But she didn't; and Moy didn't; and they both went back to work.

Dexter had made the tea and brought it upstairs, and they were drinking it side by side in the bed, their bodies not touching, the gap between them, it felt to him, solid and unyielding as a bolster.

What he usually did first thing when he got out of bed in the morning was spring, or totter, to the window, and with the hand not occupied by his genitals, invariably on full alert at this hour whatever else of him was not, fight the venetian blinds; so that on a bright day the right-hand wall, the one chest of drawers, the bookshelves on his side of the bed, their hands and faces and any other body parts that got in the way, would be barred with sunlight. Today when he came in with the tea he'd steered clear of the window. Darkness – it was not so much darkness as half-light – had seemed more tactful and in keeping. In keeping with his headache; in keeping with Moy's unforgiving silence and stillness; in keeping with his remorse.

The guilty guy – *c'était lui*.

He'd told her he was sorry. He'd done that straight away, as soon as he'd put the tray down. I'm sorry about the ring fiasco; I'm sorry I went off in a huff; I'm sorry I had to get you out of bed – I thought I had my keys on me. I'm sorry, I'm sorry, I'm sorry, I'm sorry.

What a waste of breath.

He'd stood looking down at her as he held out her tea, in the pottery mug, slate grey with a sloppy yellow glaze, she always chose to drink out of. Her eyes were shut, her arms folded on her chest, and in the greenish light she'd appeared to him still and cold as someone on a marble slab. But corpses had an elsewhere quality; when his father died it had been this, more than the gaping mouth and ghastly flesh, that had defined him. Whereas what the apparently lifeless Moy gave off was a strong and punishing presence. He had just made up his mind to leave her to her game and go in search of orange juice and Nurofen, when she'd sat up suddenly. Sat up, punched the pillows, rearranged them, sat back, straightened the duvet. *Smoothed* the fucking duvet. When she had at last taken the mug from him she'd contrived to do it without catching his eye.

Then, still without speaking, she'd begun rhythmically stirring her tea.

Say something, Moy. Speak. Give communication a whirl. Let's hear it for *words*.

He'd expected words last night, when she let him in. Questions, recriminations, sarcastic jabs. Murderous looks, also. A lunge with the bread knife. He'd pictured these scenes, alone on his bench on the Green, after Steve had gone home. He'd played around with them and developed them, allowing the bread knife lead role in a *Jagged Edge/ Basic Instinct/Fatal Attraction/Play Misty for Me* reception scenario. Finally, having frightened himself, he'd had a go at a happy ending, the sort of closure that in print as on celluloid he would normally despise as untrue. The ending he'd fixed on had opened with a prodigal's welcome – tears of relief from his lover, or of forgiveness, were they? or maybe joy? – and concluded with an urgent and clout-casting move to the bedroom. Yes. Oh yes. Yes, yes, yes, yes, *yes*.

What had happened was that Moy had unlocked the door, opened the door, shut the door behind him, bolted the door, and gone back to bed.

He'd watched her backview, in the skimpy and sexy T-shirt-style nightie he was keen on, nip up up and away, two stairs at a time. The vivid staircase, as he peered after her, had been blacked out suddenly. Seconds later the bedroom, *his* bedroom, fuck it, its afterglow just about visible from the ground floor, had been blacked out. He'd stood for a while in the shuttered living room, adjusting to the dark, debating. Eventually he'd fumbled his way to the hard two-seater under the window. *Better to sit up all night than go to bed with a dragon.*

'Okay, okay, so is there any more tea?' said Moy.

As though she had already spoken. As though the question, conversational, not unfriendly, was part of some wider dialogue they'd shared; a natural follow-on from something that he'd said, or that she'd said.

'Sure.' He got out of bed and went to the chest of drawers and checked out the teapot. 'It'll be cold, though. You're not going to like it.'

Not to worry, Moy said, she didn't mind it cold.

Handing her her tea, it occurred to him that Moy would not be so keen on what she thought of as *her* tea mug if she knew that his ex-wife had given it to him. She would refuse to drink out of it, he thought, if she could see what he himself could see: a shaky Super Eight show of

Our First Christmas, 1987. Here is Mrs Bucknell kneeling up in the rough-and-tumbled bed, her left hand splayed in an attempt to censor her breasts (no chance, they were too considerable for that), her right hand raised, toasting the camera with a festive glass. And look, beside her, snuggling in the bedclothes – only its cocky ears are visible – her wire-haired terrier, Muffin. Cut now to Mr Bucknell, in a paper hat, prodding his Christmas stocking. Feeling and squeezing, pulling a red-wrapped mug shape out; mouthing, Now what can this be? It feels like an ocean-going yacht ... If Moy had ever known its provenance, she would most likely have dropped the mug soon after she moved in with him. Into the Belfast sink, or on to the backyard concrete, from a height.

It came to him, as Moy tried her tea, that in buying her an engagement ring he had hoped to rid himself of these conjugal bedroom scenes. To annul them or, if they could not be annulled, to counterbalance them with dependable images of himself and Moy together. It was only marriage, he had come to believe, that could give their union gravitas and provide the us-against-the-world solidarity that married couples, even warring ones, displayed. My wife, he needed to be able to think when he looked at Moy. This is my wife, he wanted to be able to say to acquaintances and strangers. And drinking in the pub, he wanted to be able to grouse to Steve, in the way that Steve could always grouse with pride to him: If I don't go now, *the wife'll kill* me.

Moy ought to understand this. As she ought to understand, without his having to explain, another need he had: to get back the sense of being a family that Hyacinth had taken away. The criss-cross connectors, as he thought of them, that had once linked child to mother, father to child, child to child, mother to father (and along which all manner of conspiracies and allegiances and passions and intimacies had run), did not work effectively with some wires missing. *Give your daddy a kiss* and *Don't you be cheeky to your mother* had been on those missing wires. *Dad said I could, so there*, and *No, no, not you – I want my mummy to do it*, had been on others. Of course he could not expect Moy, who was not his children's mother, to rectify those losses, to reconnect those wires. But if they were to get married; and say they had a child of their own – He'd always wanted a daughter.

'You're right, it is too cold.' Moy handed him back the mug. She threw off the duvet and swung her feet on to the floor. 'Mind if I have first bath?'

Breakfast; and Moy was eating her cereal standing up. Between spoonfuls she was opening the wall food cupboards and checking out the jars and tins and packets and plastic, squeezy bottles. A lot of the containers were as good as empty, and she took these down and put them on the table. 'Dig and Frankie are back on Sunday,' she reminded Dexter. 'Looks like we'll have to take a trip round Tesco's. There's nothing to eat in the house. Nothing they like.'

It sounded to him like criticism – of his memory, of his housekeeping, of his difficult and picky sons – but he stopped himself. He said, 'Okay, I'll make a list. We'll go tonight. Or I can go by myself this afternoon. I'm quite happy to do it on my own.'

Not true: he dreaded it. The long walk to Tesco's. The smelly minicab ride home with the grocery bags. The boredom. The expense. And what was he to do without a credit card? He would have to borrow cash from Moy. There had been no cheques in his mail again today.

Debtors' prison, here we come.

'Whichever,' Moy said reasonably, 'I don't mind.'

'Speaking of the kids,' he said carefully, 'I had a talk with my mother yesterday.'

'Oh?' Moy had been waiting for him to mention his mother. She had been wondering how to leave for work if he hadn't mentioned his mother before then. She'd been considering whether to bring his mother up herself. She had more or less decided that if he didn't confess to her, soon, the lie he'd told his mother about them getting married, and if he couldn't bring himself to explain the lie, she would leave. She would, as miffed servants did in Ealing comedies, *pack her bags and leave.*

'I asked her if we could go there for Christmas, and she said no. Which is a bugger.'

Moy had heard nothing of her partner's Christmas plans. 'A bugger?'

After a quick mental run-through of the options, he decided to tell the truth. *Truth is the safest lie.* Whatever that might mean. 'Because of that letter I had from Hyacinth yesterday, remember? I thought if we had a plan about Christmas, if I could tell Hyacinth we were going to my mother's, that would be the end of it. She wouldn't be able to work on the kids and, you know, sell them that rural idyll in Berkshire she and her hubby have acquired.'

'What's wrong with Christmas in London? Like last year.' She was thinking, What about me? And what about Joe? Have you forgotten about Joe?

(She had explained to Dexter before she moved in with him that Christmas for her meant Joe. Meant Joe for Christmas dinner, or for the whole day. He was her responsibility, she'd explained. Since their father had remarried and moved to Washington State, Joe had nowhere else to go for festivals and public holidays. But if Dexter couldn't face the idea of having Joe, she'd understand. What she would do was go to Joe's place in the morning, cook his Christmas dinner, eat it with him, and come back to Dexter and the children after tea. There was no reason at all why Dexter should have Joe, or why Dig and Frankie should put up with him; Joe was quite capable of ruining Christmas. She felt it was only fair to point this out. Her problem about Christmas – and Easter too, unless she had some plausible excuse. The Joe problem.

And Dexter had taken her in his arms. We'd love to have Joe, *of course*, he'd said. Of course we would. He's your *brother*. And it's good for the kids to spend time with people less fortunate than themselves. We'll make him feel really welcome, I promise you. It'll be fine, darling. It'll be great.

In the event, it had not been fine or great. Joe had arrived in noisy and contentious mood, ungrateful for the presents they'd bought him – Another sweater, ha ha ha, just like last year; I've got eleven sweaters now, d'you know that? Eleven. I've got a football team of sweaters. How many sweaters do you think I need? – criticizing the goose – Call this Christmas dinner? ha ha ha; where's the turkey? – demanding beer instead of the better-than-usual red wine Dexter had put on the table; belching, laughing insanely at his own unfunny jokes; teasing the boys, who'd sat in silence most of the meal, twitching their noses – for it was evident, from the moment he stepped in the door, that Joe had been giving the bathroom a wide berth for quite a while – or whispering behind their hands.

142

Joe *had* brought presents for the kids. He *had* remembered to buy, and wrap, and bring them. But he had forgotten everything Moy had told him about the boys' ages and interests and the inexpensive suggestions she'd been careful to provide. The large friction dumper truck – for Dig – and ditto digger for Frankie – which had the advice 'Age 2–3' on their primary-coloured containers – had not met with the unreserved enthusiasm he must have been expecting. Moy had minded about this. She'd minded for Joe – though she was angry with him for the cock-up – she'd minded for Dig and Frankie, she'd minded for herself. And she'd minded for her dead mother, whose absence-presence she'd been aware of throughout the awful dinner.

After Joe left, she'd apologized curtly to Dexter and explained Joe's illness – as far as it was possible with children their age – to Dig and Frankie. Joe was not always like that, she'd told them. He could be friendly and easygoing on good days, on days when he felt well. He could be thoughtful. They might find this hard to believe, but Joe was an intelligent man. What had happened to him – and it could happen to anyone – was tragic, and a tragic waste.

Dexter, grim faced, carrying goose-greasy plates to the sink, had told her not to worry about it. To leave it alone, if you don't mind. They were going to have fun now, he said, with serious emphasis on fun. They were going to play a game of Are you there Father Abraham? – as he and the kids always did at Christmas. Then they were going to play the board game, Takeover, Frankie had got in his stocking. Then they were going to play charades, or maybe the Game. The nightmare of Christmas dinner, he said, was best forgotten.

But he had not let her forget it. When Dig and Frankie, who because it was Christmas had been allowed to stay up till midnight, had at last gone to bed, he'd fetched a plate of mince pies and the bottle of Graham's port his sister Elizabeth had sent him, and they'd sat together on the two-seater, eating and drinking. About Joe, he'd begun, between mouthfuls of mince pie. What's hard to know with him, with someone like him, is how much of his behaviour is due to mental illness, and how much to personality. What I'm really asking is, what was he like before his first breakdown, or attack, or whatever it's called? Was he a sympathetic guy up till then? Was he an easy guy? Did he have friends? Moy knew the answer to these questions, but she didn't want to discuss it; she'd had more than enough of Joe for one day. So she'd shrugged and said she couldn't remember; Joe had been ill for so long she couldn't recall a time when he hadn't been. They'd sat in silence for a while, sipping their port. Finally, Dexter had asked, Was there a history of mental illness in her family? He was interested, he said, because he'd read somewhere that these things often had a genetic origin.)

'What's wrong with Christmas at home is that the kids would prefer to spend it in the country,' he said now. 'It's more of a happening for them at the farm. And as you know, they've really gone off London. They hate the lack of freedom. I can understand it. What lads their age like doing is mucking about with water and building camps. Of course when they're older, when they're teenagers, they'll appreciate London – they'll find the country boring then. We probably won't be able to get them into the country then. But at the moment what they want is bike rides and sleeping under canvas and helping Donald around the place – the stuff I did when I was small, the stuff my mother's place has to offer – the stuff any minute now Hyacinth will be able to offer, damn her.'

Buttoning her jacket – for it was cooler today, a rackety wind was blowing, and outside the living room window the tops of the sycamores and mountain ash trees on the Green were doing a silvery, sideways dance – she listened to Dexter's speech, his pompous and schoolteacherly speech, with amazement. What he'd said about his kids' needs and desires was probably true, but he didn't need to sell those arguments to her. The number of times she'd suggested, as a result of things Dig and Frankie had confided, that they should take the kids out of London more, or at least fishing on the canal; and the number of times he'd dismissed her with, Oh no, they're fine, they're city kids. They're metropolis men, like me.

'Why does your mother say Ah?' she suddenly said. She was surprised by her question; she hadn't known she was going to ask it.

'How d'you mean, ah?'

'You must know what I mean. She asks you a question and you answer it and she says Ah. Like, Aaaaah. Like, I *seeee*. Like she knows something different. Like she doesn't believe you.'

He was silent while he tried to consider the truth of Moy's remark. He was finding it difficult to focus because of the big and weighty and unpleasant something at the back of his mind that seemed bent on interfering with his thought processes, but which, though he was doing his best to uncover it, refused to identify itself.

'Did you hear me?' Moy said. 'Did you hear what I – ?'

'Yes, I did hear you, and I was thinking about it. I was wondering why you asked that particular question, which is obviously a loaded one in some way – and then I was trying to examine, to hear in my head, my mother's conversational isms and tics, and asking myself if I really thought ah was one of them. I was just coming to the conclusion that it wasn't, that she doesn't say ah any more than anyone else says ah, when –'

'But she's always saying it. She said it to me last night on the phone. We didn't talk for long, but she must have said it three times at least.'

The big and weighty and unpleasant thing at the back of his mind shouldered its way to the front. No. He couldn't have told his mother they were getting married. He couldn't have. Oh no. But hang on, perhaps his mother hadn't mentioned any of that to Moy. He had the impression, though she'd never said anything specific, that his mother disapproved of Moy, or of his relationship with Moy. His mother's call must have been to do with Dig and Frankie, and intended for him. Perhaps she'd had second thoughts about Christmas. He said, as casually as he could manage, 'Does she want me to call her back?'

'She didn't say so.'

A van door slammed; an engine started – Dickie, the kitchen fitter from number 15, leaving for work. The back doors of Dickie's van had recently acquired a notice saying RIDGID TOOL GUARANTEED. Dexter had wanted to quiz Dickie about the spelling of rigid, but Boss-Boots Moy had said no. It would be mean to do that, she'd said, when Dickie had taken such pains with the lettering.

'I must go.'

'Did you tell her where I was?' What he meant was, what was my mother phoning about?

'I said you were out. I didn't know where you'd gone.

Have you seen my studio keys, Dexter? I really do have to go now.'

He got to his feet and went to the worktop. From the drawer underneath he took out her keys and handed them to her.

'My bike?'

'Bike, bike. Bike? Oh God yes, bike.'

Unless bad weather prevented it, Moy bicycled to work. It was one of Dexter's morning duties to fetch her bike from the shed in the yard (where all four family bicycles were housed), manoeuvre it through the narrow back door, and carry it through the kitchen and living room to the front door. It was a duty he had imposed on himself – Moy was of course perfectly capable of carrying the bike through herself – and which he ordinarily enjoyed, as he enjoyed checking the machine before she rode away. Doing these tasks for Moy allowed him to feel, what his domestic existence gave him few opportunities to feel, a functioning adult male, a real regular guy. Propping the bike against a lamp-post, he would first test the brakes and the gears and the handlebars. Then, squatting on the pavement, whistling a cheerful snatch of Mozart or Schubert or Haydn, he'd check the tyres and the chain. If oil was needed for the chain, he fetched the oil can. While he pumped tyres, or tinkered with spanner and oil can, Moy would stand with her arms folded, looking on. 'There you go then,' he'd say at last, straightening up, wiping his hands on a rag, 'all set for the milk run.'

He carried her bicycle through the front door and set it on the pavement.

'The bike's fine, you don't need to check it.' She took the handlebars from him. 'Thanks.'

'My mother isn't overly bright, you know,' he said. 'If

147

she says ah, as you say, it's probably because she hasn't got the point of something and doesn't know how to respond.'

'She has a stutter too,' Moy said. 'Some sort of impediment. Or she had last night. I don't remember her stuttering bef—'

'My mother does not have a stutter,' Dexter said.

'Mornin' Dexter.' Midge, their next door neighbour, hardened racist and oldest resident of the street, was taking in her milk from the pavement and watching them. 'You want to wear a helmet on that cycle, young lady,' she said to Moy.

'I'm always telling her that, but she won't listen to me.'

'I hate wearing anything on my head,' Moy said to Midge.

'You was makin' a fair old din in the middle of the night,' Midge said to Dexter.

'I'm very sorry, Midge. I locked myself out, and I had to wake Moy to let me in.' He had to keep in with Midge because he owed her. On all the occasions he and the kids had been out of town, staying at his mother's or bucket and spading on the south coast, Midge had watered his house plants and fed Frankie's goldfish.

'It weren't just the young lady you woke,' said Midge who, possibly because Dexter and Moy weren't married, or because Moy's skin colour in summer turned suspiciously dark, or because she couldn't get her tongue round it, never mentioned or addressed Moy by name.

'Yes, I realize that, and as I say I'm sorry.' He frowned at the pavement.

When Midge had gone inside and closed her front door, Moy said, 'Well, I'm off then,' and she wheeled her bicycle off the pavement and into the road.

148

'Midge's right you know, you should wear a helmet. It's crazy not to. How can I make my kids wear their helmets when you won't wear yours?'

'You don't have to make them, they like wearing their helmets.' She placed her left foot on the left pedal. 'Well, bye then.' She hesitated. She wanted to give him one more chance. *I love you Dexter. I love you. I will forgive you if you tell me now.* 'Was there anything else before I go?'

He looked up at the sky. A big puffy cloud, white with a black underbelly, was lumbering through the blue. Symbolic of something. He looked down at the pavement. There was a dried rivulet of dog pee at his feet. He could smell it. The stain was dark and shiny, as though it had been glazed. He moved his feet out of the way. 'No, I don't think so.'

Still she couldn't bring herself to leave. He must say something. He must. 'What've you got on today?'

I have got to take a rejected ring back to the jeweller's. I have got to waste my entire fucking morning . . . 'Usual stuff. Acquisitions and mergers in the morning, bullion broking in the afternoon. And over lunch –' He stopped. Moy's expression stopped him. 'I've got to write seven hundred and fifty words for Philip. You know, for his My London slot. He wants it by tonight. I told him I'd write something about Fun Week.'

'But you haven't been to anything in Fun Week.'

'I can make it up.'

'Good money?'

'Crap money. And he warned me they won't pay for months. Still, it was nice of him to ask me. Bloody nice.'

'He liked your last piece, didn't he, about Hackney City farm, otherwise he wouldn't be asking for more. Perhaps he's going to give you something regular to do?'

149

'I think he might.'

'Well, good luck, then.' She tightened her grip on the handlebars. She squeezed the brake levers tight, and released them.

'Good luck to *you*.' He rubbed his hands together. 'Is that Doom window section finished yet? I want to see it when it is.'

Such patronising heartiness. It reminded her of her father, how he used to sound when pretending an interest in her homework. She said, 'I'm still waiting for the Prussian blue. They promised to deliver last week. But you can see the panel any time. I'd appreciate any —'

'Just a minute —' Across the road, in the middle of the Green, he'd spotted two youths and a dog fooling around under the trees. As he watched, the smaller of the two pulled down a branch of a young mountain ash, ripped it from the trunk and, as the dog danced round him with sharp, anticipatory barks, stripped the branch of its leaves and hurled it away. The dog bolted after it. 'Stay here,' he said grimly. And crossed the road at a sprint.

Don't, Moy wanted to call. Just don't.

'Hi there, I don't know if you realize, but dogs aren't allowed on this Green.'

He had intended being a lot ruder than that. He'd been going to shout and scream at the youths. But as he got closer he saw that they were not youths but men. One white, one black. In their late twenties, he guessed. Shaven heads and unshaven faces; both in vests and Nike trainers; one wearing shorts, one wearing jeans. Both broader-chested than him, and a lot heavier. And there were two of them, he reminded himself. And their dog was a power-pack — pit bull, or close relation. When he'd taken

150

in these details, he slowed his sprint to a trot, his trot to a walk, his walk to a stroll.

'Oh yeah?' At his approach, the smaller guy, the white guy, the one wearing shorts, had grabbed the dog and slung a choke-chain round its neck. He was now squatting on the grass beside the slavering and panting and whining beast, jerking the chain from time to time and squinting up at Dexter. 'Oh yeah?' he said again, in a tone of casual interest – fake, obviously.

The black guy, who wore assassin-like shades, stood a little way off, leaning against the abused tree, examining his nails.

'There's a notice beside the gate – beside all the gates,' said Dexter, continuing in his role of imparter of useful information. 'No dogs. Perhaps you didn't see it?'

'That roigh'?' Shortie slapped the dog affectionately on the chest. 'This gen'leman says you din oughta be ere, you naugh'y naugh'y boy.' He cupped his ear to the dog's head, then turned to Dexter: 'Bomber says he ent much of a rea'er – sorry an all that.'

Dexter smiled feebly. 'You see, the kids play on his grass,' he explained, 'it's the only place for them to play, so unfortunately there has to be a no dog rule. I like dogs, *of course*,' he felt it wise to add: 'my wife has a dog, but –'

'Don' see no kids.' Shortie shaded his eyes with a hand and peered all round him. 'Can you see any kids, Melv?'

'Na, can' see no kids.' Melv left the tree and came to stand on Bomber's left (so that the dog was now sandwiched between, and protected by, his two minders). He took a little time sorting his feet, planting them, Dexter noticed, the exact distance apart for maximum stability and instant lift-off. When Melv was satisfied with his feet, he folded his massive arms across his chest and jutted his chin.

151

Group photograph – the image came to Dexter and he hung on to it like a life raft. Mass–Observation-style photojournalism, in grainy black and white, was how he saw it. And the caption: *Two Villains and a Pit Bull, Bethnal Green.*

'Well, it's a bit early yet for the kids,' he said quickly, looking at his watch. 'It's only eight-thirty. But they will be out soon. The cricket game usually gets going early in the school holidays. And the mums and toddlers will be out any minute now.' (How had he got into this, and how the fuck was he going to get out?) It was then he saw the dog turd, a walnut-whip, still steaming in the grass. He pointed. 'You may not know this, but if a young kid, a toddler, say, crawls into dog shit and the dog shit gets in the kid's eye – the kid can be blinded. There's some sort of chemical, or organism, or bacterium, in dog shit, apparently, that can cause blind—'

'That righ'? That's reelly reely interes'ing. Did you know 'bout that, Melv? Did yer know my Bomber's lickle pooh-poohs can make kiddies blind? Learn somethin new every day.'

'Yeah, y'do,' Melv said, grinning hideously.

'He's like a walkin TV documen'ary, that one, ent he?' Shortie said to Melv.

Enough, Dexter decided. More than enough. The worst they can do is kill me. He said, icy cold, 'Dogs aren't allowed on this Green, and I've told you the reason. So take your dog out now, and clean up that mess. You've already destroyed a tree. That mountain ash will undoubtedly die – you've torn the bark right down to the ground – look. That tree will bleed to death.'

In slow motion, it seemed to him – though it was probably fast; afterwards he would decide it was fast –

Shortie got to his feet. As he did so, he slackened the choke-chain, incitement to Bomber to make repeated snarling rushes at Dexter's legs and ankles.

'Your trees, is they?' Shortie sneered. 'Your park? Your private fuckin park?'

'No, of course not, but –'

'A copper, are you? Par'keeper?'

'No.'

'Well then. Well then.' Shortie spat viciously on the ground. Then he looked Dexter over, slowly, lingeringly, while snapping his fingers as though to some hidden rap, 'Well then.'

An ugly moment. A panicky laugh began to bubble up from somewhere deep in Dexter's gut.

'Well then, you can shut the fuck up and you can get the fuck outta here. The trouble wiv cunts like you is, you think you own the whole fuckin planet. You think you ave the roigh' to push the rest of us around. You wanna spoil everyfink for everybody. But you can't, not any more mate – so you can just get the fuck out of it now. Else I'm gonna let my lickle doggie off is chain.'

Before Dexter could obey, Melv stepped forward and pushed him in the chest. A hard, shoving push, a punch, that almost knocked him off his feet. As he righted himself, Melv punched him again, harder this time, and they continued like this for several yards: Melv punching him, Dexter staggering backwards (and wanting to turn and run), Melv helping him on his backwards way with another well-aimed slug. Finally, Melv let his arm drop. 'Git. Git goin, arsehole. Piss off dahn West where you belong.'

Close call. When he was able, he turned and pissed, or staggered, off.

Moy was waiting for him outside the Green, by the gate. She tugged the gate to behind him. 'Are you all right? Did he hurt you?'

He couldn't speak for panting and shaking and hurting. Everything hurt. At the same time he was aware of being on some adrenaline-fuelled high, which objectified his pain in some way and made it seem, while sharply feelable, not quite his. Which allowed him to know himself as Cock of the Walk or King of the Castle. As Hero of the Hour. 'Somebody has to have a go,' he managed to puff out eventually, 'those thugs can't be allowed to – shit. Shit, hurts like hell.' He placed the flat of his hands on his chest and began padding it all over, pad pad pad, the tender and comforting action he had employed, when they were younger, for drying his sons with their bathtime towel. He bent forwards and let his head drop to his knees. He straightened up and then repeated the exercise. 'Shit.'

'D'you think anything's broken? Tell me.'

He grinned bravely. 'It's just, huh, my breastbone, my ribcage, my lungs. But I'm h'okay. And at least he didn't manage to deck me.' He pushed up his T-shirt. 'How's it huh-huh-huh look to you.'

There were red marks on Dexter's chest and diaphragm, but no broken skin. 'It looks red,' Moy said. 'It looks sore.' She took him by the arm and led him across the road, slowly and carefully, as though he were a very old man. 'You ought to lie down. I'll make you a drink of something. What would you like?'

'No,' he said, 'you must go off to work. You're late enough already. I'll be fine.'

On the pavement, outside their front door, Moy tightened her grip on his arm. She said, 'You are never,

154

never, never to do that again. I don't want you dead. Dig and Frankie don't want you dead. They might have pulled a knife on you, you realize. If they'd had a knife –' She let go his arm. 'What you smiling for?'

He was smiling partly through shock, but also because he was glad to be alive. And because Moy was angry with him. Anger, in these circumstances, had to signal love. In between pants and groans, he went on smiling.

'Look over there,' Moy said. 'No. There.'

At the far side of the Green he could pick out his two oppressors, with Bomber still on the choke, weaving through the trees towards the corner gate. At every tree they were pausing just long enough to tear off a branch or two. The amputated limbs fell to the ground, where they struck awkward, leafy attitudes in the grass.

'The bastards, I'll report them, I'll –'

'Who to? Anyway, it's your fault. What's happening over there is entirely your fault.'

'What's that you're saying, Moy? Are you saying that thugs should be allowed to commit whatever acts of desecration they like and no one try to stop them? Are you saying we should all just stand by and let – ? Shit. Shit, it hurts.'

She said, Yes, she thought she was saying that. Yes she was.

'I don't believe you.' He glared down at her. 'I don't believe you really mean that.'

'I do mean it. I do believe it.' But she was beginning to feel less sure. 'I do.'

'Shit.' He smacked a hand to his headache, harder than he meant. 'Well, that's a great philosophy, I must –'

'Mornin, Dexter, mornin Moy.' A pushchair, with a woman attached to it, was doing its best to steer round them. 'Say hallo, Lesley.'

'Hallo, hallo, hallo, hallo,' chanted the child in the pushchair.

'Hi Angie. Hi Lesley.' They moved out of the way. Moy retrieved her bicycle from the gutter.

'Wait –' He put a restraining hand on her handlebars. 'This is important. We have to sort this out.'

'I'm tired. And so must you be.' She was very tired. It was twenty to nine in the morning and it felt like midnight. Not the time, anyway, to debate ethics or morals or whatever they were.

'You can go in a minute. Ow, ow, *Christ*' – he winced; he tried to straighten up – 'Look, I just want to get this straight. Are you saying, do you really believe, that no one should ever have a go? That there are no circumstances –'

'Can we talk about it tonight when I get home? It's impossible in the street –' But when she looked about her, apart from a gang of young Asian boys, making for the Green and carrying cricket stumps and a bat, the street was empty.

'I need to know.' He started to pant again. Maybe something was broken. Maybe – the pain in his ribs was searing.

'Well of course there are occasions, circumstances, when people should have a go, as you put it. Of course there are.'

'That's not what you said a moment ago.'

'I don't know what I said. What I think is, what I think I think is, it's okay to interfere, no, it's right to interfere if somebody's being hurt. Obviously you wouldn't be able to stand by if you saw someone being beaten up – a child, or an old person. Or an animal. You'd have to do something then. You'd want to.'

'Those maniacs allowed, encouraged, their dog to crap

156

where our kids play. And they were destroying our trees. It's trees, let me remind you, that are — oh shit — that are the green lungs of the city, the things that counteract the effects of carbon emissions and —'

Oh really, Dexter. Pack it in please. And in any case, they hadn't been destroying the trees. When he went speeding after them they'd taken *one* branch from *one* tree. They'd needed a stick to throw for their dog, and they'd broken off one small branch. Not such a terrible crime. But she'd already said as much. 'Could you take your hand off my handlebars, I've got to get to work.'

'Perhaps you think vandals should be rewarded with grants or handouts?' He kept his hand, heavily, on the bike.

'Don't be daft.'

'What, then?'

'All I know is,' Moy said, 'all I know is, if you hadn't rushed in there in that officious way and — it isn't your Green, you know, Dexter. You'd think it was, the way you carry on.' A pause. 'You've got your own green acres, anyway. Two hundred of them, or whatever it is. Maybe if you spent more time looking after —'

'*What* did you say?' He took his hand off the handlebars.

He was going to hit her, she knew it. He was about to strike her in the face.

But he didn't hit her. (He probably couldn't, he hadn't the strength to hit her, he was in too much pain.) He lowered his hand and replaced it, less heavily this time, on the bike.

'I said you were officious,' Moy said. 'And officiousness, bossiness, doesn't quite square with your bleeding-heart liberalism you're always going on about. That's all. That's

157

all I meant. Do go in now and lie down. You really ought to. Please.'

'Officious? I was incredibly polite to those bastards. You should've heard me. You've no idea how tactful I was. But you weren't there, were you. You weren't fucking there.'

A new thought occurred to Moy. A frightening thought. 'They know where we live now, you realize. They may not know what number house, but that's easy to find out. Phone, Dexter. Phone's ringing.'

'My bloody mother, I expect that'll be.' He paused. 'You said it was right to have a go if you saw someone being beaten up. But you saw me being beaten up and you didn't do anything, did you? You didn't shout at them, you didn't run for help. You didn't even come into the Green. You weren't prepared to risk anything for me.' He glared at her. He bent down suddenly and kissed her on the mouth. An aggressive and punishing kiss. 'Ride carefully,' he groaned as he limped into the house. 'Watch out for that diesel spillage by Three Colts Lane.'

WHAT ARE windows for? the inspector who visited Moy's primary school asked the Reception Class. And Moy waved an arm and shouted, To see out of. The wrong answer. The right and intelligent answer, which Mary Barnscroft, who sat next to Moy and shared her work table, unassumingly supplied, was to *let light in*. Being able to see out was useful, of course, the inspector explained to Moy, but secondary to a window's main function which was to allow light and air to penetrate what would otherwise be an unventilated and benighted building. (That was how Moy told this story against herself to Dexter, early on in their relationship, in a conversation – it felt more like an argument – they were having about stained glass. Dexter said Moy must have invented the inspector's language. He was unlikely to have used the words penetrate and benighted and unventilated in any explanation to five-year-olds, Dexter said – though it made a good story.)

The window that let light and air into Moy's rented studio, on the second floor of what was once a warehouse, looked out over the Mile End football stadium and running track and sports courts and, in the foreground, a grassed leisure and play area, sliced horizontally in two by a thin tarmac path. Depending on where you stood in the studio, there were trees to the left of this view, a grove of them; and two cut-price tower blocks, one near, one far; and a circle of giant stadium lights that perspective rendered absurdly differing sizes. What was noticeable, in daytime, about this cityscape was the absence of human life. There might be an old man walking a dog along the tarmac, or a woman with a shopping bag resting on one of the benches that measured the path, but very often when Moy went to the window and looked out and down, there was no one. No one on the sports courts, no one on the running track. No one playing, or lying, on the grass. The lack of life was disturbing – as though London had been evacuated for some bad reason – and it was depressing. When Moy felt depressed she would get down on the floor and examine the window view from there. The stadium and tower blocks vanished when you sat on the floor. Sky took up the entire window, wider than it was tall, and with a pattern of glazing bars – two verticals close together framing a six-foot-square central pane, and two horizontals, one top, one bottom, of the window frame itself – that Dexter, when he first visited the studio, pronounced Mondrianesque. The sky was a busy or colourful place a lot of the time, and when Moy felt low she often chose to look at that.

This Copperfield Road studio of Moy's differed in every way from her Battersea studio, the one she rented until she moved in with Dexter, a time when she was living in two rooms above a dry cleaner's in St John's Road. The Battersea studio, in Northcote Road, had been on the ground floor, with street frontage and commercial designation, which had allowed it to function as work-room and showroom and shop in one. It had been, and presumably still was (she had not been back to check), part of a complex of craft and design workshops-cum-selling-spaces, and her neighbours there, all ages and nationalities, some on the street and some in an adjoining alley, had been wood-carvers-and-gilders, furniture restorers, upholsterers. They had made pottery and jewellery and leather belts; also hats to order, embroidered slippers, beaded evening bags, and lampshades out of smoky glass. One of the advantages of being a member of this community had been the interactive support network it provided, the 'you scratch my back, I'll scratch yours' philosophy that had kept everyone involved in it more or less afloat. (Customers, in particular the professional stylists and interior designers who called in regularly to pick up props and ideas, were passed from shop to shop.) Another advantage of this set-up was that you could count on there being someone to talk to, if you felt like talking, any time of day.

The one bad thing, as Moy saw it then, about spending her time in a craft environment was that she thought of stained glass as art.

How do you see stained glass – as art or craft? was the question she put to anyone who asked her what she did for a living. And almost without exception the reply came back, craft. Some hesitated before answering what sounded like a trick question; most did not. A few hedged their bets: I'm not sure, Moy – how do you see it yourself?

The three artists, two young men and one woman, who rented the three studios on the floors above Moy's space, had not considered stained glass to be art. They'd made that plain. The artists had a name for the crafts people –

farty-crafties – and steered clear of them. They were not rude exactly, they were aloof – which came across as scornful and superior. When Moy encountered one of them in the passageway he or she would nod or say Hi without catching her eye, before taking the stairs two at a time. It was as though I had some revolting disease, she told Dexter, describing her life in that place. She would never have got to speak to any of the artists, she told him, had not the female one, Daria, cut her thumb one morning and come into Moy's space in search of Elastoplast. You crafties have your uses, Daria had said, as Moy bound up her thumb. She'd said it smilingly, and she'd accepted the mug of coffee Moy offered. But while they waited for the kettle to boil, and while they afterwards were drinking their coffee, she'd made no mention of Moy's work, in evidence all round the room. She hadn't picked up a tool, or quizzed Moy about the various kinds and colours of glass in the racks. She'd talked about the man in her life, who was a drummer in a rock band, and what an unreliable bastard he was, and how she was going to sack him – soon, before he got round to sacking her.

The Daria incident confirmed Moy's fears about the status of stained glass, and also of the people who designed and made it.

Dexter was one of the ones who hedged their bets. He did not have to ask her what she did for a living because Leila had filled him in about Moy before he telephoned to ask her out. But he brought the subject up anyway, their first evening together.

'Do you enjoy working in glass?' he asked politely, after he'd told Moy some labyrinthine hard-luck stories about himself and his marriage and his children. They were sitting in a pub; Moy was drinking beer, Dexter was drinking whiskey. 'Is it difficult?'

She said, Sometimes, meaning both. Sometimes she enjoyed it; sometimes it was difficult. And sometimes –

'Are you *ambitious*?' His next question.

'In what way? How d'you mean?'

He meant for fame. Or for money. Or to do something really ground-breaking. If it was possible to break ground, as such, with stained glass?

She was ambitious to design and make something wonderful, Moy said. One of the things she really wanted to make was a Doom window. Not, you know, the sort of devils and hellfire Doom window they went in for in the fifteenth century – though devils would be fun to do – but a Warning window. A global-warming Flood or New Ice Age window. A contemporary Prykke of Conscience window, if you like. She didn't see it as Christian, necessarily. She didn't want it to be read as apocalyptic in a religious, or cult religious sense – though a part of her would like to see it in a church because stone, old stone, was probably the most sympathetic setting for stained glass. But if she was going to do it, she would have to do it soon because she couldn't go on working with lead for ever. She was sure she'd already got short-term memory loss – one of the first signs of lead poisoning. 'It frightens me, if I allow myself to think about it, how much lead my body, my *brain*, must be carrying around.'

She was on the young side to be a member of the Craft Club, Dexter suggested.

'Sorry? I don't follow.'

'C-R-A-F-T,' Dexter said, 'stands for Can't Remember A Fucking Thing.' But, to be serious, didn't she wear gloves for working? Or some sort of protective gear? He sounded shocked.

She did have surgical gloves but she hated wearing them, Moy told him. She hated the feel of them – and the smell. Ugh.

She had to wear gloves, Dexter said. It was stupid and irresponsible not to wear them. 'You have very pretty hands, by the way,' he added.

But you haven't felt them yet, she thought. (They were dry and rough from all the chemicals she used.) Wait till you feel them.

It was then that she asked him the art-or-craft question. Craft Club aside, how did he see stained glass?

'Well, it depends, doesn't it,' said Dexter. 'But if you want a fuller answer I'll need another drink.'

From their table near the door, she examined his backview at the bar. He was wearing a heavy-knit fisherman's sweater – from Norway? Sweden? Finland? – off white with all-over blue dots, and with two bands of blue at the bottom, which, earlier, when he removed his jacket, had made her at once decide: *that sweater will have to go.*

She let her eye wander away from Dexter, to the left of him, to the middle-aged couple – in their late fifties? or sixties? – sitting at one of the tables closest to the bar. They were both trim and fit-looking, like the couples in the Over Fifties life assurance commercials they put out on daytime TV. They both had white hair, his thick and short and boyish, hers short and stylishly cut. She was wearing a neat lovat trouser suit; he had highly polished shoes. They were talking to each other, not in an animated way but in a comfortable and companionable way, it seemed to Moy. They were talking about their grandchildren, perhaps, or about the exhibition they had bussed into London to see, or about some domestic detail that concerned them equally. They would both be retired now, and together all day, at home. She allowed herself to imagine this home, which she saw as a semi in a quiet, tree-lined avenue. Friendly neighbours dropped in for coffee, many of them retired folk like themselves, who, like themselves, went on walking holidays in the Cairngorms or the Isles of Scilly. He would play golf, Moy thought – but only once a week because of the expense and because, being a thoughtful man, he would not want his lady love (he called her that) to be a golfing widow. At the back of their house was a colourful and manageable garden, which they both worked in – he cutting grass and hedges, she planting out the bedding plants and staking the dahlias. They chatted as they did their separate tasks, calling each other over from time to time, for advice, or to examine a blackbird's nest or some tender plant that was thriving against the odds – or disappointingly, not thriving. On summer evenings, after a long day working in the garden, they would sit out on the paved area in front of the trimmed lawn, on white garden chairs that had flower-patterned cushions, and admire their handiwork, while perhaps drinking a glass of chilled white wine. Moderate people, they would stop at one glass, except on their respective birthdays, when they might drink two.

I would settle for that, Moy thought, watching them, watching the husband, apparently without being asked, top up the wife's tomato juice from the half-empty tomato juice bottle on the table. If I could have it without marriage, I would settle for that routine kindness and safety and moderation. (Though she had never come anywhere near to settling for it so far. So far, Richard the dull exception, her affairs had been messy and extreme, involving married men, and subterfuge, and abruptly broken-off telephone calls, and lies.)

But perhaps she had misread these people. Say they were not a couple at all, but an affair. An affair of the heart, thwarted in youth, that had survived years of marriage to other people. And say —

Giving up on them, she turned her attention back to Dexter.

I want him — another decision she made as he pocketed his change, and with frowning concentration carried the full glasses to the table. *I love him. I even love that sweater because* —

Immediately, a correcting voice in her head interrupted: *You don't know him. You hate that sweater. What sentimental tosh is this?*

'Ahhhrt,' Dexter drawled, handing her her beer, 'Art Garfunkel. Art Buchwald. Art Tatum. Artie Shaw. Would you name a child of yours Art?'

It could be short for Arthur, Moy suggested.

'Art,' he repeated, 'it's such a portmanteau word. It has to do so many things. The art of coarse fishing. The art of motorway driving. Though one kind've suspects that what's meant by those *is* craft. Skills that can be taught and learnt — to a certain level at least.'

He was standing beside her when he said this; but now he sat down and shunted his chair closer to the table. 'And then there's something called "the arts", whatever they may be. And then there's bad art. Bad art always amuses me, doesn't it you? The expression, I mean. I don't mean the stuff itself. Necessarily.'

He's showing off, Moy decided. He's showing off or trying to put me down.

But perhaps it was just nervousness on his part. Perhaps he was nervous too. And he has a sweet smile, she reminded herself. (He was smiling at her at that moment.) He has an adorable smile.

'Anyway, why does it matter whether what you do is art or craft?' Dexter said. 'Or what people think? What difference does it make?'

'It doesn't matter,' Moy said. 'It doesn't matter at all. Forget it.'

'It's just that the two are so intertwined, aren't they. Think of the Arts and Crafts Movement. So okay, craft may not always result in art – in what we recognize to be art – or anything vaguely resembling art; but art can't do without craft, can it? It's there in all great art surely? Or it used to be – in music, poetry, painting, whatever.'

Would that do? he asked when Moy still said nothing. Did these truisms, these *platitudes*, answer her question?

Moy said no, it wasn't what she meant. All she wanted to know – and she didn't want to make a heavy thing out of it – was, how did he, Dexter Bucknell, off the top of his head, label stained glass? Because most people did label it.

'Could we call it coloured glass?' Dexter said.

More games. She sighed. She said, 'It sounds American.'

'It's just that when you said *stained*, I immediately saw –'

Oh no, not that. 'No, don't say it!' She put her head down on the table and covered her ears.

He leaned across and removed her hands, very gently, one hand at a time. The first time he'd touched her. He said, 'But you don't know what I was going to say, do you? Unless you're psychic, you can't have any idea.'

She thought she did know, though. She was certain she did know.

'Well then, what was I going to say?'

'Underpants' – or 'Y-fronts' – was the answer. Joe's long-standing, still-running joke. He would phone her at the studio – always when she had a customer or was in the middle of something fiddly – and say, How's the work going? How are those stained underpants you insist on making, ha ha ha? How are those semen stains? Ha ha ha. How are those *skidmarks*?

Ha ha ha ha ha.

But Dexter was not Joe. The unfunny connexion her brother unfailingly made with 'stained' would not occur to Dexter. Or to any other sane person.

'I haven't the faintest idea,' she said, lifting her head, smiling. 'I was just –'

'I was only going to tell you that what I saw, when you said *stained*, was the opening of *Don't Look Now*. When the child's running around the pond – was it a pond? Or was it a stream? – and Donald Sutherland knocks the ink over on his drawing board and the stain spreads, the *blood* spreads – eventually across that stained-glass window.'

'Oh I see. Well, if you want to know, I can't cope with the beginning of that film,' Moy said. 'Whenever they show it on TV I look away for the first five minutes, or I leave the room. And I turn the sound right down so I don't have to hear Donald Sutherland's howl when he's lifting his drowned baby out of the water. I don't want to know about it. I don't want to see it or hear it.'

Dexter said he agreed about the howl. But he supposed that, as a piece of scene-setting, the opening probably achieved everything Nicolas Roeg had had in mind. It was frightening, it let you know immediately that the Sutherland character was psychic, and it was visually stunning. A neat bit of cutting too, didn't she think? 'The way the red of the child's mac and the red of –'

168

'I can't be objective,' Moy said. 'I don't see how anyone can be. His grief is too real. And you know it must be just like that. One minute your darling happily playing, absorbed – and the next. Well. You must have had scares with your kids, I imagine? Near misses. They must have run into the road in front of lorries, or set the carpet on fire, or fallen into the deep end of the pool?'

'Of course they have. Of course. When Dig was five he – but actually I don't want to talk about it. I try not to dwell on negative things. I don't let myself go back over them.' He picked up his glass, moved the melting ice out of the way with his finger, took a long swallow.

'Something else about *Don't Look Now* I've just remembered,' he said when the glass was empty. 'Something a whole lot jollier – that sex scene, love scene with Julie Christie in Venice – remember it? Must be the most convincing – most tender, most passionate, most desperate – sex scene on film. Can you think of a better one?'

Moy said no, she didn't think she could.

'We agree. We agree.' He pointed to their empty glasses. 'Shall we?'

'My shout.' She got up from the table.

'Going back to the art or craft question,' Dexter said when she returned.

'Don't let's. We've done it to death. Really. Let's talk about what you do.'

'But I never answered you properly. I merely said it depends. I was going to say, by way of illustration, that the stained glass at Chartres, for example, has to be art – at least that's how we recognize it now, though I don't imagine the designers and makers of those windows thought of it like that – you know, as a purely aesthetic enterprise. The fear and glory of God must have been the

169

motivation for them, don't you think? Plus the need to educate, to tell the Bible story in pictures for an unlettered congregation?'

'Something like that.' She did not need a lecture, on what was her subject, from him.

'On the other hand, the stained glass you see in suburban doors and windows isn't even pretending to be art, I imagine? It's decoration or a screen to stop people looking in – a more colourful alternative to net curtains, if you like. There's nothing wrong with that. There's nothing wrong with being a craftsman, either – I'm one. At least I hope I am. I like to think I am.'

'Well thank you for that,' Moy said. 'Thanks.' She felt uneasy, nervous of him suddenly. Ninety per cent of the stained glass she made came into the category he had just described.

'We've got some good stained glass in Ludlow, in the parish church. The Palmer's window. D'you know it? And there's a stained-glass colour, I believe, called Ludlow Blue?'

'We? How do you mean, we?'

'I don't mean we. I mean, Ludlow's my home town. Where I was born.'

'Oh.' She had imagined him to be a Londoner.

'I'd like to see the glass you make one day,' Dexter said. 'And I'd be very interested to see your ideas for the Doom window if you'd let me?'

'One day' turned out to be the following week. A surprise visit, at ten o'clock in the morning. Moy would have liked some notice. She might have put on something more flattering than the black leggings and khaki tunic she wore for work if she'd known he was coming, and she would

170

have washed her hair. She would have organized her workbench and made sure he found her engaged on a piece she was not ashamed of, and that might impress him. She would have hidden away the net curtain stuff, the stuff, as he'd put it, that didn't even pretend to be art, if he'd given her any warning.

She had her back to the door when he came in. There was a customer with her and they were sitting on stools at the workbench, discussing the cartoon Moy had made for the stained-glass panel the customer wanted for her front room window (a replacement panel for the damaged one, with colours she didn't care for, the woman had inherited with her house). She didn't bother to turn round. She called over her shoulder, With you in a second! – and went on talking to the customer. It was only when she got up and went to the glass racks to fetch samples of the glass she intended to use, that she saw it was Dexter. Though it took her a moment to recognize him.

'You're busy. I'll come back later,' Dexter said.

'Okay, give me ten minutes,' Moy said, her heart beginning to thump in the old, recognizable way.

'You're not wearing gloves,' Dexter said.

'Gloves?' For a moment she pictured woollen ones. 'Oh – well no. I don't need to – I'm not leading up.' The shock of seeing him, of his being there, on her territory, had triggered a melting sensation, a weakness, that was affecting her whole body. If it was really him. For he seemed a different man from the burdened single father – in that terrible sweater – she'd sat in the pub with only a week ago; and different again from the watchful creative-writing tutor whose house she'd walked into over a month back. He was wearing a heavy brown greatcoat with the collar turned up. He had not shaved – for several days, seemingly. If she hadn't already known what he did for a living, she might have guessed him to be an actor. Or a model, who'd been roughed up on purpose for a fashion shoot.

'Ten minutes,' Dexter said. He held up both hands, and spread his fingers in emphasis. '*Ten.*'

Ten minutes turned out to be over an hour. Moy had got rid of her customer long before then, and done some speedy tidying of her workbench. She'd scraped all the loose nails and the assorted lengths of lead that littered its surface into two plastic containers, and arranged her tools – the glass cutters and lead cutters, the hammers and groziers and breaking pliers, the wire brushes and polishing brushes and riggers and mops and badgers and scrubs – that had been lying any old where, into a semblance of order. She'd marshalled her glass paints on one side of the bench, and the five small bureau drawers that housed glass fragments, jewels, roundels, lenses, tallow wax and lead calms on the other. Finally, she'd removed all the meths bottles and tubs of cement and tins of plaster of Paris and bottles of boiled oil that were essential to her work but which had no permanent business on the bench, and stacked them on the shelf behind it where they belonged.

While she was creating symmetry out of chaos and reinventing herself as a methodical worker, a middle-aged couple wandered in, glanced at examples of her stained glass, asked about prices, and left. As soon as they'd gone she filled the electric kettle, and boiled it so that there would be immediate coffee or tea for Dexter when he returned. She wanted to go out and buy a bottle of wine. But the off-licence probably wasn't open yet – and anyway, say he arrived and found the place abandoned, and the door locked? He might go away again. He might

172

decide – or the fates might decide – if she was not there, that it was too late for the two of them, that the moment had irrevocably passed. This had happened to Moy once, with a man she'd met at a party and landed up in bed with. They'd made a date for the following week. Lunch, meeting first at her workplace. Not long before he was due to arrive she'd realized she had nothing to offer him to drink, and nipped out for a bottle. Hurrying back, she'd found a note sellotaped to the glass shop door: *You weren't there – Danny.* The last she'd seen, or heard, of him.

When, after forty-five minutes had gone by, there was still no sign of Dexter, she sat down at the workbench and began picking out, with a horseshoe nail, the glass of a panel she'd leaded up, and cemented, and rubbed whiting into, the evening before.

He is not coming back. The fingers gripping the horseshoe nail were shaking so badly she was in danger of chipping the glass. *He will not come back, ever. You had better get used to the idea.*

He came in with a rush of freezing air. He had a bottle of wine under one arm, and in his other hand a bunch of lilies in a paper cone.

Relief at seeing him made Moy sharp. She told him to shut the door, for God's sake. She said she wouldn't be long, but she had to finish this process now she'd begun it. He could make himself some coffee if he wanted.

He put the bottle and the flowers on the ledge by the door and came and stood behind her. He leaned over her shoulder, so that she could feel the chill of his coat and the heat of his breath. What process? he wanted to know. What was she doing with that shoe brush?

It was a polishing brush, Moy said. She was polishing the lead to oxidize it, to turn it black. She pointed to a

173

section she hadn't polished yet, where the lead was still silvery.

Was that wise? Dexter asked. Wasn't silver lead a whole lot prettier than black lead?

But perhaps because Moy did not bother to answer him, he abandoned his facetious tone and became interested and serious, a seeker of hard information. Tools and glass had to be identified and handled; techniques not just explained but demonstrated. And after that he demanded to have a go himself – at glass-cutting and lead-cutting, at leading up and soldering. He took his coat off for this and rolled up his shirt sleeves in a workmanlike way, though he insisted on wearing gloves.

'I charge for these lessons,' Moy said happily. It was true; she did give lessons, to any who asked for them, and she did of course charge. Watching his tentative handling of the glass – a piece of green English muffle she didn't mind him making a mess of – she was aware of happiness, of its being a state, of being enveloped in it, like a warm towel.

Dexter said he hoped she might decide to waive her fee if he bought her lunch.

They went to the pizza place across the road. On their way out he stopped to look at the posters and postcards and blown-up photographs of famous stained glass that Moy had pinned up, for reference and inspiration, on the workshop walls.

'That's Edward the Confessor – at least it's thought to be.' She hoped that Dexter would see the likeness to himself that she saw in Edward, and remark on it, but he was concentrating on something else.

'That's Adam,' Moy said.

'I can see that.' He was peering at a postcard-size

depiction of a man with a long-handled spade working a patch of ground that appeared to be all stones. A tall, pale, grim-faced man with a brown beard and dirty-looking brown hair that straggled over his shoulders. A bony man – every rib showing – but muscular from toil. His spade yellow, the stones bone-white and smooth, like sea-bleached pebbles on a beach. Behind him, on an emerald knoll, against a background of exquisite blue and purple sky, a tree. A springy tree, all of it – trunk, branches, leaves – bone-white as the stones. (It was a tree that Moy had 'borrowed' many times. Anyone who asked for a tree window, or a Tree of Life window, got some version of this one, though not often in white.)

It was one of the Canterbury Adams, Moy explained. It was *Adam Delving*. He was in the clerestory originally and too high up to be seen, so they moved him to the nave – to the great west window. At least she imagined that's why they'd moved him. He was early – twelfth century. He was French, very likely. And he was number one in a series of – she stopped, remembering something Leila had said about Dexter's boredom threshold being on the low side.

'What a life,' Dexter said, 'what a comedown. What a fall.' He was bothered by the spade, he said. The shaft was too long – too long to be workable. If you put any weight behind it it would probably snap. It was a stunning design though. And the tree was beautiful. He would like to see the original glass. He'd only been to Canterbury once, a long time ago, and he would like to go again. He opened the street door and held it back for her. He said, 'Will you take me to Canterbury? To see the stained glass? I'd like to make the pilgrimage with *you*.'

Flannel. Blarney. Baloney. She was certain of it but, unaccountably, did not despise him.

In the pizza place, which was full and very noisy, waiting for their pizzas to arrive, filling her glass with wine from a bottle he had ordered without consulting her, he said he realized he didn't know anything about her, really. He hadn't even asked her about her family.

'My mother's dead. She died five years ago.' The mother she had loved, and loved still, and would go on grieving for to the end of her days, deserved better than this unvarnished death certificate. But if she were to attempt a definition, or try to tell him what her mother had meant to her, what could Dexter say except, I'm sorry? 'My father left her years ago, he's remarried now and lives in the States. His wife's American.'

Whereabouts? he wanted to know. Did she ever go and stay with them?

'They keep asking me, but I haven't. I will go some time. It's rural Washington State, his wife has some sort of smallholding. I hardly know her. I don't think I like her. Mardie, her name is. It's the way she says *we* all the time that pisses me off. We are doing this, we are going there, we are having friends over to dinner. As if my dad had no will of his own. Another thing — it's always her who answers the phone. Patrick's busy right now, she'll say, was it important? Shall I get him to call you? I don't believe she gives him half my messages.'

'I've been to California and I've been to Oregon, but somehow I missed out on Washington State.' He unwrapped a bread stick, snapped it in half and handed half to her.

'I gather it's beautiful, where they are it is. If you like pine forests. I want to go, I really want to, and Dad says he'll pay my fare. But.'

176

'But?'

'But I don't like him much. I'm not sure if I can forgive him for what he did to my mother.' She nearly added 'and for abandoning Joe', but checked herself just in time. 'I'd like to forgive him, obviously, or at any rate understand him, I'd like not to hate him – because he's my father. But I don't know. Another problem is, I hate flying and it's such a long flight.'

'How extraordinary. I love flying. I'd fly all the time if I could.'

They caught each other's eyes for a moment; looked away.

'Have you got brothers? Or sisters?' he asked next. 'Or both?'

The question she had been dreading. She would have to tell him about Joe, but not yet. She needed to know him a lot better before she tried explaining Joe to him.

But then the thought occurred: What if Leila had already told him about Joe? What if she had really gone to town on the subject – with all sorts of amusing, and not so amusing, anecdotes. Could Leila have done that? Would she? Oh yes.

'I have a mad brother.' She said it matter-of-factly, cheerfully even.

'That's okay – I have two mad sisters.'

'No, I mean really mad. I mean schizophrenic.' To her surprise saying it in this uncompromising way was a relief. Mad. Not mentally ill, as she usually described her brother. Not 'nutty' or 'loony' or 'not quite as others'; not 'bonkers' or 'a bit different' or 'out to lunch' or 'off the wall' – the jokey ruderies (or affectionate insults) she had sometimes employed in explaining Joe, for the good reason that they could be used about anyone. She did not

177

feel disloyal saying mad. Because if Dexter couldn't cope with it, and with schizophrenic (and with insane and demented and paranoid and psychotic and deranged); if her blood link to these words and their manifestations was too difficult for him, it was better to know it now. 'He's in and out of hospital,' she said. 'He's been ill for years. He was diagnosed at eighteen. He'll be forty-four in October.'

Dexter looked down at the tablecloth. 'Poor sod. What can I say? And it must be difficult for you,' he said when he finally looked up. 'I imagine it must be?'

Difficult. One way of describing it.

'Sometimes it is. It can be. Yes.'

'I haven't had any first-hand dealings with schizophrenia, so I don't quite know what to ask, though there's a guy I sometimes see in Spitalfields market who . . . Is he, is your brother – I'm sorry, I don't know his name?'

'Joe.'

'Is Joe *dangerous*?'

Not many people asked her this question, though she suspected they wanted to, and for a moment she was shocked. But then why shouldn't he ask it? Wasn't it – she had used the word mad, after all – the logical follow-up? And at least he was showing interest. He hadn't changed the subject or suddenly remembered an urgent appointment the other end of London. She said, 'To himself maybe. Not to anyone else. At least I don't think so, but you can't be sure about that, can you? You never know what pressures or circumstances might tip a person – even a sane person – into being dangerous. But no, I don't think Joe would hurt anyone.'

He had threatened to, though. Once, in a manic and desperate state, in total despair, he had threatened to go out into the streets of Tooting with a Kalashnikov and kill everyone he saw. Fortunately he had had no access to a Kalashnikov or any other firearm, and she'd got him into hospital right away. Not something to tell Dexter.

'If I met him, would I be able to tell he was – ?'

'Oh yes. Yes you would. Within minutes, probably.'

'How? Can you explain? If you want to, I mean, not if you don't. I'm really interested.'

'Well okay, you'd know from his face – his eyes especially. They don't look right – I can't describe it better than that. A few years ago you'd have known from the involuntary shaking and twitching he did then – hands, legs – he was all over the place. But they've changed the drugs that caused that – some of them, anyway, and they've changed the doses, so he doesn't shake so much now, thank God.' She stopped to sip her wine, and while she was sipping, images of her brother, in varying degrees of mania and distress and (hopeful and misleading) near-normality, began to come at her. She wanted to pick out for Dexter one image, one embodying detail, that would give him real insight into the hell of this skewed life. She wanted to confide to him about the unreasonable ambition Joe had that directed him, always always always, towards work he was unfitted for and incapable of. Work he would laboriously apply for, and not get. Work he (through some philanthropic desire, or lack of prescience, on the part of the employer?) miraculously did get – and would be sacked from within days or sometimes hours. Whereas the jobs he was capable of, that would not stress him to the point of breakdown, that would take him out into healing air and birdsong (park sweeping and mainte-nance or, under supervision, tree and annuals planting), he would not consider, as being too menial by half. Would vociferously refuse even to contemplate.

179

It killed my mother, she wanted to tell Dexter. His illness as good as killed her, it sapped all her strength and she died. It will kill me if I let it. As it is, it's ruined every important relationship I've had.

'Actually, Dexter, it's too complex. I mean he varies so much. When he's well he's pretty much okay. He works when he's well enough, he hates to be out of work – he's extremely courageous about working. And he's a talented drummer, could have been really good, I think. He plays drums in a band with a group of' (other loonies, she was about to say) 'friends. But when he's ill – no. Look, most of the time Joe is, Joe's behaviour is just, how shall I put it, *inappropriate* to some degree. Inappropriate remarks, inappropriate laughter – that kind of thing.'

She had said too much already.

'What's happened to our waiter?' Dexter said, twisting in his chair. He turned round to Moy and leaned towards her on his elbows. 'I'd like to meet your brother. I really would.'

For five seconds, Moy thought. I'll give it five.

'I've been thinking about your Doom window you told me about last week,' Dexter said. 'Your window of opportunity, as it were. You promised to show me your designs for it, by the way, and you didn't'

'I didn't promise. I haven't got anywhere with it yet. I've done some pencil roughs, that's all. And really I need a commission because decent cathedral glass ain't cheap.'

'You said you'd like to see it in a church, but I'm not sure a church – or any ancient building – is the right place. If you're making a state-of-the-globe window, or a where-the-world's-headed-if-we-don't-mend-our-ways-sharpish window, it ought to be set in a correspondingly state-of-the-art building. Don't you think. Otherwise, what's the point? But I do think you ought to include a few devils, if only as a sort of link or reference back.'

He refilled their wineglasses. He took no notice when Moy said she would not be able to do any work if she went on drinking. 'I hope you won't discount the idea of devils. They could stand in for all sorts of present-day horrors – superbugs, say, or blister packs, or voice mail. Or pizza,' he added, as the waiter set down their plates.

Silence. Which was immediately filled by a general hum and by the, suddenly unignorable, conversation of the young couple at the adjoining table.

'And I painted my bedroom red,' the woman, whose elbow was only inches from Moy's elbow, said. 'A very dark red. I used a paint swab.'

'Red? That's neat,' the man said.

'I have a sleigh bed.'

'Oh, I love a sleigh bed.'

'Me too. It's like, it's like it's way up there.'

'I have to write this down,' Dexter whispered, pulling a notebook from his coat pocket.

'Why?' Moy picked up her knife and fork and began cutting a way through the uncooked onion skins and burnt olives that decorated the rock-like crust. 'What for?'

'Shhh. Or I'll lose it.'

'Why?' she persisted, when he'd shut his notebook and refilled her glass. 'Why do you have to write it down? Are you writing a book?'

'No.' He sounded surprised.

'I should've thought someone with your background – publishing, I mean – might be tempted to write a novel. You must know all the tricks, presumably.'

He looked at her reprovingly over his wineglass. '*The Great Gatsby* has already been written,' he said.

181

Oh God, thought Moy. Please don't put me off you too soon.

He was just a compulsive note taker, that was all, Dexter explained. He wrote things down because he didn't want to miss anything.

'He left it so open-ended – know what I mean?' The young woman at the adjoining table was saying now. 'It's like, a wimpy thing.'

Dexter put down his fork and grabbed his pencil.

'Hey,' Moy said. She felt threatened by the note-taking, by his fascination with the conversation of two stranger Americans, by his not paying attention to her. 'Hey.'

'It's like, you know, a foreign language thing.' He looked up from his notebook, and grinned. 'It's like, it's way up there.'

When Moy laughed, he leaned right across the table and said, 'What's their relationship, d'you reckon?'

'Brother and sister?'

'Can't be. They don't know anything about each other.'

'Perhaps they've been separated since childhood, and have just remet. They do look quite alike. They're both blond. Or I suppose they could be colleagues. Business colleagues?'

'*Colleagues*,' Dexter said. 'That's it; that's what they are.' He went back to his pizza.

Moy hunted around for a topic of conversation.

'Do you think you'll ever hear from your creative writing students?' was what she eventually came up with. 'Do you think any of them will get published and famous and say they owe all their success to you?'

Dexter said no. They were a bunch of no-hopers, he said – except for one, except for one, very young, guy. He was okay. Anyway, he wasn't a teacher. He wasn't patient enough. He only did the course to make some money – he was always trying to find new ways of making money. One thing he'd tried was selling sheep manure door to door. He'd bagged up the manure on a visit to his mother's place in Shropshire – his mother was a farmer – and driven the load to London and tried to flog it to rich pricks with gardens in Kensington and Chelsea, most of whom had shut the door in his face. But as to the creative writing bit, he'd never do another. 'It was a killer.' He frowned. He put down his knife and fork and picked up the pizza and continued eating with his fingers.

'Leila said you were a very good teacher. She said you were good but tough.' This was a lie, Leila had said nothing of the sort. But his candour ought to be rewarded, she thought.

A grunt from Dexter. A silence. Then he said, rather sourly, 'I learnt from it, though. I suppose I did. Lessons are not given, they are taken – as someone wiser than I once said.'

'Who said?'

'An Italian novelist, dead. At least I think it was him.'

'But it's ambiguous, isn't it, *taken* is ambiguous. It could mean, it presumably does mean, *received* – on the other hand teachers take classes, don't they? So taken could mean *conducted*?'

He groaned (it sounded like a groan). 'I think not.'

'I was sorry about the girl who died – who killed herself,' she heard herself say. 'Leila told me, I hope you don't mind. It must have been dreadful for you.'

'Not for me. I didn't know her. For her family.'

Again she felt reproved. Giving up on the pizza she began to move her wineglass around, making circles with

183

it and figures of eight, guiding it over bumps and ruckles in the tablecloth. Eventually she picked up the glass and took a long swallow. *Look at me, Dexter. Don't go away. Come back. Talk to me.*

The wine speaking, she knew this. The wine giving her a heightened, or maybe lowered sense of things – of possibilities. Daring her to stretch out her hand now, and touch, or hold, his hand. To lean right across the table – knocking over the wine bottle – and kiss his mouth. To kiss it better, as her mother had done to her grazed, five-year-old, knee. To make it all right. To kiss it all better.

Or slap his face: the wine's next suggestion. Why not slap his face really hard? Not for any reason. Just for the hell of it.

'Well, that was pretty nasty.' He pushed his plate away, drained his glass. He picked up the bottle – empty. 'Shall we have another one of these?'

She shook her head. 'We've got through two.'

'A half-bottle then. Or a glass at least. Or coffee? Double espresso?'

'Nothing more for me.' It sounded prissy, or plain dreary. And it was not what she meant. No coffee, and no more wine, meant the bill, which they would fight over and pay. Then they would leave. And go their separate ways.

'Moy.' He leaned towards her on his elbows. 'Moy?'

'Yes?'

He raised his eyebrows in a questioning way.

'What?'

He mouthed, Can-we-go-to-bed? Please?

'What?' – though she'd understood him perfectly well. 'I said can we go to bed?' He said it out loud this time,

184

so loud that the American business colleagues turned their heads.

'I've been wanting you all morning,' Dexter said. 'Can we go to bed *now*?'

'I don't go to bed with men with beards,' she heard herself say, in a high and alien voice. 'I never do. I can't stand beards.'

'That's no problem, I'll shave it off. If there's a razor in your flat – presumably you have a razor? – I'll shave my beard off. Though you can hardly call this' – he rubbed his chin so that it made a rasping noise – 'a beard. I do hope you have a sleigh bed in your flat,' he added as he signalled the waiter to bring the bill.

The following day, when Moy went back to her workshop, she found the cone of limp lilies and the bottle of wine he'd brought still on the ledge by the door. He had not mentioned them, she remembered; he'd never once hinted that he'd meant them for her.

Moy did take Dexter to Canterbury to see *Adam Delving*. The visit was part of a tour they made – it was also meant to be a holiday – of English churches and cathedrals that Moy said had particularly fine, or interesting, or unusual, stained glass. The tour-holiday had been Dexter's idea. He said he wanted to celebrate Moy's agreeing, after months of shilly-shallying, to move in with him. He wanted to mark her decision to share his life – and his sons' lives – in a relevant and memorable fashion. He bought a road atlas and they spent several drunken and argumentative evenings studying it.

They argued because it was not an easy tour to plan. A week was all either of them could afford to take off from work, and the stained glass Moy specifically wanted to see

185

and to show Dexter was impossibly far-flung. Another limiting factor: Dexter said he didn't want to spend the entire holiday on the road.

'We could start off in Oxford and then go west,' Moy said. They were sitting with the atlas at the kitchen table. 'West and north – or west and south. We could start off in Christ Church Cathedral, say. Then, while we're in the area we can go to Iffley and see the John Piper window David Wasley made.' She traced the route with her finger. She wanted Dexter to see some good twentieth-century glass, she said. After that they could go north-west. There was a lot of interesting stuff round Hereford she hadn't seen and was keen to have a look at. 'Madley church has some medieval –'

Dexter said no. He said they could do Herefordshire churches any time – any time they were staying with his mother. Canterbury was where they had to go because Canterbury was the English Chartres. More to the point, Canterbury had *Adam Delving*, and *Adam Delving* was forever linked with the first time they'd made love. 'This trip is a sort of honeymoon, after all,' he said, leaning sideways to kiss her ear.

'You have to be married to go on one of those.' She thought it important to remind him of this because although she had made her views on matrimony – matrimony in general and matrimony *vis-à-vis* herself – very plain; and although she had told him that her maternal grandparents had lived harmoniously together for fifty years without being married and without feeling any need to be, Dexter seemed never to have got the message. Or perhaps it was simply that he did not believe her. He appeared unable to comprehend why a person who had declared her love and commitment, who was prepared to share his house and his life, who involved herself with his children in such positive and tactful ways, would not want to take the logical next step. The step, Dexter said, that announced to the world what two people, a man and a woman, were about (so that the world knew how to treat them). 'Most women do want to get married,' he'd told her. 'They want to get married at least once, if only out of curiosity.' When she said she was not most women, he said, with a long-drawn-out sigh, 'You can say that again.' She'd had the impression that the sigh had less to do with her resistance to marriage than with her unnatural − his word − feelings about motherhood: 'I don't want babies. I like kids, some kids anyway, I like yours, but I don't want any of my own. I've never wanted kids.'

What she had meant was, I don't want to have kids who *might turn out to be mad.* But she didn't want to tell him that, so she said, Anyway, I'm too old.

That was nonsense, Dexter had retorted at once. Women were having their babies later and later, often not starting till their mid-forties. Moy was only forty-one − she couldn't use age as an excuse. The trouble with you is, he said, you're not prepared to take a risk − any sort of risk. You are, as they in military parlance, risk-*averse.*

'I said *sort of* honeymoon,' he said now. 'Honeymoon means more, or maybe less, than you seem to think. Business partners can have a honeymoon, you know. Companies do when they merge, they usually go through what's known as a honeymoon period. You and I are, in effect, merging − and this is our honeymoon period. Would you believe.'

In the end they agreed to make for Canterbury, stopping at various churches along the way. Kemsing and Nettlestead and Marden were musts, Moy said. And they had to see the Marc Chagall designs at Tudeley, in particular the memorial window he designed for a girl who died in a sailing accident. The glass for this window was made at Reims, she explained, by a French glassmaker named Charles Marq, and it was very very beautiful – the blues were quite incredible. Oh, and they had to go to Selling. That would take up Day One. Day Two they would spend in the cathedral. They would spend a second night in or near Canterbury and the following day drive north. North to Essex and Cambridgeshire and Suffolk and Norfolk and –

Dexter stopped her at this point. North meant driving back the way they'd come. Did she really want to spend two days of a very short honeymoon on the M20 and the M25 and the Dartford Tunnel? Because he did not.

Honeymoon. That word again.

Okay, Moy said, re-examining the map, after Canterbury they'd go south and west. They'd take in Winchester and Salisbury. If they went to Salisbury they'd be able to go to Wilton, there was some exceptional stained glass at Wilton – and at the end of the week they'd go back to London via the M3 or the M4. Or if they did manage to get as far as Oxford, they'd go back on the M40.

'A motorway honeymoon ours is going to be,' Dexter said. 'A Welcome Break and Little Chef honeymoon. Oh goody.'

The car Dexter hired for their trip was a Toyota Corolla. Only a year old but with a lot of mileage on the clock. Comfortable but not gutsy. He drove and Moy read the map. The conventional division of labour didn't bother her: not having driven for over a year, she didn't relish the idea of negotiating seven-exit roundabouts and complex one-way systems in towns with Dexter agitating in the passenger seat.

They stayed in bed-and-breakfast places and in back-street hotels that had thin walls and powdery wallpaper and carpets with kinetic patterns in orange and brown. Not booking in advance meant that the bedroom they would inevitably be shown to was on the top floor, up four flights of breathtaking and fire-hazardous stairs, with the nearest bathroom and lavatory – lavatory paper by no means guaranteed – on the floor below. Giggling, they agreed that there was a sameness about these bedrooms, about the grubby candlewick bedspread, musty nylon pillowcases, quaggy mattress, dysfunctional miniature TV (in any case fixed too high on the wall, and at the wrong angle, for successful viewing from the bed), and absence of bedside lights that implied a mischievous monopoly of decorators and furnishers at work. And there was a sameness about the smell in these places, an all-day smell of Full English Breakfast (cooked in diesel oil or re-used badger fat, Dexter suggested), overlaid by spray-on laven-der furniture polish.

They made love in these rooms – in this one room, as it seemed – in the afternoons. They would get up early, spend the morning looking at stained glass, eat a sandwich lunch, go back to their hotel, make love. At six, Dexter would telephone his sister Elizabeth's house, where his sons were staying, and talk to Dig and Frankie. Then, after a shared whiskey, drunk from a tooth-mug in their room, they would walk round the now deserted town, or drive out into the country and walk in lanes or fields before finding somewhere to have supper.

It seemed to Moy, standing at the window of the

Copperfield Road studio, looking out over the deserted sports stadium, looking back on that holiday with Dexter, that he had been right in calling it a honeymoon. Looking back, it was their lovemaking she remembered best and that had impressed her most: the unhurried sweet caresses that had prefaced a frenzied urgency and intensity; a warmth, so delicious and intoxicating it had to be fuelled by something more than exercise and body contact; actions and gestures and cries and murmurings that no matter how often they were repeated she had each time understood as new and miraculous. For the ugly surroundings and impossible bed had never managed to put them off at all. Sights and smells that by rights should have been detractors had turned out to be a spur, positive contributors to their pleasure and responsible for much of the laughter she remembered – laughter (it had been more like giggling, like fits of giggles) that had made the very idea of post-coitum blues absurd. Once, pausing between licks and kisses, he had lifted his head to enquire, Who am I? Don't ask me, Moy had said, I haven't a clue, who are you? I am Adam, *delving*, he'd said.

Whereas the cultural aspect of their trip had been a disappointment to her, if not to Dexter. She had wanted to share her passion with him, to fire him into feeling a comparable ardour of his own (which they would then be able to talk about); but it was soon clear that, *Adam Delving* aside, his attention span for stained glass was short. He seemed to be more interested in tombs and stonework and carved misericords and medieval floor tiles than in the windows they had gone specifically to see. After only a few minutes of silent staring up at a window, he would melt away to look at these other things, or wander outside

190

to examine flying buttresses, chamfered plinths, head-stones. At Tudeley, he had not found much to say about the Chagall window that Moy so admired – for its colours, for the daringly free and vigorous line – and found so heart-rending. Afterwards, as they sat on a bank eating their sandwiches, he told her he had a confession to make. He wasn't sure he liked modern stained glass, twentieth-century glass, very much, he said. And he'd decided he didn't like nineteenth-century stained glass *at all*. He only truly liked old glass, he realized, ancient glass – not just because the colours were more gorgeous, or more subtle, was it, than modern glass, or because its uncluttered designs spoke directly to you in a way more recent stuff never did, but because it *was* old. Because it had survived centuries. It was this sense you got of endurance and history that moved him, the knowledge that people in tunic or doublet and hose had looked at it too.

Glancing up from his sandwich, seeing her wounded expression, he clapped a hand to his mouth. Oh lor. When he said he wasn't keen on new stained glass, he didn't mean the glass *she* made, he said. He didn't mean *that*. Her stained glass was *wonderful*, he *loved* her stained glass.

There was a muffled warbling from somewhere in the heap of stuff on Moy's workbench. She ignored it. After a short silence, the warbling began again, and she left the window. Because it might not be Joe. It might be a customer, or a potential customer, and she needed work. She had frighteningly little work on at the moment, and no new orders. Not *one* new order.

'It's me,' said the meek voice in her mobile phone.

'Oh,' Moy said. 'Oh. You feeling okay now? Had a lie down?'

'I'm ringing to apologize,' Dexter said.

Moy waited. What was he going to apologize for? There were several contenders that she could think of.

'Are you still there, Moy?'

'I'm working, Dexter. I'm trying to make up for a lost morning.'

'Yes. Of course. You must be. Look, I'm not sure if you know, because you didn't say, but I told my mother the other day that you and I were getting married. I've no idea why I did that, it was wrong of me, and I'm sorry.'

Moy didn't say anything.

'Did you know about this?' Dexter said.

'Yes, I did know.'

'Well, as I say, I'm sorry. Really am. I'll phone my mother and tell her it isn't true.'

'Okay. Thank you.'

'You don't sound as if it is okay.'

'Well, it was embarrassing,' Moy said. 'I felt very embarrassed talking to your mother.' And angry, she thought. And angry. 'I didn't know what to say to her. She kept quizzing me about our wedding plans.'

'I'm sorry.'

Moy was silent. She couldn't say 'okay' again. In any case, it wasn't okay, not yet. She wasn't going to forgive him quite yet.

'I'm taking the ring back to the jeweller's later on this afternoon, when I've finished my piece for Philip Cartwright. Just tellng you in case you needed to get hold of me for any reason. If you phone and get no answer, that's where I'll be.'

'Okay.' After a pause, she said, 'I might not be back tonight.'

'What d'you mean?'

'Thought I might stay here – you know, if I'm working late. Haven't decided.'

There were plenty of things for her to sleep on, if she did decide to stay. A sofa, rugs, a choice of chairs, a mattress. All the furniture, save one armchair, from her old Battersea flat was stored in this studio. Dexter hadn't wanted it in his house. There wasn't any room for it, he'd said.

'Moy, don't sleep in the studio. It isn't safe for you to sleep there. Please come home.'

'I'll see. I might just go and check out my godson. Haven't seen him for months – Leila's quite pissed off with me. If I do go to Leila's when I've finished work, I'll probably stay the night. But I'll let you know.'

'But aren't they coming to supper here next week? I thought you said they were. You'll see them all then.'

'Leila and Robert are coming for supper. But not the kids. They'll get a babysitter for the kids.'

He said something she couldn't hear, that she wasn't meant to hear. Fuck, it might have been.

'Did you say *fuck*?'

'I didn't say anything. Didn't say anything at all.'

'Bye, then,' Moy said. And rang off.

THE BARS of the cattle grid make a hollow rumbling clang, like some crude percussion instrument, as the pushchair bumps over them. (Tubular bells, it comes to him. Or a primitive version of glockenspiel?)

He and the kids are on their way to the farmyard to check out the two tractors and their absorbing attachments, and to chat up such animals as are not out to pasture. An after-breakfast routine on these visits to the farm.

The pushchair, with Frankie on board, is bloody hard work to push. It's an old one, forty years old at least, the one his mother ferried him about in when he was a two-year-old. Its rusted wheels repeatedly buck and lock, as though the brake's on. He stops, bends down, lifts the chair over the final three bars of the grid, sets it on the cobblestones. 'You weigh a ton, Frankie boy. Why not get out and use your fat little legs?'

'*No* walk, *no* walk, no *walk*.' The few words his younger son knows how to say, or is prepared to say, are delivered with force and in triplicate.

Ahead of them in the yard, his Mig-fighter elder son

zips criss-cross over the cobbles, swept back arm-wings dipping and tilting. 'Eeeeeeeeeeeeeeow.'

'Keep away from the slurry pit!' he warns Dig. Or Mig. There is danger everywhere in the farmyard. Crunching machinery, vicious teeth and hooves – danger everywhere for a small, curious, boy.

A freezing, but sunny, morning. Voluptuous clouds, surreally still in a hard blue sky. Hens and ducks and pigeons pecking the yard. A stench of dung so overpowering he can almost taste it. In the distance, a line of prick-eared horseheads framed in the dark openings above loosebox doors. Below him, in the pushchair, fat man Frankie, fatter than normal in a bulky orange dufflecoat, a hand-me-down from Dig.

There's a toggle missing from Frankie's coat. He's aware of it, of the rip in the cloth, under his son's chin, where the toggle ought to be. He can't see the rip (or the front of the coat) but he's anxiously aware of it. What he can see is the top and back of the dufflecoat's hood. And its sleeves, and Frankie's blue-mittened hands gripping the sides of the chair. There are blotches on the back of the hood, streaky stains from the time his son's machine-washable coat shared the Hoover *logic* with a purple shirt of Hyacinth's.

Where *is* Hyacinth? She was there at breakfast (he thinks she was, he's pretty sure she was). So where is she?

He steers towards the stable block, forces the unwilling pushchair over ill-matched stones. *This is the way the farmer rides, bumpety, bumpety, bump.*

The stable block rears up in front of them, crazily, at a crazy angle. Novice's cine film, it reminds him of. Hand-held-camera documentary. Visual cliché, either way.

He lifts Frankie out of the pushchair, swings him up on to his shoulders. *There you go, cowboy.* They move along the line of horseheads. He hangs on tight to Frankie's straddled legs as the child leans wide of his shoulder-perch. 'Hello *horse*, hello *horse*, hello *horse*.'

The horseheads throw themselves up and down, out of Frankie's reach. 'Byebye *horse*, byebye *horse*. Bye*bye*.'

'Hi, Dad.' Michael Bucknell fills the tack room doorway, a dubbin cloth in his hand. He has on the green and brown check cap he always wears, a collarless shirt with rolled-up sleeves, a green, padded waistcoat. The ends of his corduroys are crushed into black Dunlop boots. The tops of the boots have been turned down, builder or farmworker style, to reveal cuffs of cream lining.

'Dad. We're looking for Mummy.' By 'mummy' he means his sons' mother. He means Hyacinth. 'You seen her anywhere? Hi there, Raider.' He's spotted his father's black Labrador dog, on guard beside the tack room door.

(*Raider.* He knows something about Raider. Some, secret or distinguishing, fact about the dog that his father does not know. Something he ought to tell his father? If he could remember what it was.)

There's a metal notice nailed to the wall above Raider's head. Black lettering on a strong yellow ground. It says:

Welcome to Hackney City Farm
Wheelchair access through Farm yard
Surfaces may be uneven Please take care
No dogs please except guide dogs

'Mummy?' – Frankie, from his shoulder-perch. 'Mum, Mum, Mummy?'

'You seen Hyacinth anywhere, Dad?'

His father lifts his cap, smooths his thin hair, slings the cap back on his head. His eyes are very blue. 'She was in the hay barn, earlier,' his father says, 'helping Billy shift bales.'

What?

'I've got something to show you,' his father says, smiling. It's a sweet smile, a smile of unbelievable sweetness and benignity.

He follows his father's backview through the doorway. Inside the tack room, there's a muted gleam of steel and leather − otherwise, darkness. He can't see his father, though he can hear him, pounding ahead. Wait for me, Dad! Don't go so fast!

The tack room is a low-ceilinged tunnel. If he keeps his head down, there's just space enough to stand upright. But the tunnel's narrow, his progress along it frustrated by snagging bridles and bruising saddle racks. Wait for me, Dad!

'There,' his father says, triumphant. He slides back the bolt from huge double doors, kicks the doors outwards, flattens himself to the tunnel wall, points at the opening. 'Go on, D, take a look,' his father says. 'Take a good look.'

He's alone, on the threshold, looking out. Taking a good look. What is there? Water. A river, a torrent, a flood. Brown and boiling. Headlong. Numinous.

Water. He watches it career towards him. Uprooting trees, sweeping away bank, bearing its spoils on crests of dirty foam. Tossing them, dragging them, sucking them down. Water occupies the field of his vision, fills, to its four corners, the entire wide screen. For it seems to be a screen. Or a picture window? Or a picture *show*. Whatever, he senses a saving barrier between the drama out there, its tumult, and himself. He is above the drama, or in some way separate from it. At a soundproof remove from the fury he can see. Able to absorb, with interest, not terror, the ornate and credible details that rush by: a patch of moss, like a saturated black sponge, gripping a boulder; a dizzying branch spun whirligig by the current; a twist of orange cloth, caught on a reed.

Orange cloth?

Frankie. Where is *Frankie*?

Where is *Dig*?

Where are *my children*?

He's in the farmyard. In bright, horrible sunshine, turning himself in panicky circles, searching the yard with his eyes. The yard is clean-swept and empty. No life visible at all.

He runs alongside the stock sheds, the lambing shed, the milking shed, the tractor shed, tugging open doors, screaming through the doors. Dig! Frankie! Where the fuck *are* you?

He's running back the way he came. But slowly now, exhausted now, hopeless now. He's running back, banging the doors shut, slamming them in turn, when he remembers: *I've done this before.* I know this bit about the doors, I know what I have to do to find my kids because *I've done all this before.*

What he has to do is stop, and stand absolutely still. Then, facing east, he has to look out over the yard to the easternmost corner, the place by the stock fence where the elder tree and the cattle trough are. If he can find the elder tree and the cattle trough, he will find his kids. His kids will be there. Splashing their hands in the trough, he seems to remember. Mucking about with the ballcock.

He stands absolutely still and looks out east over the yard.

And there they are. The elder tree, the trough, and Dig and Frankie. There they all are.

Dig is bent over the cattle trough, hands in the water, sailing a piece of bark. Frankie, in the pushchair, is preoccupied with the buckles of his seat belt, trying to slot them.

Oh, the relief. Oh God, thank God, thank you God, the relief.

'Not like that, Frankie boy. You'll never do it that way. Watch.' He squats in front of the pushchair, extracts the buckles from his son's fat fingers. 'Like this, sweetheart.'

He's squatting there, hunkered down, untwisting the straps, sorting the buckles – piece of piss, no sweat – but there's something wrong.

It's the pushchair. It's the pushchair wheels. The size of them (the size of adult bicycle wheels), their doubleness, their double *rim*. It's the spokes. The clinical, terrifying, glint of them.

Wheelchair wheels.

But he knows about this. He knows – what? What does he know?

Keep your eyes on the buckles. Don't look at Frankie, don't dare look up at Frankie.

But he has to look. He always looks, he's compelled to look. He does:

A white, feeble elbow, propped on pitiable knees. A wasted arm, and wrist, and hand, supporting (attempting to support) an insupportable head. In the head, a black and scabious –

The screaming woke Dexter, or the shouting did. 'No no no no *no!*'

He lay on his left side, in the recovery position, eyes wide open, and waited for his backbone to unlock itself. Nightmares had this physical aftermath for him – a locking, or tightening, or stiffening, or gripping, of his spine, neck to coccyx, which lasted as long as the worst of the horror lasted.

When his spine had more or less returned to itself, he rolled over, cautiously on account of his bruised chest, and lay on his back. He did not dare to shut his eyes. Then, after a minute or two of wide-eyed staring into the dark, he rolled again, the other way, towards the centre of the bed and Moy. Moy always held him when he had a nightmare. She would crush his sweat-drenched face against her little beestings and hold him in silence, stroking his head until the fear retreated.

But the bed was wide and empty, and in mid-roll he remembered: Moy was at Leila and Robert's. An overnight stay because tomorrow morning she was going to take her godson, Aaron, on an outing to the Natural History Museum – or the Science Museum, or the zoo, or wherever Aaron most wanted to go. She'd phoned from Leila's to tell him these plans. 'Should be home around seven,' she'd shouted, cheerful against a backdrop of laughter and John Coltrane. 'Love you,' had been a rushed afterthought, as he understood it, before she rang off.

On his back once more, in Moy's side of the bed (some comfort in that), he let his eyes close for a second – and the wheelchair came at him. Accelerating down a steep grass bank, mustering terror as it –

He opened his eyes. Dad. Oh, *Dad.* He could not

know, for sure, who it was in the wheelchair; his subconscious never allowed him to know (or he did not want to know), but it had to be his father. Some, grotesque and sickening, version of him.

He began to weep. The tears chased over his cheeks and nose, streamed into his mouth; they poured sideways over his cheekbones, and collected in his ears. Oh, *Dad.*

'WHAT A weeny house.' Frankie stared round the living room. It was clear he couldn't believe what he saw. 'This room's shrunk. It's weeny.'

Frankie always said this, or something like it, when he returned to Bethnal Green after a fortnight at his grandmother's. He never failed to be amazed by the smallness of the London house rooms and doors, the low set of the door handles, the narrowness of the stairs. He always accused the place of having shrunk.

'Frankie has a microbial brain,' Dig explained to David Mullins.

'What's that?' David Mullins said. 'Can't hear you. You'll have to talk up.'

'I didn't think microbes had brains.' Moy hoped to put Dig down the way he, in public – though not in private, she had noticed – put his younger brother down.

'My point precisely,' murmured Dig.

They stood in an awkward knot just inside the front door, the boys' luggage spread out on the painted floorboards at their feet. A tent bag, an army kitbag, an ancient holdall with leather handles and trim. A black nylon backpack with white plastic buckles, a camera in a hard blue case, a leatherette briefcase that concealed a backgammon board and evenings misspent. Anoraks, cagoules, rubber boots. A Maxply tennis racquet, *circa* 1968 and with three bust strings, that the boy Desmond had knocked up with. Toys in a ripped supermarket carrier that had *Lightening the load* in looped, pretend handwriting on the front. *Lightening your wallet* was Dexter's usual amendment of this. *Lightening your pay packet. Increasing your debt.*

'I'm sure you could do with a drink after that drive? Or a cup of tea or something?' Dexter patted the two-seater, wincing because his punched ribcage was giving him hell. 'David, Enid, come in and sit down.'

'We ought to be getting on, we're already an hour later than I told the daughter to expect us,' David Mullins said. 'I could use the Gents, however, if someone would be good enough to point me in the right direction.'

David Mullins was a red-faced, stocky man, with white eyebrows and a crest of shockingly white hair. His small blue eyes were made smaller by puffily protective lids. He had big square hands that gave the impression of being bigger than his feet, and he walked in an effortful, unbalanced way – the result of an accident, involving a tractor and a ditch, twenty years or so ago, Dexter had told Moy.

An awful old bore, was how Dexter had described David Mullins to Moy. A tactless old fool, a reactionary old buffer. Typical farmer type, he'd said.

He can't help being old, Moy had said.

Dexter said he thought he could help it. He thought in David Mullins's case, he could.

What about Mrs Mullins? What was she like? Moy had wanted to know.

She was all right, Dexter had said. She was harmless except for one dementing habit – she always called him Desmond. He didn't think it was mischievousness on her part because she was a kind woman in other ways, but he couldn't be certain it wasn't.

'Show David the loo, Dig, and take your clobber up to your play station at the same time,' Dexter said, in the tones, hearty and firm, he employed for his sons when visitors were present. 'And you, Frankie boy. Take your stuff up now before we trip over it. Before we break our legs. What are you doing with that tennis racquet? It shouldn't be here, it belongs at your gran's. We're a wee bit pushed fer space, as you can see,' he explained to David Mullins.

'I wouldn't mind a cup of tea if you're really making one, dear,' Enid Mullins called over a blue-cardiganed shoulder from the two-seater. 'What an interesting room this is, Desmond. *Very* modern and with it.'

'Dexter,' Dexter muttered, 'my name is Dexter.' To his younger son he said, 'Go on now, Frankie, remove your kit.'

Frankie had not followed Dig and David Mullins up the stairs. He was sidling round the living room, running a hand over surfaces, picking up objects, weighing them in his hand, putting them down. Peering into the fish tank to check that his fish were still alive. It was another habit of his when he returned home after a week or so away – to touch things, check up on things. He did it to re-establish himself, Moy had suggested to Dexter, who found Frankie's rituals irritating and disturbing. He was marking his territory the way cats did.

204

Dexter had said Frankie was not a cat. But that if he wasn't careful he was in danger of becoming a radical misfit. And we don't want another one of those in the family, do we, he'd added.

Moy had not asked who the primary misfit was, though she'd had the feeling he wanted her to ask.

Fishing a tea bag out of a mug, adding milk, stirring, adding more milk, she could hear Dexter's jolly-uncle voice saying, 'Go on, *Monsieur Touche-tout*, get on with it. Carry what you can and I'll give you a hand with the rest later.'

'Would you like sugar, Mrs Mullins?' she called from the kitchen doorway.

'No thank you dear,' Enid Mullins called back. 'Just a drop of milk.'

'We don't seem to have any cups, I hope you don't mind a mug,' Moy said, handing it over. She sat down beside Enid Mullins on the sofa. She felt she had to do this because Dexter, who had known Mrs M for ever and whose duty it surely was to chat the old lady up, was now standing in the front window with his back to them, staring into the dark. A pose, Moy thought. An attention-seeking and ill-mannered pose, best ignored. 'Would you like to phone your daughter?' she asked Enid Mullins, 'In case she's getting worried about you?'

'Oh no. No thank you dear. Jenny won't be worried, she's not a worrier. She'll expect us when she sees us. Goodness, it's close in London – so much closer than in Shropshire – how do you manage with the lack of air?'

'I haven't seen Jenny for a hundred years,' Dexter said, swinging round abruptly, coming over. 'I haven't seen her since –'

Since? Since she'd tried to get into his knickers at a

Young Farmers' barbecue. Jumping Jenny the lads had all called her in those days. She'd managed to get into several pairs of knickers that barbecue evening, by all accounts, but not his. He'd never found her remotely fanciable.

'She hasn't changed,' Enid Mullins said. 'She's just the same friendly old Jenny. My daughter and Desmond were supposed to get married, you know – to each other, I mean,' she explained to Moy. 'We parents had it all worked out. They were going to get married and run the two farms together and have half a dozen sons who in turn would . . . that's what we planned. That's what we did our best to engineer. But you can't decide those things for people, can you? Our kids had other ideas.'

'First I've heard of this,' said Dexter, smiling in horror, raising his eyebrows in horror at Moy. 'I was never aware of any matchmaking going on, Enid.'

There was a commotion at the top of the stairs. David Mullins, coming down, had collided with Frankie on his second, laden, journey up.

'It's like living in a Whitehall farce living here,' said Dexter, who had never seen one of these farces but had heard plenty about them. Before he was born and while he was growing up his parents and the Mullinses had made a joint annual trip to London to 'do a few shows', as David Mullins had put it. A Whitehall farce, apparently, had been the highlight of these jaunts, which had included shopping at Debenhams for new outfits for the wives, tea at Lyons Corner House (until it closed), drinks at the Trocadero (ditto), dinner at an Angus Steak House, one morning in the National Gallery, one afternoon at the Royal Academy Summer Show. They went to the summer show specifically to see Stanley Anderson's farm scenes and Alfred Munning's racehorses and hunters. Also Dame Laura

Knight's gipsies and clowns. Dexter had disparaged these trips to Moy and mocked his parents' notion of culture, even going so far as to pull down from his bookshelves the RA catalogues his father had collected so that Moy could see for herself the 'unspeakable' Royal Academicians his dad had approvingly marked. He and Moy had spent an enjoyable evening with the catalogues, whooping over the plates they contained, in particular the mawkish Stanley Andersons with their children's-book titles: *Feeding Time*; *The Farm by the Brook*; *Oats, Potatoes and Hay*. It's as if modernism had never happened, Moy had remarked, turning the pages in disbelief. It's though Matisse had never existed.

But on another occasion, late at night, in bed, in the dark, Dexter had talked tenderly about these London excursions. He could picture the foursome boarding the train at Ludlow, he told Moy, he could picture the scratched-leather luggage and their excitement. He could see them *on* the train, unpacking their sandwiches, pouring celebratory, ready-mixed gin and tonic into cardboard cups. He could imagine the private jokes and the laughter, the leg-pulling of the menfolk by the womenfolk, who in his vision had swapped their habitual windcheaters and worn corduroys for Gor-ray skirts and Peter Scott fully-fashioned knitteds, as advertised in the RA catalogues. It moved him to think of these four hardworking people let off the leash for once, determined to paint the town red. They deserved their little holidays. They bloody well deserved those once-a-year breaks, he'd said, suddenly loud and aggressive, as though Moy had argued against this wisdom, which she had not. They worked so fucking hard all year, they really deserved their bit of fun. Sitting up, punching the pillows, he had gone on, astonishingly, to defend his parents' taste in art, singling out the Stanley Andersons for special commendation. At least they weren't pretentious, he said, at least they were *about* something. At least they were an honest attempt at –

Oh come off it, Dexter – Moy had been a sympathetic listener up to this point, but his latest volte-face was one too many. Those farm paintings are crap, they're biscuit-tin stuff, there's nothing truthful about them. You said so yourself, only last week.

To her relief, he had leaned back in the pillows and laughed – at himself, she imagined. Just testing, he'd said eventually, finding her mouth in the dark and kissing it. Just testing, sweetheart. Only testing.

I will never know where I am with him, Moy had thought. I will never be able to get at the truth of anything. I will never know what he really thinks or feels.

'Oh those Whitehall farces – Brian Rix – did you ever see him, Desmond? He used to make us weep. I remember your father –' And Enid Mullins began to laugh at the memory of whatever it was.

'What's all this?' David Mullins, who had been standing at the bottom of the stairs, absorbedly fiddling with his left ear, came over to join them. 'What've I been missing?'

'Desmond was reminding me –' Enid Mullins began.

'Dexter,' Dexter said crisply. 'I haven't been Desmond you know for –'

'We ought to be on our way.' David Mullins was still fiddling with his ear, now emitting a high-pitched noise, part whistle, part bleep. 'My hearing aid's on the blink, I can't hear a word any of you are saying. Ah, that's it. That's better. Now, what's happened to those lads of yours? We must say goodbye to 'em.'

They'd be reacquainting themselves with their computer, Dexter told him. They'd been deprived of it for a whole fortnight, and would be making up for lost time. 'I'll go and get them down,' he said, crossing to the stairs.

'Young Dig tells me he's thinking of becoming a Muslim,' David Mullins said. 'He's quite a card, that lad, isn't he. Quite a joker. Comes out with the most extraordinary things. A Muslim, eh?'

'Oh no, I assure you, he's serious. If he doesn't embrace Islam he'll be one of only three non-Muslims in his class next term. So he's thinking about it. Quite properly in my view.' *That should sort you, you racist old fool.*

David Mullins shook his head. He looked puzzled, or upset. He said, 'Before you get the youngsters down, could I have a word? Is there anywhere we can go where we can't be overheard?'

The boys wouldn't hear anything if their door was shut, and it usually was, Dexter said. But they could go into the kitchen if he wanted. Or they could go out the back, in the yard.

The telephone rang.

'Excuse me just a moment' – Dexter dived for the handset – 'Philip? What? *Who?* I can't hear you – what did you say? *Sorry?* Oh. Oh – it's for you Moy.' Frowning, he held out the receiver. 'No prizes.'

Moy was shaking her head furiously and holding up a warding-off hand. 'Tell him I can't talk to him now. Tell him I'll call him back later.'

'You tell him' – frowning, rubbing his sore chest, handing her the receiver. 'I can't get any sense out of him.'

You're a bastard, Dexter. 'Hello Joe,' she said wearily.

'Moy, is that Moy? I want to speak to my sister Moy Colley, is that my –?'

'Yes, of course it is. But I can't talk to you now, Joe.' She said it loudly and slowly and firmly, as she always did when Joe was upset. When he was manic and paranoid. 'We've got some friends here at the moment so I can't talk, but I'll phone you back in half an hour.'

'Basically, I'm not having a good day, basically things are against me, right? and —'

'I can't talk now, Joe.'

'— basically it's this flat that's the problem, I'm having problems, very serious problems with this flat, not for the first time I might say, because the toilet's leaking and the plumber they sent round was useless, right, he knew nothing about plumbing, in fact he was a spy and a thief and he broke my CD player, right, smashed it, and he stole a lot of my things, basically he stole my new wallet, right? and my travel card which was not in my wallet at the time, it was on the chest of drawers in the bedroom, and he stole my cigarettes and my keys, the keys to this flat, right? So I'm a prisoner here, I can't get out to see my girlfriend or —'

'Joe, are you taking your pills?'

'I was taking them. Obviously I *was* taking my pills, right? I *have* been taking the lithium, but these new pills they've given me, prop something, it begins with a p, give me a headache. Can you believe it, the medication they've given me to stop the palpitations and calm me down gives me a really bad *headache*, right? So I can't get any sleep and I can't think straight and I —'

Not right, Moy wanted to shout. Nothing right about any of it. She said, 'Joe, we've got visitors.' He had to be reminded, she always felt she had to remind him, that there were other people on the planet besides himself. Not that reminding him made any difference when he was on the downhill slide: a steely self-centredness was one of the first indicators. 'I'll phone you later on,' she said, 'and if you still haven't found your things I'll come over and help you look for them. In the meantime, make yourself a cup of tea, put your feet up and try and calm down. Watch something silly on the TV, get your mind off it.'

'Basically, there's no point in looking for my keys, right, when as I say they're no longer in this flat, when as I say they've been stolen by a Mafia hit man, right? When he —'

'I'll talk to you later. Go and have a lie down. I'll ring you as soon as I can.' She replaced the receiver, then took it off so he couldn't phone again. 'Sorry about that,' she said to Mrs Mullins, as David Mullins and Dexter emerged from the kitchen.

'Night was quite come when we came in view of the house of Shaws. Ten had been gone some time; it was dark and mild, with a pleasant, rustling wind in the southwest that covered the sound of our approach; and as we drew near we saw no glimmer of light in any portion of the building. It seemed my uncle was already in bed, which was indeed the best thing for our arrangements. We made our last whispered consultations some fifty yards away, and then the lawyer and Torrance and I crept quietly up and crouched down beside the corner of the house; and as soon as we were in our places, Alan strode to the door without concealment and began to knock.'

A bit mean to stop there, but it was the end of the chapter. Not only that, he'd been sitting on a child-size chair with his knees under his chin for the past half-hour, and it was painful. Everything hurt and ached today, not just the part of him that had taken Melv's blows. His back hurt; his calves and thighs ached; his whole body felt weighty and immovable. The only consolation he had was the rainbow bruises that had come out on his ribs. He'd decided not to show off these trophies to Moy but she couldn't have avoided seeing them. She hadn't mentioned them, but she must have seen them.

'That's yer lot.' He shut the book and got up to put it away in the shelf, the special shelf – 'Dad's shelf', his kids called it – where his own childhood books were kept. These old favourites, which included poetry, some of which had a number on the spine and a Ludlow Public Library stamp on the flyleaf, were the only books he was prepared to read to Dig and Frankie. Current authors, annuals, comics and other trash, he reckoned they could read for themselves.

'Go on, Dad, go on go on go on go on' – Frankie, from the top bunk.

'Don't push it, Frankie.' He suspected that his sons were finding *Kidnapped* a less compelling read than *Treasure Island*, a book he had had to read three times, and that all Frankie really desired was for his father to carry on reading. To carry on until this book was finished, so that another book, one more to his taste and understanding, could be begun. Or simply because he enjoyed being read to, whatever the book, and found the story-telling voice comforting – as many people, not just children, did.

'Go on go on go on,' Frankie chanted. 'I want to know what happens next.'

'You wanna know what happens next?' – Dig, from the bottom bunk. 'Pop, like, losing his temper is what happens next. Pop, like, really losing it – woof!'

Gales of giggles from both bunks.

They sounded like a couple of girls, their father told them. They sounded like a couple of silly giggling girls.

'Girly, girly, that's me,' said Dig. 'Where's my Barbie doll? Can't sleep without Barbie. Oh, Barbie darlin', where are you hidin'?'

Pretend sobs from Dig. Pretend hysterical searching under the duvet. More giggles.

'Enough!' Dexter screamed.

While his children looked on from their pillows, he moved stiffly round the room tidying up, scooping discarded clothes from the floor, folding jeans on to chairs, making a pile of dirty socks and pants and T-shirts for the washing machine. A woman's job, this, like so much of what he did. A wife and mother's — or stepmother's — job. He had hoped, when Moy first moved in, that she would relieve him of some of these chores; that an instinctive female need to nurture, buried for years, would push to the surface, propelling her towards the house-cleaning, say. Or the washing, or the routine cooking, or the shopping. All of it was what he had secretly anticipated. In these secret hopes he had envisaged a slow but accumulating change of attitude and of priorities in Moy. It would begin with her one morning picking up a duster or unpenning the vacuum cleaner. Then, by degrees, without her even being aware of what was happening, her metamorphosis from selfish artist to caring homebody would gather speed. She would find herself wanting to spend more time in the house, less time in her studio. She would insist on collecting his kids from school herself. *I feel they are my kids now*, is how she would have explained it. *You know, Dexter, I love your kids as though they were my own.* Around this time marriage would be mentioned, not by him but by Moy, who desired it. *I want to be a proper wife to you, my darling.*

Soon after, she would decide to give up her studio life

213

altogether. *My heart was never really in stained glass. I realize that now.*

Soon after that – or did this happen just before? – he would go back into publishing or some multimedia outfit, having been head-hunted to power over the ambitions and expectations of the guys and gals already on that global company's ladder. *Welcome on board, Dexter. Good to have you on the case/heading the team.*

But at this point, the point where he should have been able to envision his working day, his imagination refused to cooperate. He could just about get himself through the plate-glass and steel doors of Colossus House or whatever the building was called, and, once inside, to acknowledge the respectful nods of the receptionists and the security guard. But his legs would not carry him across the hushed carpet to the lifts, whence to ride, in air-conditioned chill, to his penthouse office. The things he knew this office must exhibit – refrigerated drinks cabinet, limited edition prints or original art works on the walls, designer desk and chairs, personalized coffee-maker, widescreen view of the capital – failed to come into focus. He could not get a proper sense of himself in that office and in that organization; he was unable to picture his present or future there.

Not a corporation man, a voice in his head would warn. Not a team player. Not a player *per se*, any more.

'Where's Moy?' Frankie was leaning over the edge of his bunk, peering about as though he expected her to come out from under the bunk unit or from behind the curtain.

'I don't think much of the job you've made here, Frankie.' He pointed to the outdoor clothes and games his younger son took away on holiday and had dumped any old how in a corner. 'Your idea of putting your gear away is —'

'Where's Moy?' Frankie said again.

'Gone to see her brother. You'll see her in the morning.'

'Oo er, looney time.' There was a muffled, snorting noise from Dig's pillow.

'What? That's not kind, Dig. Not kind — or funny.'

'I like Moy,' Frankie says, 'I like old Collie Dog.'

'Oh yes?' Reaching into the clothes cupboard to hang up his younger son's anorak, he waited to hear more and to learn more; but after a minute or two it became clear Frankie had nothing to add. He debated asking, In what way, Frankie? or, Why do you like her? and decided against it, partly because Dig had said nothing. It astonished him, and could make him feel uneasy, that neither child had ever quizzed him about Moy or his relationship with Moy. Are you two going to get married? would have been a natural question when Moy moved into the house and into their daddy's bed, but they had not asked it then or at any time afterwards. Naturally, when she had moved in, he had talked them through this big change in all their lives. Squatting beside them on the play-station floor — it had seemed important to get down to their level — where they were building a track for Formula One racers, he had been careful to explain that just because he had fallen in love with Moy and wanted to share his life with her did not mean he no longer loved and needed his boys. It did not mean that at all. On the contrary.

They had sat back on their heels and listened to everything he had to say, or they had appeared to listen; and then, after a polite pause, they had carried on handing each other pieces of track and fitting them together on the floorboards. He'd braced himself for tears and sulks and dramas, even for the nervy jauntiness Frankie sometimes displayed, as he'd braced himself for the eye-rolling sexual innuendo Dig had recently tried out in mealtime conversations. Squatting beside them, he'd waited for the import of his news to sink in, for a sign that it had sunk in.

I said a curved bit, dickhead, Dig had admonished Frankie, chucking back the piece of track Frankie had just handed over.

Ignored, dismissed, he'd eventually pushed himself up off the floor and left the room. Can you shut the door, Dad? Dig had called after him, without looking up.

'How was Gran, by the way?' was what he could and did ask now. His sons were very fond of their grandmother.

'She was okay,' Dig said.

'Sort of okay, only sort of,' Frankie corrected him.

'What does that mean? Explain.'

'I can't explain. I don't know. Well, she's old, isn't she? She can be a bit strange sometimes.'

'She's always strange,' Dig said. 'Gran's always been strange.'

'How strange?' He directed his question to Dig. He made himself defer to Dig, when he remembered to, because Dig was the elder and the one, he believed, most damaged by their mother's defection. And also because Dig was, *au fond*, less bright than Frankie. Most people who met his kids did not guess this, or imagined it to be the other way round. They were taken in by Dig's knowingness and quick-fire repartee and misled by Frankie's babyishness and inarticulacy — as Moy had been before she moved in with them and had had a chance to suss it for herself. Academically, for his age, and particularly at maths, Frankie was streets ahead of Dig, about whom his class teacher had confided at a parents' evening, Bright and breezy within his limits, but gives up easily when difficulties loom.

'Try and think of an example,' he said to Dig.

But Dig couldn't think of one. It was too complicated, he said, after he'd thought for a while, it was too hard to describe.

'I tell you what,' Frankie said to the ceiling. 'She gets names wrong. She can't say some words, or she can't remember them. She gets stuck in words, at the beginning of them it usually is, and then she stops. Then she starts again.'

'But sometimes she doesn't start again, does she,' Dig called up to Frankie. 'She just changes the subject to something quite different.'

'That often happens to people when they get older,' Dexter said. 'It's called short-term memory loss. It's normal. It even happens to your old dad sometimes. It's beginning to happen to your old dadda already already.'

Senile, he thought. His mother was getting senile, or she had Alzheimer's. The beginnings of Alzheimer's. Oh great.

'When are you going to take over the farm?' Dig propped himself on an elbow to ask this.

He was not prepared for this one. For this, impertinent, subject change. 'I don't think I want to discuss that now, Dig. It's late, you should have been asleep hours ago. And it's not really your business, is it?'

Though he was aware that it was Dig's business, in a way. If he should ever be forced to take over the farm, it would be everybody's – Dig's and Frankie's, and Moy's –

business. Change of schools, loss of friends, isolated life, these were some of the reasons why Dig might consider a move to the sticks his business.

But he had no intention of taking over the farm.

'I was only asking because Don asked *me*,' Dig said. 'He said, when's your dad taking over then? He said he couldn't go on much longer, he wants to retire this year before the farm kills him. He said he was only staying on for Gran, he said he couldn't stop working till she stopped. And he said that Gran —'

'Okay guys, bedtime.' He leaned over the safety rail of the top bunk and kissed Frankie, who gripped him in a neck hold to kiss him back. 'Nightnight, sweetheart. Glad to be home?'

'I am,' Dig called from below. 'I want to see my friends. I want to see Jordan and Ravi.'

'Lemme go now,' Dexter said to Frankie.

'I feel sick,' Frankie said. 'My tum hurts.'

'Since when?'

'I don't know. Now.'

'Show me where the pain is then.' He pulled back the duvet.

'Here. No, here. Ow.'

'It's because we had supper so late. Much too late. You'll be better in the morning. *If* you go to sleep now.' Pulling up the covers, he caught sight of the photograph on Frankie's bedside shelf. White-haired baby Frankie smiled fatly from his mother's knee; plum-haired Dig stood, serious and protective, beside his mother's chair. The professional photograph, one of a series, some of the prints finished in trendy sepia, had been a surprise Christmas present for him. *From your little family*, Hyacinth had written on the card. As so often with group portraits, none had managed to capture all three sitters equally well, and he'd been disappointed with his present.

Christmas. The thought of it reminded him, as he stood by the door, his finger on the light switch, that there was a question he must brave himself to ask: 'Oh, by the way, I wanted to ask you both about next Chrimbo – where d'you think you'd like to spend it? Any strong feelings? Because your –'

'The South Seas?' Dig's suggestion.

'– because your mother has written to me –'

'Oh, we know. She phoned us at Gran's. She wants us to have Christmas with her and whatsisname.'

How stupid of him not to realize that that's what Hyacinth would do – write him a spurious letter asking if she could have the kids and then, before he had a chance to think about it let alone talk to them, phone the kids *at his mother's* and put the emotional screws on.

He would kill her one day. Oh yes.

'So. So what did you both, kind'v, like, decide?'

'Nothing,' Dig said. 'I told her it was up to you and her. I said where we went for Christmas wasn't something me and Frankie could decide.'

What rectitude. He could hardly believe it. What astonishing rectitude, or was it diplomacy, from someone of ten. But Frankie hadn't spoken yet. 'What about you, Frankie? Any views on next Christmas?'

'Don' mind.' Frankie was indistinct, sleepy. 'Don' mind.'

It was only when he was out of the door and half-way down the stairs, that he began to question these exchanges, to have doubts about his reading of them. By the time he'd reached the kitchen and was pouring himself a glass of wine, he'd decided it was probably not rectitude, nor

219

diplomacy, nor even priggishness had made Dig answer his mother in that way. No, Dig had probably been motivated by something nearer self-protection, by a need to protect himself and Frankie from an impossible choice and its consequences.

Sitting at the kitchen table, drinking his wine, a chillier solution, a chillier word, one that fitted with Frankie's 'don' mind', presented itself: indifference. Don't give a stuff, one way or the other, was what his kids were telling their mother and then himself. Not for you, not against you, either of you. Neutral. If Dig and Frankie had a desire about Christmas, it was probably to spend it in the South Seas, on their own. And at once he could see them, two tiny figures moving deftly about the decks of a white schooner as it sailed, on a blue sea under a blue sky, towards –

'Dad.' It was Frankie, in the doorway, shivering and clutching himself. 'I been sick, Dad. I didn't get to the bathroom in time. Sorry.'

When Moy let herself into her brother's flat, she found him, dressed in T-shirt and jeans and trainers, lying face down on the living room divan. There was a bad smell in the flat, and Joe was not alone, there was a girl in the armchair, slumped forwards with her head tucked into her chest, so that her long brown hair hung down, like a grubby string curtain, in front of her face. She did not look up when Moy pushed open the door or acknowledge her presence in any other way, and Moy thought, They're dead, they're both dead.

I've arrived too late. She knew it, standing in terror in the doorway. Double suicide, she thought, suicide *pact*. An overdose, it had to be – there was no blood.

Best thing for them, a voice from nowhere suggested. Dexter's voice?

They were not dead. As she stood there, unable to move, the corpse on the divan rolled over on to its back and began to snore in a snorting and familiar manner – a manner that suggested it was most likely beer, not pills, had put her brother to sleep. Next, there was movement in the armchair as the owner of the string curtain crossed, and immediately recrossed, her legs.

Moy knew who this girl was. She had met her at least twice, though the little she knew about her she had had to learn from Joe. Her name was Kirsten, she was twenty-six, she was out of work, she lived somewhere off Streatham High Road. She and Joe had had some sort of affair, though not a satisfactory one from Joe's point of view because, as he'd told Moy in more detail than she wanted to hear, Kirsten did not enjoy sex. She could believe this – Kirsten did not look as though she were capable of enjoying anything very much. Moy had never managed to have a conversation with Kirsten. On all the occasions she had met her, Kirsten – or Kitchikoo, as Joe called her – hadn't volunteered one single word, not even to Joe.

It was only recently that Joe had confided that Kitchikoo was a clinical depressive, and that it was the psychiatric patients' day centre they both attended from time to time that had been the venue for that lucky first meeting.

Once she was sure her brother and Kirsten were not ill, or no more so than usual, she took off her jacket and set about clearing up. In Joe's frenzied search for his stolen possessions, drawers and cupboards had been emptied on to the living room floor. Clothes and shoes and music and porn videos were jumbled together with empty beer cans and full ashtrays. The standard lamp that in an earlier life had shed light on her mother's chair in the old Plymouth flat was horizontal in a corner, its tassled parchment shade battered and split.

Similar upheaval met her in the bedroom and the minuscule kitchen. The lavatory in the minuscule bathroom had not been flushed for some days, by the look and smell of it. She climbed on to the bath ledge and opened the window. Then, having got the flush to work (the plastic handle mechanism inside the cistern had snapped, which meant plunging a hand in to release the ballcock), she went back to the living room to open another window and let out another smell, the sealed mustiness sharpened by sweat the place always reeked of because Joe, even in hot weather, refused to raise the sash so much as an inch. He did not feel safe with the window open, he said. (Paranoia, she had always put his fears down to. That is, until last January, when Joe's neighbour on the ground floor – a mental patient like himself, and also, according to Joe, a crack junkie – had been bludgeoned to death on his own doorstep. Joe had phoned her countless times about the frightening goings on – the bangs and thumps and screamed threats – he said went on nightly in that flat and in the street outside it, and she hadn't believed him. The police hadn't believed him either.)

It took her over an hour to put the flat into habitable shape, and in the course of it she uncovered the missing items Joe said the Mafia had stolen. His wallet and travel card she found in a pair of jeans on the bedroom floor. His door keys were in the tin army mug on the mantelpiece, the place he always kept them when he remembered to.

Joe and Kirsten came to when she switched on the vacuum cleaner. Kirsten pushed her hair out of her eyes and got up and meandered through to the bathroom. Joe sat on the edge of the divan, mumbling and coughing and pulling at his ear.

That was half an hour ago. Since then Moy had shown Joe how to work the ballcock to flush the lavatory, and she had spread out on the table all his missing things so that he could check them out for himself. She had made coffee for herself and Ovaltine for Joe and Kirsten, and they had drunk these in the living room. Between them, Joe and Kirsten had smoked the packet of Marlboro Lights she had bought for Joe on the journey here. She had phoned Dexter to tell him she was on her way home, and she'd phoned for a minicab to take her home. (Though Joe had warned her not to do this. All the minicab drivers in this area were Yardies, according to him.)

It was now a quarter to two in the morning.

'Think I'll wait downstairs,' Moy said. 'Minicab'll be here any minute.' She needed to be on her own in order to digest the news Joe had told her when he was drinking his Ovaltine. The news that he and Kitchikoo were going to get married and start a family 'because, basically, right, Kitchikoo is very fond of babies, aren't you, my Kitchi-koo?'

'By the way, he says he wants to have a drink with you. He said, tell that boyfriend of yours we'll go out for a drink and he can give me some tips on the fair sex. He wants advice from you on how to keep his little woman in order, he says.'

Ye gods. 'I wouldn't know, would I? I'm the last person to ask.'

It was twenty past four, according to Dexter's digital radio clock. They'd given up all idea of sleep and were sitting up in the bed, drinking tea. There was a mosquito in the room – it might be two mosquitoes – and in any case they were listening out for Frankie. Every so often there was a retching noise from the next room, and one or other of them had to rush through and hold Frankie's head as he strained over the bowl. Then empty the bowl of what for some time now had been a frothy bile that looked, though did not smell, like the dregs of a banana milkshake; and afterwards tepid-sponge Frankie's burning face.

When Moy arrived home she had offered to sleep downstairs so that Frankie could sleep in the big bed with Dexter – which would be a lot less disruptive for Dig, and nicer for Frankie surely? – and Dexter had said no. No, because the sight of Moy pulling off her shirt and kicking her pants into a corner had given him other ideas. Frankie preferred to sleep in his own bed, he'd insisted. And lying back on the pillows he'd patted the bed in a lazy and encouraging way.

You are very beautiful, you know, Moya, he'd told her when she was in bed beside him, you are very, very beautiful. I love your hair, he'd whispered into it, I love your eyes. I love your little breasts, he'd added bravely. And he'd touched her nipples with the uninsistent, fingertip pressure Moy liked and had long ago instructed him. I love –

But Moy was too done in for anything of that kind, she'd said.

Disappointed and at the same time relieved (for the act of rolling across her had wounded his sore ribcage), he'd slid away from her and kept his hands, unobtrusively, to himself.

So for the past hour they'd been drinking tea and

224

talking. About Joe and Kirsten, and their marriage plans. About their plan for having babies.

Lung cancer, was his solution to the problem. A double dose of lung cancer before the banns could be read. Failing that, a vasectomy or female equivalent. Kirsten could have her tubes tied, or her ovaries removed.

Moy said it wasn't funny, though she did smile, he noticed. She said it was serious and awful and tragic. She said that Joe might have made a good husband, a good father even, if it hadn't been for his illness. She said, 'It's odd how damaged people are drawn together, don't you think? As though two wrongs might somehow, conjoined, make a right.'

He said, Sure, sure, to this. Then he said, okay, so Joe and Kirsten couldn't have babies, babies were out obviously, but why shouldn't they get married? Handicapped people did get married. It might be a good thing for Joe to have someone to live with and look after, someone who would look after him. It would be a lot less lonely for both of them, wouldn't it?

Moy said she doubted if Joe would be able to handle a live-in anything for more than a week. She said that the budgerigar she'd given him as a present once, on the premise that caring for a pet was said to be excellent therapy for the disadvantaged, was still on her conscience. Anyway, what would happen to Kirsten each time Joe was sectioned? How would they manage when they were both out of work? And what comfort, really, could a *depressive* be to Joe?

Still playing devil's advocate, he said they'd have something in common at least, there'd be something profound and serious to bind them. Understanding each other's difficulties, they'd be able to give each other

225

sympathy and support. 'For richer, for poorer,' he added dangerously. 'For richer for poorer, in sickness and in health.'

'Why *are* you so keen on marriage, Dexter?' Moy said. 'Why do you go on and on about it? I really don't get it, especially after –'

'Because it makes a couple work harder,' Dexter said. 'That's one reason. It means there's more at stake than just the two people involved. There's this third person, thing, rather, at stake called *the marriage* – so they have to work harder.'

'What about gay couples, though? Aren't you being a bit rough on them? They can't get married. They have to get by without this third –'

'Yes, they can. In some countries they can get married. In some states of America they can.'

'Oh, bullshit. Those aren't proper marriages, are they? They're –'

'Well, actually, I think they are. If marriage means making a commitment, vows, in public, in front of witnesses, then a gay couple ought to be able to feel just as married as any hetero couple can, however bizarre the ceremony they choose to do it in.'

'You don't really believe that.'

'I do.'

'Something you haven't mentioned. If you don't get married, you can't get divorced either, can you. And the divorce rate is high. Even among gay couples, I imagine.'

'What have you got *against* marriage, Moy? Because you're just as much against it as I am pro. Against it in principle, I mean, leaving you and me out of it.'

'Well.' But she couldn't tell him. There were so many reasons, not just to do with her parents or because of Joe.

She did not want to tell Dexter about the girlfriends she knew who had married seemingly generous, easygoing, flexible men. Men who, after the wedding, as soon as the ceremony was over, had become high-handed and tyrannical, their faces suddenly set like concrete. Who had said, We are going to the beach today, and brooked no argument.

After that they sat back in silence and drank their tea. Then Frankie was sick again.

'I know what I wanted to ask you,' Moy said. 'What did David Mullins want to talk to you about? You know, when he took you off into the kitchen? I liked him, by the way. You said he was awful, but he seemed okay to me. You shouldn't have said those things to him about Dig becoming a Muslim. Did you see his face?'

'Oh. Oh, that was just Farmer Giles stuff. We were talking agri-environment schemes and woodland planting schemes. We were talking biodiversity and set-aside and arable wild flower reserves and country stewardship payments for not using herbicides. We were talking sheep scab and, and. Or rather, he was. It was just like *The Archers*, except nobody put the kettle on.'

He could sense Moy thinking about this, turning it over. Eventually she said, 'But what's so private about that? Why did he have to take you on one side to talk about that?'

'Oh. Well, he did mention my mother. It seems he's a bit worried about my mother for some reason. So I said I'd check her out when I go and see Mark on Wednesday.'

'Mark?'

'Bank man.'

'I didn't know you were going to see your bank man.'

'Told you I was.'

'No.'

'Thought I had.'

Silence. Then she said, 'What is going to happen about the farm, exactly?'

Jesus, not her too. He shrugged and spread his hands. 'Search me.'

'It isn't me who wants to know, Dexter, it's your mother. She asked me to ask you what your plans were. She —'

'When?'

'Don't shout at me,' Moy said. 'The other night, on the phone. When you were in the pub.'

'Okay, I'll talk to her about it on Wednesday.'

'Talk to me about it now. We've been living together for over a year, you know, and you've never really talked about the farm or told me what's expected of you. I reckon I have a right to know if the guy I live with is going to go off and be a farmer. But you always change the subject when I —'

'I could do with a spliff. You haven't got a spliff anywhere, I suppose?'

There was a packet of cigarettes downstairs, Moy told him.

But ordinary cigarettes did nothing for him; he shook his head.

'The farm,' Moy said.

'It's like this,' he said. And speaking fast, rattling the information off to get rid of it, he told her that before his father died, after his second stroke, when it was clear he wasn't going to last much longer, he'd agreed to take the place over when his mother decided to retire. When she felt she couldn't cope any more. He'd signed his name to

228

that. His father couldn't speak by this time, he explained, he was incontinent and helpless – but he could read. Michael needed reassurance, his mother said, so they'd concocted something and written it down to show him, and he, Dexter, had signed it. In front of his father. And a week later his father had died. He stopped at this point, expecting some sort of reaction. 'You asleep, Moy? I'm not going on with this if you're asleep.'

She was not asleep, she was listening, Moy said. She listened better with her eyes shut, she said.

'Dad must have decided he could let go when I signed. He felt reassured, as my mother said, and let go. But of course I didn't mean it. I can't think of anything worse than being a farmer. I only signed the thing to comfort Dad – as my mother well knows.'

'Doesn't sound to me as though you had a lot of choice.'

'I had *no* choice. Though at the time I didn't worry too much about what I'd signed. I was in my twenties, the farm was doing okay then, my mother was energetic and strong as a horse, she had Don to help her – not just Don, come to think of it, there was a part-time cowman then, and extra hands at harvest etc. – and I suppose I thought, it won't ever happen. Or not for a very long time.'

'What will you do, then? Can you sell the farm?'

'Not till my mother dies. Then I will. If anyone'll buy it. If anyone wants farmland any more. I suppose when she does die I'll sell out to a conglomerate, or to a housing developer, or to some arsehole who wants to turn the place into a golf course or a theme park. That's what my sisters would like, Elizabeth, anyway. She's dead keen on me selling because if I do the proceeds have to be split between the three of us. Whereas if I decide to keep the farm and work it, my sisters don't get a penny.'

Silence. Then Moy said, 'Why haven't you told me any of this? It's really insulting. I mean, it's a huge thing, a hugely important thing. And it affects *me*. It makes me wonder what other huge things you've been keeping to yourself. I don't think I know you at all.'

I didn't tell you because I thought you might leave. I didn't tell you because I thought you would never agree to move in with me if you knew.

But he wouldn't tell her that.

No, hang on, he would. 'I was afraid you might leave. It was very wrong of me. I'm sorry.'

'Your mother said if you weren't going to take over the farm soon, she was going to sell up herself.'

'Ah but she doesn't mean that. She can't anyway – it's not in her power. She's just trying to goad me into taking action. But there's no possibility she would sell my father's land, even if she could. Over her dead body, she would say about that. Which is how it will be in the end. In the meantime, it's what happens when she packs it in that's making me sweat. We can't afford to have a manager in – so who's going to run the place? If it isn't me?'

'You're quite split about it, though, aren't you,' Moy said. 'I mean there's a side of you that's proud of your roots, that thinks of Shropshire as home. That time we went to Wenlock Edge, remember? It was as though you owned the woods and the escarpment, the way you went on. And it's just the same with Ludlow. You're extremely rude about the town, you dismiss it as heritage –'

'It is heritage. It never used to be but it is now. It's like Bath, you know, a graveyard of ambition and full of fancy eateries the locals can't afford.'

'– but at the same time you get a kick out of it, out of its history at any rate. You get a kick out of having such a stunningly beautiful place as your local town, as your home town. The most beautiful town in England, you told me Betjeman called it. Stop shaking your head. We only have to drive in to the chemist and you're giving me a history lesson, lecture, rather, on the castle and Sir Philip Sidney and the Council of the Marches.'

He hadn't realized he'd been so boring, he said. He hadn't realized he'd been so incredibly dull.

'It wasn't boring. I liked it. I actually like it when you're enthusiastic and communicative. I love it when you tell me things.'

'Bethnal Green is where I feel at home.'

'And you've got mixed feelings about the farm as well. You're rude about the place, you complain the whole journey there – and then, when we do get there, you pull on your boots and your dad's old cap and turn into the country boy. Just like that. It's quite scary to watch. I find it scary. I watched you and Don stripping down the tractor engine, and I remember thinking –'

'Well, of course. Of course, I can do those things. I was brought up to do them. It's easy for me. I don't even have to reinvent myself. But that doesn't mean I want to be a farmer. That doesn't mean I want to join an industry that's dying on its hooves. Well, do *you* want to be a farmer? Do you?'

Silence.

'I got *away* from it, Moy. And I've always had this idea, conviction, that going back equals failure.' If he had the energy, if he weren't so tired, he'd have a go at explaining his feelings better, tell her that, as he saw it, the so-called journey from cradle to grave ought, ideally, to be just that

– an actual physical journey, or a series of journeys. A series of jaunts and excursions or, more critically, of expeditions and pilgrimages – and no going back in between. In itinerancy lies true progress! Or something of the sort. Or some nonsense of the sort. Perhaps all he meant was, I was born in Ludlow and have *no desire to die there*.

And there's something else he wouldn't tell her: his desire for fame. He'd been almost famous once, as an editor he had. He hadn't given up on the idea of fame, it was still out there. But, whoever heard of a famous *farmer*?

He kicked his feet free of the duvet. 'Can we now stop this conversation. Can we now try and –'

'What about Wednesday? Are you planning to take Dig and Frankie with you?'

Oh God, here we go again. 'I don't know. Why? I don't *want* to take them, obviously, they've only just come back from there. I don't want to ask Hyacinth to have them. If you must know, when I made the appointment I thought they'd be back at school. I got the week wrong. I was going to ask you if you'd pick them up from school for me.'

He didn't have to worry, she'd look after them, Moy said. They might go on an outing. If Fun Week was still on, they –

Had he heard her right? 'What about your work, though? You'll miss a whole day. Two days if I stay the night with my mum, which I ought to. I probably ought to.'

'I haven't got much work at the moment. Dexter, I've had enough of stained glass. I've done it all my life and it's time I tried something else.'

He had willed her to say this and she had and he ought

232

to feel triumphant. But now that she was lying back (with her arms behind her head) saying it, what did he feel exactly? Guilt, was it? Or something like fear?

It was the lead thing, partly, Moy explained. She was getting more and more frightened by it, by what it was doing to her brain. By what it might have already done. 'And then there's the cement I use. I mean, look at my hands, feel my hands –'

He had felt them. He did feel them, every day. Old Lizard Hands was how he thought of them – but then she refused to wear gloves. Taking her hands now, he felt sad for her, sad for both of them. 'I don't like you using lead either,' he said. 'It frightens me too. I worry about it too.'

And perhaps that was the truth. Perhaps that had been his reason, all along, for wanting her to give up stained glass. Nothing to do with wanting to reinvent her as a hausfrau, but a fear for her safety so profound he'd had to suppress it.

'Also, not much work means not much money – I'm not earning anything like the amount I used to earn. Apart from that Healing Chapel window I got sponsorship for, I've earned peanuts this year. I didn't tell you because you've got your own money worries, but since May, I think it is, I've been paying you my share of the mortgage out of the little bit of money Mum left me. I can't go on doing that, it –'

'You should have told me.' He stroked her lizard hands. 'Yes. Well.'

'You're not to worry about money, you hear? I'll keep you. We'll be all right. I have a feeling my journalism career is about to take off, you know. I really do. Philip Cartwright says –'

He stopped because Moy was coughing, she was having

a sudden fit of coughing. When the fit was over, she said, 'That's really nice of you, I appreciate it, but I have to work. I *like* working. I *like* paying my own way. It's a need. I've always done it.'

'Of course.' A soothing murmur, into her hair.

'I don't know what I could retrain for at my age, but there must be something I could do. Incidentally, you know that interview I went for? I didn't get the job. Told you I hadn't got it. Didn't.'

'Oh, sweetheart. I'm sorry.' He meant it. He was sorry, truly sorry, for her disappointment, and, releasing her hand, began to stroke her naked shoulder, very tenderly, with the tips of his fingers. 'When did you hear this, Moyse?'

'Saturday. They didn't waste much time. Only comfort is, they've decided they don't want stained glass at all. Not mine, not anyone else's. So it's not just me. I can tell myself it's not just me, my work, they didn't like. They've decided on *reflection*, the letter says, to have a piece of sculpture for their vista point. To put an eye-catching heap of whatever in the middle of their hall or courtyard. Or on the building itself.'

'But that's outrageous.'

'That's what I thought.'

'Are they going to give you a kill fee? Or some sort of compensation?'

'They didn't say so. But then there's no reason why they should pay me anything, is there? They hadn't commissioned me. I hadn't done any work – except for a few cartoons.'

'Bastards.'

'I don't know why you say that when you agree with them.'

234

'What?'

'You don't like stained glass, do you. Modern glass. You told me so. You certainly don't like the stuff I make. You think it's naff.'

'That's not true.'

'Of course it's true. If you did like it, if you were even vaguely interested in it, you'd come down to the studio occasionally and see what I'm up to. But you never do come.'

'You don't ask me. I'd come if you did. I'd come like a shot if you did. But you're very private about your work, you know, and I don't like to intrude.'

'That's such a lie. Dexter. That is such a lie.'

He made a sudden dive across her, clapped his hands. But when he opened his hands and examined the palms there was no blood smear, no sign of the mosquito. 'Missed the bugger.'

'Anyway,' Moy said, 'it's not just the lead or because I've been turned down for something that would've been prestigious and well paid, or because I'm bored of what I do, or because you don't rate it −'

'Bored *with* what I do.' It slipped out before he knew it. Before he could stop himself.

'− it's not just because I'm bored *by*, *with* and *from* what I do − I'm lonely. It's bloody lonely in that studio. I don't see anybody all day. From the moment I park my bike till the moment I leave, I don't see anyone − not even out of the window most days. And of course the reason I'm broke is I don't get any passing trade. There is no passing trade in Copperfield Road. And even if there was − or should it be were? − I haven't got a shop window, have I, so nobody knows I'm there, stuck on the second floor.'

'You should never have moved to that place.'

'Could you repeat that, please?'

'I said —'

'Dexter, it was you found it for me. It was you said it was too far for me to travel from here to Battersea every day. You insisted on me moving.'

'The journey was too far. Is too far.' Then he remembered. 'Anyway isn't there something you've forgotten in all this? You asked me to find you an artist's studio because you wanted to be seen as an artist. You went on and on about that. It was vital for your image, you said, to get away from all those eco-Sloane types in Northcote Road and the whole crafty —'

An angry flounce of duvet as she leapt out of bed. 'I'm hungry. I didn't have any supper last night. I'm going to make myself a sandwich.'

Jesus. 'Come back to bed,' he said wearily. 'Come on now. This is a very heavy conversation for this hour of the morning. I think we should try for some sleep. Frankie hasn't thrown up for ages and I think we should try and get at least an hour's sleep.'

Or cut our throats. Or jump out of the window. He dragged his pillows down into a sleeping position. He turned on to his side, facing away from her. The world behind his shut eyelids was a hot orange-pink. It was like a hot pink field, or a hot pink painting of a field.

'I haven't finished what I wanted to say.'

Jesus. 'Say it at breakfast.'

The mattress sighed as she sat down abruptly. 'I want to go and see my dad. He keeps asking me, and I want to go.'

'Well, of course. *Of course*, you must go and see your dad.' Not at all the reaction she was expecting, he was certain. Not at all what she'd been hoping for. 'How are you planning to get there?'

'Sorry?'

'You hate flying.' Though he remembered that that was not quite how Moy had explained her fear to him. Flying was okay, she quite enjoyed flying, she'd explained. It was *not flying* she was afraid of. The aeroplane all of a sudden deciding it didn't want to fly, or take off, or land; finding itself, all of a sudden, unable to do those crucial things. The aeroplane stalling and dropping; and flipping over, and spiralling maybe. Before going into an endless screaming nosedive.

Not endless, he'd corrected her, laughing. And he'd held her tight against his chest and kissed the top of her head. Not an *endless* nosedive. I promise you, Moya darling.

'Obviously I've got to fly. But it's okay. I'll drug myself with tranks and booze.'

'D'you want me to go with you? Would that help?'

'No. Look, I do want to see my dad, that's one reason for going. But I also want to get right away on my own so that I can think about what I'm going to do. We need a break from each other, don't you think. We're on top of each other all the time. We fight.'

'We don't fight. Okay, we argue sometimes, but everyone does that, all couples do that.'

'Also, I don't like living with Hyacinth.'

'What did you say?'

'You're obsessed with her. She's still *there*, Dexter, you've never got rid of her. She's there all the time, in your head.'

'I just don't know how you can say that. I don't understand how you can even –'

'You'd be extremely pissed off if I went on about Richard the way you –'

237

Unfair. Monstrously unfair. She was never married to Richard. She hadn't had kids with him. She didn't get nightmare letters from him. She didn't have to *deal* with him.

'You even call me Hyacinth. I don't know if you can imagine how that feels.'

'*Once.* I only did that once. And at the time – listen to me, Moy. I would give anything to get Hyacinth out of my life, out of our life. I would give anything. But it's the thing about divorce, isn't it, where there are children of the marriage. You can't make a complete break – as you'd like to, as you *need* to – and move on. You can't do it because of the kids. But you know all that. We've talked about it. You've told me, many many times, that you understand it.'

'Maybe.'

'Maybe? *Maybe?* What the fuck does –'

A noise, like an explosion downstairs. A crack-crash shatter of glass, a hard-edged thump and rumble. A splintering. All these noises together and all of them over in seconds (though they would hear the individual sounds – as you can hear the individual instruments in a symphony – long drawn out, long afterwards).

After that, silence.

'*WHERE DID you heart hat?*' Dexter read. And read it again. It was eleven-thirty, Monday morning, and he'd had no sleep. He would have liked to lay his head on his work table and drowse the morning away, but he couldn't do that because he was waiting for the police. An officer will be with you shortly, don't touch or move anything, he'd been told three hours ago, when at last he succeeded in getting through. But it's *raining*, he'd argued, and my window is, like, *smashed*, and the rain is coming *into* my *front room*. Can't I put a bit of cardboard up to keep it out? – Don't touch or move anything, the electronic or digitally remastered voice had repeated. As I say, an officer will be along shortly. Click.

Officer, eh?

Apart from the rain, drumming on the one unbroken pane, driving through the three empty panes on to the two-seater and his painted floorboards (and on to the dazzle of ice-like glass, in splinters and chunks and daggers and shards, that littered the entire room), the house was quiet. Moy and Dig, bored with hanging around for the fuzz, had taken themselves off to a Fun Week event in the

Museum of Childhood. Frankie, pale and awful-looking, but feeling better he said, was upstairs in his room. Surfing the net for adult material, according to Dig.

'*Where did you heart hat?*' Wake up now, laddie, concentrate. Was *hat* a literal here, a mistype for *hit*? Could heart-hitting be a sport of some kind? A winter sport, say, like curling? Or did it just mean shooting up? Heart *hit*. Or could heart hat be a noun, shorthand perhaps for the plastic chest protector amateur boxers wore under their vests (and gutless batsmen under their shirts), in a sentence that had two words missing and was intended to read: *Where did you get your heart hat?*

He turned back a page to check the preceding line of dialogue, and found ' "Alan's been promoted to area manager," Roger told Gerald as, in gathering dusk, they speeded from Gatwick on the M25.'

'Oh of course. Oh how *dull*,' he said aloud. 'I really liked heart hat. I really *need* a heart hat.' And at once he could see it, a purple, miniature version of a cyclist's helmet, shaped to fit snugly over his bruised and vulnerable heart. He put a separating pencil stroke between the r and t of heart, then joined the t to the h of hat. In the margin he wrote, '*Speeded*, did they? In the rush hour? On the *M25*?'

Sitting back, yawning, he was aware of a tightness in his nose, of something pressing against the inside of his left nostril. His investigating finger located the something and levered it off, and at once there was a sweet sharp pain that made his eyes water. A sizeable black twig was lodged under his fingernail. Your average nosepick? Or a scab? Or an insect, maybe? The twig appeared to have legs. Examining it more closely, he saw that the legs were in fact hairs, presumably his own.

I am an old man. I am a gross old man.

The telephone rang; he put out a hand. 'Welcome to Nosepickers International! None of our advisers is available at present to answer your call. If your problem is chronic, press your star button *now* –'

The line went dead.

You are a child, Dexter. I am married to a silly child – the words, in his ex-wife's sorrowful voice, echoed in his head. Well, screw her. She had never got the point of silliness. Silliness for its own sake, or as a cover for sadness and embarrassment. Or as a way of managing pain. *And if I laugh at any mortal thing, / 'Tis that I may not weep* cut no ice with her, though he'd pointed out that it wasn't just Byron who felt like that: the lines wouldn't be famous if they hadn't struck such a chord. Throughout history, he'd told her, all sorts of brilliant men and women had exhibited a silly side – Read Robert Louis Stevenson's letters! Look at Mozart! So, childishness being an integral part of the creative/artistic mind-set, he would take her remark as a compliment, he had told Hyacinth.

The telephone rang again.

'Debtors' prison, Governor's office.'

Silence. Then a man's voice said, 'Hallo, hallo? Have I got the wrong number? I'm trying to get hold of Dexter Bucknell.'

'C'est moi,' Dexter said. 'It is I.'

'Dexter, hi – it's Scott here.'

Scott. Scott? Scott Fitzgerald? F. Scott Fitzgerald? Francis Scott *Key* Fitzgerald?

'Scott?'

'Scott *Marchant*,' Scott Marchant said. 'How many Scotts do you know?'

'Oh. Marchant. Hi.'

Scott Marchant, whose appointment as CEO of Orpheus Dexter had read about in a recent issue of *The Bookseller* he'd picked up, and gutted, and replaced on the stand, in a Piccadilly bookshop a few weeks back, had once been a colleague of his, but he hadn't seen Marchant for years. Hadn't had smell of his aftershave since Hyacinth left and his own publishing career had been pulped. A year or so ago he'd found himself sitting next to another old workmate, Dan Peterson, in an outpatients' waiting room at the Royal London Hospital; and during a swap of news and views and complaints – Dan was out of work, having been a casualty of what he described as a 'downsizing stroke rationalizing stroke restructuring programme' following his company's takeover by Maxton Multimedia – Scott Marchant's name had come up. That fling Scott had with Hyacinth, Dan went on to ask, was it responsible for his marriage bust-up?

Dexter hadn't known that his ex-wife and Scott Marchant had had a fling, and he went cold. (It was as though the temperature in the overheated waiting room had dropped twenty degrees, he decided afterwards, descending the hospital steps, dodging the four-lane traffic to Whitechapel tube. It was the chill you get in the supermarket, when you leave the warmth of Cereals for the Cooked Meats and Butchery aisle.) He went cold, and his teeth began to chatter, and he couldn't answer Dan. He kept his attention on a poster on the wall in front of him which said PREGNANT? AND DON'T WANT TO BE? COME AND TALK TO US. IN CONFIDENCE.

Dan had been embarrassed by Dexter's reaction. He'd said he was very sorry if he'd spoken out of turn.

'How *are* you, Dexter?' Scott Marchant was asking.

'Tolerably well.'

A pause, before Marchant said, 'So. It's been a long time. How's that deer park of yours? In Shropshire, right? A Shropshire lad is how I always think of you. A well-heeled Shropshire lad.'

Deer park – shit. He felt his face redden and burn. He had buried this reinvention of his roots along with all the other grandiose terms – landowner, estate, home park, ancestral seat – his youthful, editorial-assistant self had variously applied, in the belief that he would not be found out, to his parents and his parents' farmhouse and his parents' trifling acres. But he had been found out. A publicity girl with social connexions in all the counties of England had quizzed him about the exact location of the deer park and –

'What are you up to these days, Dexter?'

'Sorry? Oh – this and that.' Marchant wasn't interested in what he was up to, that's for sure. Marchant wanted to tell him what Marchant was up to. He remembered suddenly that in the days when the two of them had done a brief stint together at Plane Tree Books (axed some years ago now), Marchant had been in the habit of referring to Hyacinth as a trophy wife. How's that gorgeous trophy wife of yours? Marchant had been in the habit of shouting over the partition wall as they settled down at their desks in the morning.

Why hadn't he guessed what the scumbag was up to?

'I hear you're writing a book,' Scott Marchant said.

'Where'd you hear that?' (Or, Where'd you heart hat?)

'Bad news travels fast. No, seriously, I got it from Philip Cartwright. I read that piece you wrote for his rag and I have to say I was impressed. I hadn't any idea you could write.'

'Thanks. If you're interested, there's a second piece going in this Sunday, I think it is.'

'Great, great, look forward to it. Anyway, I phoned Philip for your address. He's an odd guy, isn't he, chippy. A bit too New Labour for me. Whaddya make of him?'

'Philip's okay,' he said, defensive. 'I like Philip.'

'Perhaps it's just his manner. Anyway, he told me he'd had great difficulty persuading you to write the piece. He said you'd told him you were writing a full-length fiction and didn't want to waste any of your East End material on a bit of pisspot journalism.'

Fuck. Had he really told Philip that? No of course he hadn't. Marchant was making it up. Unless of course Philip, who he suspected had no time at all for Marchant, had been having a bit of fun with the guy?

'By the way, I don't know if you've heard, but I'm at Orpheus now. I've got Elaine Arnold's old job. Old job, new title.'

'Congratulations.'

'Yes, well, I am very pleased of course. The competition was pretty steep. I know for a fact that Jenna Harrington was after it. And Mike Edwards. Of course I'd feared it would be an in-house appointment, and the interview merely a matter of –'

'Did Elaine get the chop?' He had been Elaine's assistant once, years and years ago, his first job in publishing. She'd been kind to him and covered for his mistakes. She'd fed him up on doughnuts and chocolate bars. And she'd given him a generous reference when, against her advice and interest, he'd decided it was time to move on. He'd liked Elaine, even though he hadn't thought too much of the books she published. He saw her teeth suddenly. Her big, jutting teeth – too big and too jutting for her mouth to close over them.

'Not exactly, though by all accounts her departure was something of a relief. The official line is that she left to have a sprog. At forty-nine! What sort of biological clock can she have?'

'What indeed.'

'Fortunately, I've always had a blue-skies attitude, as you know, and I'm taking the helicopter view of this one – but, Jesus, it's going to be a challenge. Do you have any idea what this list is like? Eighty per cent of the stuff we publish does nothing at all. We need to get some new blood in. A couple of authors I looked after at Pickaxe are joining me, I'm glad to say, and I'm working on Tom Cameron – I gather he's not at all happy at Stylus – wasn't he one of yours?'

'You know he was.' He'd been the first person to recognize Tom Cameron's talent and to publish him decently. More than that, they'd been friends. When he first started editing proper, at twenty-six, he had naively imagined that working with an author – an author he admired – would automatically lead to close friendship with that author. But Tom had been the exception, he had been friends with Tom. Cricket was the chief bond; boozing another. And squash, which they'd played together on Sundays, to work off the effects of the booze.

But Tom would never move to Scott Marchant's crummy outfit, would he? Marchant wasn't even a book man, for God's sake. He was Marketing and Sales. Or had been at Plane Tree.

Tom. Tom. He hadn't been in touch for quite a while. Why hadn't he been in touch? Whose fault was it? Well, he must do something about it. He'd phone Tom and ask him over to supper so that he could meet Moy. He'd give Tom a call. He'd do it today.

'When I've got this company on course I plan to have a party,' Marchant was saying. 'It'll be a double celebration – I've got a serious birthday coming up this year. Maybe you'd like to come along?'

'Sure.' Either Marchant reckoned Dexter knew nothing about the Hyacinth episode, or he'd forgotten it himself. Or the arsehole didn't give a damn.

'I'll make sure you get an invitation. Haven't decided on the venue yet. I suppose we could have it here, though as you probably recall this building is hardly –'

But he wasn't really listening, he was picturing Marchant's party. He could see himself arriving – at the Soho Room in the Groucho, or some such. Chucking his coat at an overloaded portable coat rack in the passage, he pushed open the ante-room door. And then, as a publicity babe ticked off his name and a waiter proffered a tray, the sound from the main room reached him. Engulfed him. An unmistakable sound. The sound of a thousand egos clashing.

'I've bought in a couple of American names but I still need more young blood,' Marchant droned on. 'Young *male* blood. This list – Elaine's list – is top heavy with female novelists of a certain age. Unfortunately a lot of them are under contract, so it's going to take a bit of –'

Marchant was going to offer him a job. So that was it. Marchant was working round to ask him to be his assistant – but with a fancy new title, natch. The bastard was chicken; he had to have a fall guy to do the slash-and-burn business for him.

'What I'm phoning to ask,' Marchant said, 'is have you

got a publisher for your novel? Because if you haven't I hope you'll consider us.'

Well. Well, here was a turn-up. He swallowed hard. 'I'll remember that, thanks. But, um, young blood – aren't I just a smidgen on the old side?'

'Thank you, Natasha. Thanks. Just put it there. No, there. Sorry, Dexter. Look, can you tell me anything about your novel? There'll be some thriller interest, I imagine, remembering your list – ?'

'Well. Well, yes, I suppose there is that element. But in fact.' In fact what? 'In fact, my book, my novel, is essentially a, a *thanatopsis*. And I'm not sure at this stage whether I really want to go into it in any detailed way.'

Silence. Presumably while Marchant wrote down 'thanatopsis' so he could look it up afterwards.

'Forgive me asking, but your novel couldn't be described as *domestic*, could it?' Marchant asked eventually. 'Given that you work from home and, as I understand, look after your kids yourself – ?'

'Do me a favour, Scott.'

Marchant laughed, the laughter of relief. 'Look, you don't have to tell me much now, not now, but if you felt like sending me an outline – or preferably a chapter or two – I'd be really interested to see it.'

'I appreciate that.'

'How far have you got? Is that a permissible question?'

'Sure.' Fuck. How far had he got? How far was he likely to have got? 'Third draft of – ?'

'Third draft? Are we talking typewriters here? Don't you use a computer or a word processor?'

He had a quick rethink. 'As a matter of fact I write in longhand. Not in a notebook, as it happens, but on yellow legal pad paper. You know, like a lot of American writers do. Like some of the big guns do. Harold Pinter too, I believe.' Don't let Marchant ask where he got these yellow legal pads from. Did he get his supplies flown over? Did he get a chum on business in NY to collect a stash? Did he fly over himself and –?

'Sounds like hard work. Title?' Scott Marchant continued. 'Do you have a title yet, or a working title? Just to give me some idea of –'

'London Fields? Anna Karenina? Novel on Yellow Legal Pad Paper?'

There was a rude noise in his receiver.

'Well why not? There's no copyright in titles, Scott, as you know. And with one of those we'd be pretty certain to shift a few copies before –'

'In a minute, Natasha. Tell him to wait. Look, I haven't the time for arsing about, Dexter. I've got a meeting in just five –'

'Okay,' he said quickly. 'Okay, okay, I do have a couple of titles I'm tossing around if you'd like to hear them.'

'You'd better be quick. If not, we can talk again after five. I'll be tied up till then.'

He got to his feet and scanned his paperback shelves. Help help help – ah. 'Well snow seems to go down well with readers – *Miss Smilla* did brilliantly, remember? And those *Cedars* of Guterson's didn't do badly. Oh and there's a book on my mother's shelves called *The Snow Goose* which apparently made selling history in the fifties. And anything on polar exploration's always a winner. So, bearing all that in mind, I thought a really snowy title would –'

'Is there snow in your book?' Marchant sounded suspicious.

'Not yet. Not as yet. But there's a big fall coming, I promise you. I'm working towards a really big snow. A *Fargo*-type snow. A *Groundhog Day*-type blizzard.'

'I don't think I remember a blizzard in *Groundhog Day*.'

'It was forecast.' Don't mess with me, pork chop.

'A big snow. But we haven't had any appreciable snow in the south for years, have we, and I thought you said your book was set in the East End. Are you serious?'

'I'm very serious.' He was on a roll now, enjoying himself. 'As you must be aware, once global warming has melted the ice floes and fucked the Gulf Stream entirely, this island's going to be in for some pretty hard winters – a new ice age in fact. So that accounts for the snow. But then I thought, hang on, horses are big right now, there's Jane Smiley's *Horse Heaven* – and *The Horse Whisperer* of course, and Cormac McCarthy's trilogy and Annie Proulx – and it occurred to me that some sort of combo would make for a hit title. *Snow and Horses*, say. Or, *The Snow Horses*. Or, *Horses in Snow*. Or *Horses Falling on Snow*. What d'you reckon?'

'*The Snow Horses*,' Marchant said ruminatively. '*The Snow Horses*. Could be. I take it there are horses in your novel?'

That night, after weeks of threat, the snow came, Dexter wrote in his notebook when Scott Marchant had rung off. *At daybreak the wind swept savagely across the hills, blowing snow down into the highways in twenty-foot drifts. On the lower slopes the snow came up to the horses' chests, and the beasts floundered and plunged, making for higher ground –*

He dropped his pencil to grab the phone, warbling again. 'Yes?'

'Dexter. You said you'd get back to me. I really must talk to you. It's very, very important –'

'I can't talk now, Elizabeth. Look, we've had a break-in, okay? I'm waiting for the police. I can't possibly talk now.'

'Well, I'm sorry about that. But will you ring me as soon as they've been. Without fail. I mean that. I must –'

'Okay okay okay.'

The phone rang again, the moment he replaced the receiver. Before he could say anything a male voice, a benign and friendly voice, said, 'Dexter?'

'Philip! How *very* nice to hear you. Get my piece okay?'

'Well yes I did. That's what I'm calling you about.'

'And?'

'And I'm afraid to say I don't think it works. I really don't think it does. You know I thought the piece you wrote for me about the city farms was ace. I loved it, we all did here. But this new piece –'

'But the new piece is better, surely. It's better written, it's funnier. A lot funnier, I think. It's a superior bit of writing altogether.'

'Now that does astonish me – that you should think that. I hoped you were going to tell me you were having an off day. As anybody can.'

'So what's so wrong with the thing then? In your opinion? D'you want me to rejig some of it? I suppose I could have a go.'

'It's partly a matter of tone. I found the tone, when it wasn't irascible, how shall I say? *Aware. Knowing.* Quite horribly so in parts. I got very irritated by it. There was none of that nudge nudge feeling about the first piece, was there – that assumption that everybody out there is bound to think as you do. Are you with me? D'you know what I'm saying?'

'No. Can't say I do.'

250

'Okay, then. Okay. But it's not just the tone. There was that episode in the park — you with me? With the two guys who beat you up? That didn't convince me at all. So much so I wondered whether you'd made it up? Not that it would matter if you had made it up if it worked. But the black guy, in particular, was little more than a stereotype — a sort of cardboard cut-out figure.'

'If it interests you, Philip, those two stereotypes came round to my place early this morning and put a brick through the window. I can see it from here. That's how cardboard they were. Are.'

Silence. But Philip's discomfort, if that was what it was, gave him no feeling of triumph. He felt sick.

'Oh. Well, I'm sorry, Dexter. I'm extremely sorry about your window. Did they do a lot of damage? Did they take anything?'

'It doesn't matter.'

'Look, I don't want to fall out with you, you can write good stuff. But I'm not going to run this piece. It wouldn't be in your interest, you know, apart from anything else. You come across as a kind of latter-day Kingsley Amis, which I can't think was your intention. But do please keep in touch. And if you have any other ideas, let me know, won't you. Oh — you'll get a kill fee of course. I can't say when, but I'll do my best to hurry it up.'

'Da-ad' — It was Frankie, shouting from the top of the stairs. 'There's a police car outside. Filth's just getting out.'

The pub was dead, no one in there but him and Yvonne, and the pub cat, Pasta, asleep on a chair. Early evening was always a dead time, particularly on a Monday, on an end-of-summer Monday. The younger regulars must have easyJetted off for a last minute dose of melanoma 'n' chips,

251

he supposed, or else braved the M4 and the M5 to spend a waterlogged week in a caravan park. Or they'd died of boredom, here, in Tower Hamlets, in the checkout queue.

Watching Yvonne pull his pint, in the deft and careless, fag-in-mouth, eyes-shut way she contrived, he thought, I need a holiday, I deserve a holiday – and immediately he had a picture of himself, dressed in top hat, frock coat and gloves, strolling along the Promenade des Anglais in Nice. Somewhere in his house, unless he'd binned it, there was an old postcard of the Promenade, postmarked *mai, 1914*, that Hyacinth had bought for him in a junk shop once, and doubtless because of this card everything he now pictured – himself, the ebony cane he carried, the spiny palm trees, the ornate lamp-posts, the pretty women in hobble skirts and burdensome hats who were promenading with him – was in black and a yellowing white. (We'll go there one day, Hyacinth had promised him, slipping her gift into his pocket, pecking him on the cheek. You can take me there, Dex. We'll stay at the Majestic, *n'est-ce pas?*

But of course they never had. Before they knew it, Dig had come along. And then Frankie. And then –)

Back in the pub, Yvonne was setting his mug on a beermat, knocking ash into the black glass ashtray beside it, taking another pull on her Berkeley kingsize.

'You had your holiday yet, Vonny?' He leaned towards her encouragingly on his elbows.

'Nah. Don't reckon holidays. You always need another, don't you, just to recover from the first.'

'Where's Ken?' He liked the barman; a good-natured and hospitable guy, he'd always found.

'Gone down his mother's,' Yvonne said. 'He'll be back.'

'Well, what are you drinking then?' He wanted to keep her there, talking. If he could get her talking it might stop him thinking – and hearing. What he kept hearing was the crash and splinter of glass; that, and his phone conversation with Philip, endlessly replaying itself in his head.

He should have told Philip he *was* having an off day. That he'd written his piece only hours after being punched senseless. He should have told him that.

'S'bit early for me,' Yvonne said. 'Oh, okay then, if you're buying, I'll have a gin.'

She stubbed out her cigarette, squashing the butt down, moving the butt around in the ash. Her fingers were small and thin, like the rest of her, the nails manicured and carefully lacquered an aubergine colour. He imagined it was aubergine.

Her eyes were large and brown. She might have been pretty once, in a sharp-chinned, darting, Jenny wren way.

'You ought to give that up, you know.' He said it kindly and concernedly, pointing at the open pack of cigarettes on the counter.

'Why? What's it to you?' She snatched up the pack and stowed it out of sight beneath the bar, then turned her back on him while she shot gin into a tumbler, snapped the cap off a tonic bottle, added two chunks of ice, daintily, with the ice tongs.

'No lemon then?' he asked genially, smoothing a wrinkled ten-pound note and sliding it towards her. There was lemon on offer, he could see it, ready-sliced in a saucer, next to the ice bucket.

She removed his ten-pound note. 'No lemon.'

No smile, and no explanation, either.

You load sixteen tons — and whaddya get? Another day older and —

Isn't it time you got some slightly more up-to-date compilations? *Hits from the Seventies*, say?'

'Why?'

She didn't like him. He'd known it for a long time, intuited it the first time he'd walked into this bar. He could not console himself that ice-queen was just her style, so don't be paranoid, boyo (though he had tried that tack with himself to begin with), because she wasn't chippy with everyone. Too often he'd seen her, having taken his order unsmilingly and delivered it with bored impatience — palm held out while he sorted his change — greet the next customer with 'Hello there, my old lover.' He had witnessed her, up the other end of the bar, laughing her head off in a semicircle of teasing admirers. He'd spotted her, having left her post for a moment, chatting up octogenarian Stanley (arm round his shoulder, whispering in his ear), parked at his table in Old Folks Corner, next to the toilets.

Why didn't she like him? Was it because he tried too hard? Or because he didn't try hard enough? He'd asked Steve once what he thought the problem was — she was always lovely to Steve — and Steve had laughed and said, 'Pr'aps she fancies you, and can't handle it.'

If only Steve would walk in. Now. But Steve never came in on Mondays.

He pocketed his change, glanced at his watch. (Just a quick one, he'd promised Moy. No need to hurry back on our account, Moy had assured him. We're fine. We've got a Scrabble championship lined up.)

He raised his beer mug. 'Cheers then, Vonny.'

'Cheers.' She said it, he'd forced her to say it, but she

254

avoided his eye. After a quick sip of her gin she picked up a sponge cloth and began wiping a stack of brown plastic trays, restacking them as she wiped, on a shelf behind the bar.

It's a very terrible thing when someone dislikes you for no good reason, Vonny. For no bad reason. (He had never been rude to her, or fresh with her, or smart-arse, or out of order in any way.) It's a very terrible thing to be disliked for one's face or one's voice or one's walk, or for some invisible, unknowable – and therefore untreatable – real or imagined, character defect. You hurt me, Vonny. You cut me to the heart. Thinking it, watching her wipe the last-but-one tray, he wanted suddenly to challenge her, to ask, What is it you've got against me? Out with it, Yvonne, please.

But perhaps it was not too late to win her over. Or to get her, at least, to address him by name. 'Was Steve in yesterday?' he called out – because she liked Steve – and then, when she shook her head, said, with an effort at breeziness, 'Don't quite know what to make of these new Exit signs – what you think of them?'

'What new Exit signs?' She put down her tray, came back to her gin, took a sip, eyed him briefly over the rim of her glass.

There were two Exit signs in the bar, one above the main door, the other above the, not in use for months now, corner door. He pointed at them. 'Those ones.'

'They're not new.'

'They are.' He frowned. 'They must be.' They had to be because he was observant, and it was only recently he'd become aware of them. The first time, a couple of weeks ago, had not been here in the pub but in Carlton House Terrace, where he'd gone to hear a one-time author of his lecture the Royal Society on 'Science and Literature – a marriage made in Heaven?' Abandoning his attempt to catch the words of a speaker who clearly felt under no obligation to share his wisdom with the no-count-pups in the back row, he'd relaxed and stared about, absorbing, with pleasurable awe, the grand proportions and decoration of a drawing room George IV would surely have had a fit to learn was now a lecture hall. Sizing up the immense and immensely grand Nash windows, his eye had been affronted by a hideous, illuminated, green and white Exit sign high up on the wall. Next to the words 'Fire Exit', an arrow, pointing downwards. Next to the arrow, a man, or symbol for a man (he had no hands or feet), running to escape the flame-shapes leaping behind him. Hot on his heels, it had occurred to him about the flames – if the symbol had had heels.

After that evening, Exit signs, plain, emergency and fire, the arrows and the running men (who were green on white, or, in the case of the illuminated kind, white on green), invisible to him previously, began to leap out at him. He saw them everywhere. In public toilets, supermarkets, department stores, train stations, cinemas. Everywhere.

'If they're not new, or newish, Von, when did you get them?'

'I dunno.' She shrugged. 'Can't remember. A twelve-month ago? Two? Could be two.'

'You're joking.'

'If you don't believe me ask Ken when he gets back. It were Ken dealt with the bloke who came to put them up, so he'll know.'

'I do believe you. Of course. It's just –' no, better to

start again. 'Look, doesn't it strike you as a wee bit odd to show someone *running* for the exit?'

'How d'you mean?'

'Well it's giving the wrong message, isn't it. We're always being told, in the case of an emergency, to walk to the nearest exit. In an orderly and calm fashion, as you might say. And then the safety guys come up with a sign that shows someone really *legging* it. Now if everyone did that when there was a fire or a bomb scare or what-have-you, there'd be pandemonium, wouldn't there? There'd be a stampede. People would get trampled and crushed and —'

Her look and sigh stopped him. A look and sigh that said bonkers, or boring, or both.

'Haven't you got anything better to worry about?' she said, and then, as the door burst open and old Stanley and his walking sticks fumbled into the bar, 'Go and sit yourself down, my love, and I'll bring you your pint.'

Dexter drank up quickly, and left.

'OKAY, SEE you at the Buttercross four-thirty. I should
be through at the bank well before then.' Then he
had second thoughts. 'No, don't bother to get the car out,
it's a sweat for you. I'll get a taxi. There's no reason at all
for you to pick me up.'

Nonsense, his mother said. It was no trouble. One of
them would be there.

One of them. His mother or Donald. He hoped it
would not be Don. When his mother fetched him from
the station she always allowed him to drive them home.
He didn't even have to ask. She would greet him,
sometimes on the bleak uncovered platform, more often in
the station car park (she was almost always late), help him
stow any luggage in the boot, walk round to the passenger
door, get in. An instinctive move. His mother knew he
minded not owning a car and grabbed every offer of the
steering wheel. But it was not just thoughtfulness on her
part, he was certain. He had a feeling that women enjoyed
being managed, even bullied, by their male offspring, and
that his mother – who, when he was thirteen had spent

jolting hours on the farm tracks teaching him to drive – got a kick out of being driven by her only son.

It was very different when Don met the train. Don did not even bother to get out of the Land Rover. He stayed in the driving seat, reading the *Advertiser* or *Racing Post*, propped on the steering wheel. After a grunted greeting, he would fold and refold his newspaper, slide it under the seat of his overalls, and reverse hard out of the car park. In clouds of exhaust and gravel dust. He never asked Dexter if he wanted to drive.

A road drill, working immediately outside the bank's double doors, accompanied his interview. Mark apologized for the noise and shut the window, though this did not make a lot of difference. The whine and frenzied judder continued, interrupted now and then by a misleading silence. They had to talk up to hear each other.

The interview did not go as badly as Dexter had feared, partly because there had been a couple of work cheques to pay in. Plus a cheque from the jewellers for Hyacinth's ring. Eight hundred pounds, they'd given him in the end. Which made a paying-in total of £1,863.75. For once he did not have to deal with Miss Pinsett. A friendly, smiling Janet Jones, who looked all of sixteen, received his cheques and slip. Between smiles she called him Sir, twice.

And he was owed more than the £1,800, he reminded Mark, who was tapping away on his keyboard, his eyes concentrated on the computer screen. He was expecting another two cheques any day now.

Mark stopped tapping and told Dexter he could use his cash card again. With caution. But he had got to get his overdraft down. Seriously down, before Mark moved on. No spending sprees. The bank was changing to a central telephoning system in October, he said, and when that happened Dexter's queries and requests would be answered by whichever customer services official happened to take his call. In future, Dexter would not be able to speak to anyone in the Ludlow branch. He would not be able to negotiate overdraft facility or discuss his financial problems on the telephone in quite the same way as he'd been used to doing with him, Mark. There would be no one to fight Dexter's corner the way he had. However, the new, scale-economic, system would be advantageous to customers, Mark added. There would be considerable benefits and savings to customers in the long run. As Dexter would discover.

Dexter said he would almost certainly change banks. If he could no longer deal with a human being, one for whom the name D.B. Bucknell meant more than just an account number and a password and a disembodied voice, he would move his account. To a bank that still believed in the personal approach. To a bank like Coutts or Hoare's.

Mark inclined his dark head and smiled down at his folder at what had to be Dexter's little joke. He had an old-fashioned haircut, short at the back and sides but long and vigorously wavy on top, the style favoured by servicemen in the Second World War and that you saw in old newsreel footage. Nobody had that sort of hair now, Dexter thought, examining Mark's rippling waves. Curly hair, okay; but not wavy hair – except for Mark.

Mark closed his folder and placed his black and gold ballpoint on top of the folder.

Now they could talk about things. Mark asked after Dexter's mother, also a customer of the bank, but who, when she needed to talk to anyone (or when anyone needed to talk to her) about the farm overdraft, saw the manager, not Mark. He had not seen Mrs Bucknell in the bank recently, Mark said. Dexter asked after Mark's wife, Janice, and their two daughters, Claire and Lucy, who were seven and five. Dexter had not met Janice and the little girls, but had been shown a snapshot of them. They were fine, Mark said. They were all fine, and Janice was looking forward to the move to Birmingham. There was only one disadvantage about his promotion, Mark said – apart from leaving their friends of course, and Janice's mother, who was diabetic, and apart from Janice having to look for another job, which, with her qualifications, she should not have too much difficulty finding – Claire was doing well at school. It wasn't ideal for Claire to have to change schools when she was enjoying life where she was. But, onward and upward, he said.

Mark drew back a white cuff to check his watch. One minute to four. Unfortunately, he had another customer to see at four. He got to his feet. He was immensely tall and stooping, and even with the stoop towered over Dexter. They shook hands. 'Final Test begins tomorrow, hope it keeps fine at the Oval,' said Mark, who did not follow cricket himself. Dexter had forgotten about the Test Match, and his spirits lifted; fell again when he realized he would be on the train tomorrow morning and without his Sony Walkman.

'Nice to be back in the old town?' Mark said, holding open the door. 'You've got a good day for your visit, anyway. We've had some weather these past weeks, I can tell you.'

Dexter said, Yes it was. Just before the train pulled into the station, tumbling his holdall from the rack, he had glanced out of the grimed window and caught a glimpse of

Titterstone Clee in full noonday sun. Shunting along the aisle to the door, carrying the holdall high in front of him, he'd looked right and seen the tower of St Laurence's, and the Marston Brothers warehouse with its familiar yellow bands in the brick, and the Scots pines he loved, all floodlit by sunshine. And for a brief moment he'd felt that there were worse places to be.

Dexter walked up Broad Street towards the Buttercross. Towards, behind the Buttercross, the church. Towards, his first port of call, Victoria Wine (to the right of the Buttercross as he faced it, in King Street). He walked slowly, having half an hour to kill, peering in windows. Past the Wool Shop, the name in olde worlde lettering to match the façade's, truly old, beamwork. Past the Angel pub. He had never, even as a child, cared for the black and white late-medieval architecture that characterized this end of Broad Street and for which it was famous. Its jazzy patterning was as much to blame as the tourist-aimed shops, in his view, for the street's being choked always by jay-walkers and by parked and crawling cars. He preferred the colour-washed eighteenth-century town houses, enormously grand, some of them, further down the street, that continued handsomely right on down to the Broad Gate (and beyond the Broad Gate into Lower Broad Street to the bridge). He preferred Mill Street, which ran parallel, and was less commercial and quieter, and was, almost, black-and-white free. Though he didn't dislike *all* the black-and-white stuff, he'd told Moy on her first visit, walking her round the town. Castle Lodge, he admired, on the corner of Mill Street. And the Reader's House in the church close. But Broad Street was too much. So many lozenges and diamonds and zigzags and stripes fighting each other – enough to give you a migraine. Moy hadn't had a problem with the patterns as such. But the buildings themselves did make her think of the panto-mime. The opening scene of any pantomime. Any minute now, Moy had said, girls in tight-laced bodices and puffed sleeves would lean merrily from the jutting casements. Or burst, singing and dancing and flourishing dainty-waisted flower baskets, out of the oak doors. Remembering this, he wished Moy was with him. Giggling up the steep pavement. Pointing, with feigned approval and desire, at figurines in gift shop windows. Hiding from him behind pillars or in overhung doorways. Talking nonsense about pantomimes.

He had not wished this earlier, on the train. Settling himself into his seat, forgetting his imminent ordeal at the bank and the ding-dong, over the farm, he would later have to endure with his mother, he'd opened his newspaper with a feeling of contentment, almost, and relief at getting away for once. Away from the house, and the street, and the kids, and Moy. A natural feeling, he thought, that commuters, men and women, must experi-ence daily, abandoning the shambles of breakfast and lost school shoes and cereal-smothered highchairs for the ordered world of work. Out of sight, out of mind, these commuters must say to themselves. Go for it.

But the good feeling had not lasted long. He had not been able to concentrate on what he read, had found himself reading the same sentence over and over and not making sense of it. So he'd put the *Independent* down on the laminated table top and stared out. At brambles and stunted sycamore and silver birches on the embankment. At blackened hazel bushes and landslides of tipped rubbish. 'Oh, we can do those too, no problem,' the guy in the seat opposite was shouting into his cell phone. 'But you'll see the full range at the presentation-of-product session on Friday. Cheers.' Automatically, he'd felt in his jacket pocket for his notebook. Not there. Then he'd remembered that he'd been on his way to get the notebook, last thing before leaving the house for Euston, when Moy had stopped him. Had he forgotten Leila and Robert were coming to supper tomorrow? He had forgotten. Something else Moy had mentioned, as he was checking his wallet, trying to get out of the door: she was going to find out about air ticket prices to Seattle. Today. Before she and the kids set out for Fun Week she was going to phone round, see what sort of deals were on offer, call her dad, make a date with him. Who's going to look out for Joe while you're away? he'd asked her, mischievously. And she'd said, Kirsten is. Quite firm, no hesitation. *Kirsten* is. Not, as would be normal, surely, with your partner, *You* are, Dexter. (Or, you are, I *hope*. Or, you are darling, please.) So then he'd known she was serious about this trip, and at the same time learnt she was not going to ask any favours of him. Staring at the embankment – not so steep now, bigger trees, brighter grass, less litter, sun-freckled – he'd felt uneasy. It came to him that if Moy did go on this trip, she might not come back. Or if she did come back, to England, it might not be to Jesus Green.

He stopped for a moment outside the old-established gentlemen's outfitters. The window was full of tweed and wool and waterproof. Tweed overcoats and jackets and plus-twos. Green all-wool socks, ankle and calf and knee-length, lightweight and double-knit, draped over a cartridge bag. A deerstalker in noisy check. A bottle-green waterproof fisherman's hat and jacket with, alongside them, a rod, and waders, and a display of flies.

He walked on. The pavements were busy still, though the pace was laggardly. No reason in the world for hurry down here. No elbowing and jostling and trotting. No manic ducking and weaving and sprinting for the – non-existent anyway – Tube or bus. A lack of urgency that infected everything and everyone, so that meals and drinks and electricians took for ever to arrive. It was not just Ludlow, it was all small country towns, no doubt, all out-of-the-way communities. Whatever, he deplored this slowness, which seemed, like the outfitters' window, like the circuitous minor roads and lanes outside the town that led nowhere of consequence, to include a deal of resolute self-satisfaction. (On first arrival he deplored it. But within a couple of hours he would find himself – it was as though a brake were being applied – adjusting to the new and undesired rhythm, falling in step with it, unable to withstand it. Turning into a slowpoke himself.)

In Victoria Wine, using his restored Switch card, he bought two bottles of red. New Zealand Sauvignon, £6.99. Not-so-special offer, two for £12. He bought a bottle of Black Bush also. His mother would have whisky, probably, somewhere in those kitchen cupboards, but it would be Scotch. Then, as the assistant was rolling his bottles in tissue paper on the counter, the champagne cabinet caught his eye and he asked for a bottle of Veuve – boxed, if possible. His mother liked champagne, he seemed to remember she did, though she never got to drink it except at weddings. And when had she last been to a wedding? A treat for her, then. A softener-up before they went through the farm accounts – or, if he plied her with enough, a way of avoiding the farm accounts altogether. He stowed the bottles in his holdall, separating and protecting them from breakage with his clothes.

A quarter past four. His mother would not be early. It was a truth, or a paradox, that the closer you lived to a place – it was only eight and a half miles from the farm to the Buttercross, a journey that took twelve minutes on a good day, twenty five on a bad – the less likely you were to be there at an agreed time. He wandered into Market Street, narrow and dark as anything in Whitechapel. The Globe pub, one of the few uncompromisingly working-class pubs left in the town, had no lights on and was not open for business, clearly, though its door was open. Through it he got a glimpse of a pull-along vacuum cleaner abandoned on turbulent carpet.

It occurred to him, as he turned out of Market Street into Market Square (out of the dark into the sunshine, old-gold now), that he had been in the town since lunch and apart from Mark had not encountered one face he knew. Another thing: he had not seen one black face in all that time. Not even among the, obviously foreign, sightseers. It was like being in Canada. Or Eire.

No market today, and the centre of the square was given over to car park. More cars than people, he reckoned – except in the far right-hand corner, where a stream of visitors was leaving the castle, or maybe only the Castle Souvenir Shop. Hesitating outside Woolworth's – he'd meant to have a wander in the church, but there wasn't enough time now – he saw the Job Centre sign, and crossed over. Machine operative, they could offer him. Meat packer. Wood machinist/bench joiner. Poultry catcher. Community Home carer. Waiting staff. Chamber person. Cleaning operative. Poultry catcher – yes. That was the one.

He stood on the steps of the Buttercross, his holdall and a carrier bag of groceries at his feet. Dead centre between the pillars, dead centre under the clock tower, head erect, heels together. A guard outside a Royalist stronghold. He was looking out for his mother's ancient blue Peugeot estate, with the caved-in front bumper. Or for the Land Rover, originally green but so mud and dust-coated always – the registration plates and headlights entirely obliterated – he saw it in his head as brownish grey or greyish brown.

In Broad Street a man in a long white catering apron stepped out of a doorway and stood with arms folded, looking up and down the street. A sudden breeze caught the apron and it flew and billowed, skirt-like, above the man's black-trousered knees. Marilyn Monroe's skirt, in *The Seven Year Itch*, in that famous still, it made him think of. He was trying to recover details of that still – the breast-dividing halterneck; the hands, locked on her crotch in some laughable stab at modesty; the peep-toe spindle-heels; the *legs* – as a Toyota pickup, maroon with silver go-faster stripes, hooted past and pulled into the kerb. A head leaned out of the cab, a face screwed round at him. Don's head and crumpled face. Don's pickup. Newish, or new to him at least. The Toyota revved. He gathered up the carrier, hoisted the holdall, and ran.

'Smart pickup. Had it long?' He had always fancied owning a pickup, or a side of him had. The side that felt cinematically at home with a dust road and a gas station, a motel and a diner, and considered *The Last Picture Show* second only to *Chinatown* as the best film to come out of the Seventies, *Paris, Texas* the best from the Eighties. 'Thanks for coming out for me.'

'S'orl right. Gets me about.'

Don was a man of few words and no explanation. It was hard to know whether he was referring to the pickup, or to Dexter's thanks. He and Don did not like each other much, an old antipathy that went way back and showed itself in wary looks and mistrustful glances. Or it did with Don. A papering-over affability was what Dexter usually tried for, if only because his mother and Don were thick as thieves. There was nothing to be gained from falling out with Don.

Don's braking style – last minute, fierce, not too much interference from the gearbox – was sending Dexter sliding around the bench seat, even with his seat belt fastened. He kept his left hand on the door-hold, his right hand at the ready to fend off the windscreen. Or the roof. They were out of Ludlow now, heading east towards Cleehill, the sun behind them. The hedges on either side had not yet been cut back and above their tight dark thicknesses the year's new growth showed scrannel and uneven.

'A lot of elder in these hedges,' Dexter said, farmerly critical, conversational. 'Bad that. Hell to get rid of.'

'Yerse.'

Taking his eyes off the road for a second, he caught sight of Don's thighs and knees, beside his own on the bench seat. Old man's thighs and knees, wasted in their drill overalls. Old man's hands on the wheel, the skin shiny and loose, spotted and purple-veined. The veins squirming under the skin. As a child, he had thought of Don as a big man, with big shoulders and powerful hands that smelled of animals – of udders, primarily. He smelled of tobacco now, all of him did. And he was a small man now, not just thin but short; half the size, surely, of the robust shepherd–herdsman Dexter remembered. How old would Don be now? Seventy? He glanced at his profile. Big fleshy nose (something big about him, at least), fallen-in cheeks, criss-crossed with lines and cracks in a way that reminded him of Auden – of Henry Moore's drawings of that 'wedding cake left in the rain'. Even the lobe of Don's ear had these painful-looking furrows and cracks. The man looked eighty at least.

'Hey.' He was flung forward as Don stamped on the brake. A bale truck was coming at them. Top heavy, swaying load, crashing through branches, scattering straw; filling the width of the lane with diesel fumes.

Don slid to a stop, then backed, blind, round the bend he had just negotiated. It was some way to a passing place, and the reversing pickup swung all over the road while the bale truck pursued them, slow but relentless, breaking branches, spilling straw.

On track again, they passed a dead badger lying by the side of the road. Flung clear by the impact, presumably, unless it had managed to crawl as far as the verge. The injuries had to be internal for, from what he could see, it was unmarked. It lay, foetally curled, its head on its paws. Asleep, you might hope, if badgers were not notably shy animals; if they were ever in the habit of taking roadside naps in broad daylight. Earlier, just before the signpost Moy had enjoyed for the choice of destinations it offered – Bitterley (left), or Bedlam (right) – the Toyota had bumped over a pulped fox. He'd known it was a fox because its head had somehow escaped injury and as they

269

approached reared obscenely, ears pricked, from the mangled rest of it. From the sumptuous entrails and flattened pelt. This sort of slaughter, a common, if not daily, rural sight, sickened him, as he'd told Moy, even though, as he'd confessed to her, he had killed animals himself in these lanes. Not with the drive-straight-at-it intention of local delinquents, who considered road-killing a sport, and pheasants fair game; and not, so far, a badger or a fox – but rabbits, a hare, a hedgehog, birds. Impossible to avoid it, he'd told Moy. Birds, fledglings the most vulnerable, would fly straight at your windscreen, or into your radiator, and be imprisoned and roasted there. At night, zigzagging in front of your dimmed headlights for a mile or more, a hare or rabbit would finally dart to the safety of the hedge. Only to dart out again, further along, when you had picked up speed.

He had not told Moy that he had killed a roe deer once, a young buck. Driving to the farm around midnight with Hyacinth beside him in the Golf GTI they had owned in the early days, the car had been struck by something hard and soft and heavy – stone block in a blanket, was the nearest he could get to describing it – and slewed off the road into the ditch, missing the trunk of a mature oak by inches. Neither he nor Hyacinth had seen the deer, which must have sprung from the hedge. It hit the Golf's offside wing, was thrown up on to the bonnet, died instantly. Nobody's fault.

He had kept this story from Moy, not simply because the recounting of the death, in such violent circumstances, of a vivid and graceful and *large* wild animal might have upset her (it would have done); nor because she might secretly blame him as driver (that too); but because the

270

nightmare of it had been shared with Hyacinth. Quarrelling at the moment of impact, they had afterwards sat in shock in the listing car before feeling steady enough to deal with practical things – finding a torch; inspecting the dead deer (which had a gash in its flank and a deeper, more terrible and unforgettable gash in its stomach, running from genitals to ribcage). Taking a foreleg each, they had dragged the warm, head-lolling, deadweight into the depths of the ditch and covered it. After that they had walked, supporting each other, the three miles to the farm. In bed Hyacinth had wept for the dead deer and from relief at their own, miraculous, escape. Clinging together, they had made vows, and eventually love. They had counted their blessings, thanked their lucky stars.

'What's going on there?' He jerked a thumb to the red-brick terrace of cottages on their left, a landmark in his schooldays, one that, if you came by this route – there was a network of lanes to choose from – meant *almost home now*. Don pulled over on to the verge to let Dexter have a look. The terrace roof slates were off and a roofer, on all fours, toured the rafters. There were no windows to the terrace front, just holes, ragged dark squares and rectangles in the brick where the curve-topped, white-painted wood casements, that Dexter had always liked, as being English cottage traditional, had been knocked out. The smashed remains of these littered the grass, along with a heap of old curtains they had pulled down, and a dog bowl, and a child's plastic tricycle. A bigger hole on the ground floor of the middle cottage marked the place where Jack Martin's front door had been. He thought of it as Jack's place and Jack's front door because the Martins had lived there throughout his growing up, but at the same time was

271

aware that Jack had died in '85, the same year as his own father. Also that Linda and Billy and John Martin had moved out into a council bungalow – where Billy had died – years ago now. The tricycle and the dog bowl, that seemed familiar, must have been left behind by the most recent tenants, people he did not know; they could have nothing to do with the Martin family.

Don swung the pickup off the verge. A youth in vest and jeans, shovelling sand beside a slowly revolving cement mixer, looked up for a moment, and nodded, and went back to his spade.

'Sold 'em, didn't he,' Don said. 'No use for 'em. One weekenders' place they're making out of 'em. Pricey, it will be.'

'Yes.' He could imagine the finished result. Comfortable, at any rate. Easy maintenance. A place of double-glazed warmth and louvred hanging cupboards. With a pine-panelled breakfast room or 'country-style' kitchen-diner. Carriage lamps.

'Linda's going on all right, after that knee replacement,' Don said. 'But you'll know about that. Herself will have told you about that.'

Herself. Don's way of avoiding saying 'your mother', or 'Mrs Bucknell', or 'the boss'. The name Don always used, speaking of Dexter's mother. He called her nothing to her face.

Linda. He hadn't seen her for years. When he was small, before Billy's accident, Linda had helped out with house-cleaning at the farm – and for a moment he saw her, cheery and pink-faced, drinking her elevenses cup of tea. He saw himself, perched on the kitchen table, swinging his legs, watching Linda break off pieces of her ginger nut and feed them to the dogs. Linda was not supposed to feed the

272

dogs sweet biscuits, she was asked not to many times, but she could not bear the dogs' disappointment. Don't you tell on me, D, she would say, snapping her ginger nut into three, dropping the pieces under the table; looking up at him through her hair (reddish and wild, as he remembered it); laughing.

She would not look like that now, though, would she? merry and wild-haired. It was unlikely he'd recognize her now.

One mile to go. Bucknell hedges, Bucknell fields and trees, on both sides of the lane.

From the pickup cab he could see into the fields, was allowed distressing glimpses of the thistles and ragwort his father would have knocked out in April, at first showing. Set-aside, these neglected fields resembled – or a chicken farm. He hated chicken farmers. Reading *Seize the Day* as a student, he'd come across a passage that had put him off the chicken industry for ever. 'Sinister', Bellow had described it, among other things. It was not just the weeds made him think of chicken farms (of chicken *prisons*); it was the sickly grass and the bald earth that randomly patched the grass. Red earth, a rich sandstone red, his side of the lane, whereas in the Lower Pasture, on Don's side, a dark chocolaty loam. The whole acreage was like this, made up of abrupt and seemingly random soil changes. He was used to them, had thought nothing of them till Moy pointed it out.

Moy. He missed her suddenly. He'd phone her from his mother's, first chance he got.

Don was slowing now, thank Christ, slowing and changing down into second for Breakneck Hump. At the bottom of the hump the pickup roared and slipped

273

backwards. This happened three times before a change into first gave the pickup the gumption to climb Gray's Rise.

Jessie, the border collie who slept in the stables and was not allowed into the house, was lying in the farm entrance, head watchfully between her paws. Like a bad farm painting, like a Stanley Anderson daub. She got up, barking, as the pickup approached; saw who it was, yawned widely, sank back on her haunches.

Don pulled up beyond the entrance, alongside the sandstone wall.

'You not coming in, Don?' It was not much after five, and Don never knocked off work before seven or eight in the summer months. But maybe a less taxing, winding-down-to-retirement, timetable had been agreed with herself?

'No. Hens is fed. I'll be off home now.' Home was a couple of miles away, at Cleehampton. He had been to Don's place many times on errands. Had on each visit made the obligatory inspection of Don's back garden, given over entirely to vegetables save for the dahlia bed and a wigwam of sweetpeas. You had to have time on your hands, visiting Don's place. You had to have time to spare to examine every tomato plant and cabbage leaf and marrow and runner bean. Also the ornamental pond in the front garden, and the reconstituted-stone wall, with impressive castellations, that Don had made.

'Well, give my best to Mary. She going on all right?' As soon as he said it he had the awful fear that Don's wife was dead, had died months, or even years, ago; that his mother had told him this.

'Yerse. Will do.' Don seemed to be about to expand, or

to ask Dexter a question. He opened his mouth wide and began squeezing his chin between fingers and thumb in a sideways motion. He still had his own teeth, Dexter saw, a few of them, yellow and crumbling, like lumps of ancient Cheddar.

'Thanks again for the lift.' He reached for his holdall and carrier, on the floor of the cab; remembered, as he yanked them on to the seat, that he was going to have to tell his mother that he and Moy were not getting married after all (something he'd promised Moy was already done). *Shit.* What a fun evening this was going to be.

He was on the ground, about to shut the cab door, when Don leaned across the bench seat. 'Tell 'erself she knows where to find me if she wants me,' he said. 'She can call me if she needs to, tell 'er.'

'Okay.' But he was here now, wasn't he? He could do any chores herself needed doing. 'Fuck you, Don,' he shouted after the pickup, vanishing into a line of oaks along the ridge.

'It looks great,' he told his mother. 'It looks *terrific* – almost how it used to look in Dad's day. Can't get over it.' He meant the farmyard. On his way round to the back door he'd taken a peek through the brick arch that led into the yard, and, beyond the yard, on the left of it, to the cattle sheds and open-fronted farm-machinery sheds, and found the yard cleared, the concrete swept. Just like in his dream. No old wheels and wire and stacking pallets and empty fertilizer bags in sight.

He'd stood under the brick arch, on the cattle grid, shading his eyes against the glare. There were no cobbles in the yard, as in his nightmare; his subconscious had invented the cobbles; had stolen them, along with the pigeons and the metal notice, from Hackney City Farm. Even so, standing there, he'd sensed his nightmare lying in wait; had the feeling that if he were to take just one step into the yard, its terrors would enfold him. So he'd turned his back on the yard and made for the kitchen door; told himself that the place was cleared, that was the important thing. He'd been wanting it cleared for ages.

Don had done it, his mother said. Don had got hold of a couple of young lads, school leavers, and set them to it. Four skips, the biggest-size skips, they'd filled. They'd made a bonfire of the burnable rubbish. And Don had got a breaking firm along to remove the harrow and other defunct machinery. Don was responsible for the job, Don had organized it all.

She didn't tell it like that though, in a chattily running-on and natural way. There were bothering pauses and stops in her account. There was frowning concentration before she came out with certain words. 'Harrow' and 'machinery' were two.

'I'm surprised he didn't tell you about it,' his mother said. 'I imagined he'd take you round the yard. He's very pleased with himself. Quite – damn, what is the word? Chuck. Cock. It's there somewhere, but I can't *reach* it. Cock, cock*hoop*. Got it. We shall never hear the end of it, I imagine.'

He had that problem too, he assured her. He was always losing words, starting sentences he couldn't finish. And he was only forty-one, for God's sake! He drained his tea mug, held it out for a refill. This was the moment to get her to talk about her health, but as soon as he did that she'd be on about the farm, and how it was too much for her, and how it was too much for Don. 'How are you, anyway, Ma?' he said, leaning against the table, not

276

looking at her, looking round the kitchen – a tip as usual, with a finish of coke dust on every littered surface. No makeover inside the house, then. 'David M tells me you're not feeling that grand. He says he's a wee bit concerned about you.'

What Mullins had actually said was, Your mother is not well, y'know. *Not* well. It's your job to talk to her and get her to see her doctor. Enid and I have tried and failed.

'I have to tell you you don't look too bad,' he said, looking at her now, smiling; 'you never seem to get any older, Ma. It's not fair.'

His mother was at the stove, filling his tea mug. She laughed at his flattery, which was abdabs, she said. 'I found "abdabs" anyhow – did you notice, D? Abdabs didn't get away.'

It was true she did not look too bad. Thinner, possibly, than on his last visit, though she had never been fat. Strong-looking still – her forearms below the rolled-to-the-elbows check shirt, while wrinkled, looked strong to him. Despite the arthritis, in her lower back, he knew troubled her from time to time, she hadn't shrunk the way Don had; was still roughly the same height as himself, five foot nine. (Sons were supposed to outstrip their mothers, but he had never managed to outstrip her.) Her hair looked okay to him. As okay as that fly-away white wool ever did look. Her blue eyes were cloudy and smaller than they had once been, but they'd been cloudy for a couple of years, he thought. Not so surprising: she was seventy-four.

Seventy-four. Fuck.

'Let's sit down,' he said, 'let's drink our tea sitting down.' He pulled a chair out from the table, screeching it on the red–tiled floor; then a second chair, lifting it this time.

They sat down beside each other at the table. Less hazardous than face to face, was his thinking. Less chance of an argument. Even so he felt awkward with her. There was always this awkwardness with his mother, notably at the beginning of a visit and when it was just the two of them with no likelihood of interruption – as in some crap two-hander play. It did not help that she was not demonstrative and backed away from any show of affection, as she had from his kiss of greeting earlier. More critically, he simply did not know what to say to her, or what to ask, that would please, or be believed, or not be ridiculed. It wasn't that he didn't love her. He'd examined his feelings a hundred times and come to the conclusion that though she infuriated him – and he her; it was a reciprocal business, obviously, he knew that – and though he could hate her viciously when she mocked him, he was, basically, as Joe would say, very fond of her. Admiration came into it. He admired her resilience and resourcefulness; the way, when one aspect of farming failed, or looked like failing, she would try other, quite risky and long-term, things: planting acres of grazing land with cider apples, converting half the lambing shed into a dark house for specialist mushrooms. Projects which, if he did not feel so threatened always, he might otherwise be interested in and supportive of.

But the real difficulty he had with his mother, and there was nothing to be done about it, was difference. They were different sorts of people, who responded to things, to just about everything, in very different ways.

'Nice tea,' he said, sipping it. 'You know, seeing the farmyard like that, all cleaned up, was weird because I dreamt about the yard the other night. I was in the yard with Dig and Frankie, and it was swept and tidy – just like today.'

'Oh?'

'There were horses in my night, in my dream. How long is it since you kept horses here, Ma? Must be years. Twenty years?'

'Livery horses, you mean? Or the ponies? I'm not sure. A long time.'

'Dad was in my dream. He was just like himself, how he was before the stroke. Do you ever dream about Dad?'

'Well, I don't know, D. I may do, I used to dream about Michael. But these days I don't seem to remember my dreams. They um, you know. Vanish.'

Silence, while he thought up some other, innocuous, topic.

'Seen anything of the Morgans lately, Ma? Or the Calverts?'

'The who? No, no I don't think so. Not recently.'

He tried again. 'Dogs okay?' The dogs were lying on their beanbags by the stove. Neither of them had raised a nose when he came in. Nor moved since.

'Trouble has a, an ear thing, an infection, but it's not serious. Dick's put her on some drops.'

'Right. Oh, Ma, I forgot to tell you – Raider came into my dream. He didn't really look like Raider, he looked more like Trouble, but it was meant to be Raider. I know, because he was with Dad.'

Too late to unsay what – he suddenly saw – might wound her. Raider had been with his father when he died. Had remained at the foot of Michael's bed, still as a stone dog on a tomb, the whole ten days of his dying. He should not have mentioned Raider.

279

'Before I forget, Frankie left this behind.' His mother leaned across him, patted a red T-shirt folded in front of him on the table. 'Better put it in your, in your whatsit. Holdall.'

'Sure.' Not Frankie's T-shirt, though, Dig's. It had his name, DIG, in press-on capitals on the chest, letters that stuck to the iron, and smoked, and gave off a vile smell.

He sipped his tea. He said, 'Look, Ma, if you're not feeling that great – how's about having a check-up? I have check-ups sometimes. It's a good idea to have one every now and –'

'Why not put the T-shirt in your holdall *now*.'

Fuck. Because I'm drinking my tea now. But he got up and fetched the holdall. 'Oh, I've got some goodies for you, Ma.' He took the bottles out, unwrapped them, lined them up on the table. It was not his fault if she refused to see her doctor. It was up to her what she did – or did not do. He would tell old Mullins that.

'Goodness me.' She fingered the bottles, picked up her specs, peered at the labels. 'I'm on the wagon at the moment, you know. You'll have to drink these all by yourself.'

'Rubbish. I've got champagne for you – look, this in the box. Champagne can't do you any harm. Champagne's a tonic, it'll do you *good*.'

His mother smiled.

'And I've got some nice things for our supper.' He took the carrier bag over to the sink and cleared a space for it on the draining board. 'I'll wash the spinach in a minute.' He always brought the supper with him on these visits. Very often it was fish – from Lea's Fish Bar in Columbia Road, or, when he troubled to bike as far as Islington, from Steve Hat in Essex Road, the best fishmonger he knew. He brought the supper partly to save his mother from having to cook for him – a sort of treat for her – and partly to ensure that he had one decent meal at least while he was under her roof. His mother's cooking, as he'd warned Moy before bringing her down on that first visit, was 'something else'.

'You shouldn't have bought spinach. That's daft. We've got spinach in the garden. Why spend money on – ?'

'Thought it would save time. And this is really nice. It's quite fresh – look.' He held out a few leaves for her to see. 'I got it in Farmers' market, you know, in Mill Street.'

Farmers' market was not a produce market supplied by local farmers. It was a greengrocer's, owned by people whose name was Farmer.

'Daft.' His mother shook her head. 'Crazy.'

'I tell you what we're going to have.' He rubbed his hands. 'We've got some delicious duck pâté to start with, it's really good, I brought it with me from London. That's the meat course. Then I'm going to make a Provençal tian – a tian of spinach and raisins. That may sound a bit dull, but it's not, I promise you. It's got egg yolks in it and double cream, and er, *pine-nuts*, and nutmeg. Damn, I forgot to get any chervil. Have you got any chervil?'

Of course she hadn't got chervil. He knew that herb patch of old. Parsley, gone to seed by August, and a clump of chives, choked to death by lemon balm.

'We'll have a look,' his mother said. 'We'll go out and look.'

He came back to the table, sat down. Leaned towards her, sideways, on his elbows. 'That sound all right to you?'

'Sounds good. Bit fancy perhaps. But you know me.'

Yes indeed. He looked at his watch. 'Okay if I ring Moy? Just to tell her I've arrived okay, that we didn't get derailed or whatever.' A quizzing about his wedding plans was coming up now, now that he'd mentioned Moy. He made a quick decision: if she asks me about the wedding, I'll tell her. If she doesn't, I won't.

'Of course. Go ahead.'

The telephone was in the kitchen, on the wall, beside the dresser. But he was reluctant to ring Moy from here, in his mother's hearing. There was an extension in the junk room, and a separate line in the farm office, out through the scullery and the boot room. But wouldn't it look a bit rude to leave the kitchen now? Unfriendly at least.

'Might call her a bit later, when she's sure to be in. She's doing something with the kids today. Ma, are you going to take the dogs out? Because if you are I'd like to come with you.' She usually walked the dogs after tea. It was not a dog walk as such, but a tour of the farm, a checking-up tour of water troughs and fencing and gates and fruit trees and grazing animals, that the dogs accompanied her on. She did the tour on foot, or, when her back was painful, on the quad bike.

'They've already had a walk today, and I've got some pec, pac – blast it! – *paperwork* to do before we go through the accounts. But you go if you want to, D. Take Jessie with you. She needs the. Oh you know what I mean.'

'Half an hour, then. Back by seven. Then I'll start cooking.'

He was aware of her watching him as he washed the spinach, drained it, tipped it into the pan of boiling water on the stove. Boil for one minute only. He took it off. He drained the spinach again, ran the cold tap over it, squeezed the leaves dry with his fingers. (The window

282

frame above the sink was rotten, you didn't need to stick a knife in it to see that. Something would have to be done. He would tell her this later, tactfully, while they were eating.) He checked the onions, softening in butter – mustn't let them brown – on the cool plate, leapt to the table to grab a swig of whiskey. 'Are you sure you won't have a drink, Ma?'

'I'm fine. Might have a sip of your fizzy with supper.'

'Well, it's very dreary of you to be so abstemious.'

Whistling, he took the onions off the stove, tipped them into a bowl, added raisins, allspice, nutmeg, salt, pepper. He felt better now he had something positive to do. Something he was good at. He chopped the spinach and herbs – thyme and parsley, no chervil – on a salmonella-friendly chopping board, chop chop chop chop chop, with a blunt and pitted knife. Using this knife, he scraped the spinach and herbs off the board into the onion mix. Then he poured in the cream and the egg yolks and the pine-nuts. He stirred the mess around, bent his head to it, sniffed. *Yes.* 'Have you got an oven dish, Ma? About this size' – he showed her with his hands the size he wanted. 'That old brown earthenware one would prob-ably do. It's a bit big, but if you haven't anything better it would do.'

She got up from the table, fumbled around in a cupboard. Came towards him holding out a colander – an old plastic colander with clogged holes he'd instructed her to bin years ago. (He'd bought her a stainless steel one to replace it, had told her to dump the plastic colander in the bin right away.)

Oh no, Ma. No.

Fear. Fear, like a sudden pain in the gut, as she came confidently towards him. He tried to banish it, tell himself

283

she hadn't been listening, was thinking about something else. We can all do that, can't we.

'I said an *oven dish*, Ma.' He tried to say it lightly, so as not to alarm her. 'I've got a colander already. See. Over there.'

She hesitated, continued towards him — less confident now, anxious now — holding out the red plastic colander. Or oven dish, as she saw it.

Please God.

He took the colander from her, put it on the draining board, led her back to the table, sat her down. He said, 'Don't you think it'd be a good idea for us to go and see Doc Barker? If I give him a call now he could probably fit us in at the end of surgery.'

'I have seen him,' his mother said.

She had seen him. Not just him, she had been to see a specialist, a brain man, at the hospital, that Doctor Barker had straight away referred her to. She'd seen the specialist within a week of seeing Sam Barker, she thought. ('So you see the NHS can move quite speedily at times.') She had had a brain scan, blood tests, a — she had to search around for this — *biopsy*. Anyway, it was cancer. A large, fast-growing tumour. In the frontal, or temporal, was it? lobes. Not sure, she'd written it down. Nothing to be done about it — but she was quite relieved about that, didn't want nasty treatments, didn't want to lose her hair, didn't want to be in *that place*.

It hadn't been too much of a surprise, she said. Not when she thought about it. Not when she'd looked back over various, puzzling, happenings, and thought about it. Tried to think about it.

In fact, to tell the truth, it was quite a relief to know it was cancer. It might have been something a lot worse.

He sat close beside her at the table, put his hand over hers (she did not stop him), held it. What made her go? he eventually asked. What made her go to the doctor in the first place? Did she have headaches? No, no headaches. It was Frankie. Something Frankie had said, the first evening of their stay with her. They'd finished supper, and Frankie asked for an apple, and she'd gone to the fruit bowl and chosen him a nice one. Which he'd stared at and turned around in his hand. Funny sort of apple, he'd said, looks more like an orange to me. What do you think, Dig? Dig said it was a racing car, definitely. Both boys had laughed – but nervously, she thought. Uncomfortably. She'd sat them down in front of the television, taken Frankie's unwanted fruit out to the hay barn and showed it to Don, asked him what it was.

The following day, while the boys were fishing with David Mullins, Don had driven her down to the surgery. Incidentally, she didn't drive the children anywhere during their stay, in case he was worrying about that. After that first day she hadn't taken the car out at all. Don had driven them everywhere they had to go.

'I'm getting hungry,' she said, 'aren't you? Think you ought to put that spinach thingamijig in the oven before we starve to death. I'll make some toast for the pâté.'

Over supper, in a stop-start way, she told him more. To begin with, whom she had told about the cancer and who did not know. Don knew, he had to know because the illness was going to affect him, and anyway he had taken her to the hospital for the tests (and again, later, for the results). Elizabeth knew – she had told her yesterday, on the phone, quite easy to do because Elizabeth had been after her for weeks about going to the doctor and knew something was up – but Anna did not know. She could not face telling Anna. So Elizabeth was going to tell her; Elizabeth had invited Anna down for the weekend, and was going to tell her then. The Mullinses she had told this morning. They had been upset, and showed it, which she had found hard to cope with. No one else knew. But how do you tell people that sort of news anyway? You can't just ring up and say, Thought you might like to know I've got cancer, and it's terminal. She hoped the news would just get about, that the Mullinses would do the job for her, or that Elizabeth would.

Dig and Frankie. His job to tell them.

He pushed his plate to one side, the spinach tian still on it, rearranged in a heap, his fork disguising some of it. His mother had eaten hers. Between them they had drunk most of the champagne. Not the right drink, he had suggested, but she said it was.

The mind is what the brain does. (He'd read that somewhere.) Losing your mind. Out of your mind. Mindful. Mind out!

She looked normal. But behind that familiar forehead – black mole above the right eyebrow – and woolly hair, the tumour was eating her mind up. Closing it down, gobbling and consuming.

Of course she was terrified really, whatever she said. Of course she was.

He was.

She was telling him her plans now: where she was going to be, what she was going to do with the time she had left. (Which was not long, the *oncologist* had told her. No one could tell her exactly how long, it was impossible to be

286

precise about it, but not long.) The oncol, the *specialist* – Mr Sav, Mr Sa – oh dash it, it doesn't matter – had not wanted to tell her anything. He said he liked patients to have a relative with them for these sorts of chats, as his letter had indicated. But she had insisted on knowing. Not just what was wrong, and how long she had, but what was in store for her along the way. So in the end he had told her.

In store for her along the way. Dan Peterson's first wife had died of brain cancer. Aged twenty-seven. Along the way for her had included blindness and deafness and speechlessness. Incontinency. Finally – almost finally – paralysis. And before all that, a personality change. Ungovernable rages, Dan had told him, in which sweet-natured, temperate Ellen had attacked the dog she adored, smashed plates and furniture.

But it did not have to be like that, surely. Not any more, not now. It could be peaceful now, with the new drugs they had. A gentle drifting, with no pain or anger or anguish.

Please God.

God. She had Him, didn't she? She had her religion. An old-fashioned, very English thing, as he thought of it – church on Sundays when not lambing or harvesting or simply too done in to go; the significant festivals observed. A solace, it must be? A comfort. Not something she ever talked about.

A good death. The expression people used. How could there be anything even half-way good about death? About dying?

'I'm going to Elizabeth's to start with,' his mother said. 'End of next week, she's coming up to fetch me. I've got a lot of sorting to do first. Enid's going to help me with that.' Then, just as he was about to ask, What can I do? Tell me what you want *me* to do, she brought up the farm. David's son Robin would caretake the farm, keep it ticking over until a permanent decision could be made. David had offered that right away. And Elizabeth had come up with another suggestion. If her mother preferred to stay in her own house, Elizabeth would move in and look after her, and help Don run the farm. Jerry retired in November, she had reminded her mother, and was looking for something else to fill his time. He might like to try his hand at the agribusiness, Elizabeth said. So later on, afterwards you know, and as her brother showed no inclination to do his duty, she and Jerry could run the farm together. If Dexter was agreeable, naturally, and if her mother liked the idea of that.

Jerry? Run the farm? Live in this house? *Over my dead body.*

'Are you going to open that bottle of red?' his mother said. 'I've been told to keep off the booze, but, really, why not?'

After

D EXTER TRUDGES along the hazel track that runs beside the Upper Pasture, Jessie at his heels. Heavy stinging rain for the third day in a row, and his boots so freighted with mud – more adhering at each laborious stride – he's having to stop all the time to scrape the clag from the tread of his boots, and – vicious down-jabs with his crook – knock the clods off the backs of his heels. Not weather to be out in for sure, but Robin Mullins phoned earlier to say he'd heard a ewe in trouble as he was driving along the ridge. The bastard had not bothered to get out of his warm Land Rover and investigate the ewe himself. As Dexter would have done, had it been one of the Mullins's ewes. As he has done, God knows how many times.

The ewe he is seeking is not one of many. He has only a small flock now, a minute flock. After the foot and mouth epidemic, a true baptism of fire for a novice farmer – though it is the smell he remembers, that and the smoke, from those open crematoria, that remains at the back of his nose – he told himself, no more sheep; finished with sheep.

But as time went on, the empty, still pasture and silence

of the lambs, as London headline writers had been quick and pleased to describe it, began to get to him, and he bought in two dozen ewes and a couple of rams. Hardy cross-breds, Border Leicester crosses and the new Charollais crosses, that don't require mollycoddling. If these do well, he thinks, he may add to them. That is, if he does not sell the farm.

He has made few changes about the place so far, is biding his time. But then there have been other, more pressing, things to do this first year: sell the Bethnal Green house in a dicey market, move the whole shebang to Shropshire, manoeuvre the kids into what the locals are agreed is the best, most academic, school. (Two terms in, Frankie finds his new school okay, or okayish. Dig does not.) Removing the boys to such an inaccessible place sparked a big row with Hyacinth, a row so wearisome and litigious that in the end he agreed to her solicitor's demands. These days, Hyacinth has Dig and Frankie for the whole of every half-term, plus ten days at a stretch in all school holidays. He resents these arrangements; is still looking for a way round them. Is still planning to subvert or reverse them.

One good thing in the past year: Hyacinth no longer writes him letters. Two months ago she had a baby – 'a dear little sister for Dig and Frankie', ran the legend in the *Telegraph* births column she sent the kids – since when she has been too busy, with breast-feeding and nappies, to write letters, even short ones. No letters from Hyacinth is good news, but her giving birth to a girl child, one that was not his, wounded him. He had known Hyacinth was pregnant and not minded that, had been inventively rude and crude about *that* – but when her daughter arrived (news relayed to him by Dig, after a call from his

290

stepfather), he had a sudden picture of Dig being born, and Hyacinth's exhausted, triumphant face – and left the farm office, and the house, and sprinted to the end of the garden, and attacked the nettles with a scythe. Fuck fuck fuck fuck *fuck*.

He is over all that now, is used to the idea; doesn't give a toss how many girl babies Hyacinth and her 'man' have. The more the merrier, and good luck to them.

He is still determined to sell the farm. Most days he is. But he cannot do it yet; he has to wait for better days than these to sell, for a time when agriculture and global markets and consumer confidence are on the up and up.

No sign of that.

In the meantime he has plans. To let the land to a conglomerate and turn the farmhouse into a hotel/restaurant, which he and Moy will run. To convert the farm buildings into a complex of country-craft workshops. (Moy to teach stained glass.) To convert the house and the buildings into a way-out-of-town conference centre, with Jacuzzi and gym and swimming pool and outdoor sports facilities. (He has publishers in mind for this.) To convert the house and buildings into an Arvon-type creative writing and reading centre. (He and Moy the administrators.) To turn the farmhouse into a holiday home for disadvantaged, preferrably black and Asian, East End children. (But what about child abuse? How would he be certain that he and Moy had picked the right staff?) To turn the place, a part of it, into the Bucknell Cricket School; so that in time, in no time, Shropshire will be ready to take on the best, springing from nowhere – as Leicestershire did, as Glamorgan did – to win the County Championship. (Steve might be the man to help with this one. If Steve is as keen to get out of London as he always said he was, he might be the man.)

Most of his plans aren't workable, as he now and then accepts. Given the size of the farm overdraft, it would take a gargantuan grant or loan, or serious sponsorship, to get even one of his plans off the ground. But thinking about them keeps him going – as the thought of Moy keeps him going. She's away at the moment, in Washington State, a visit she delayed when his mother became ill.

During the three months his mother took to die, Moy stayed at home with Dig and Frankie. He did not have to ask her to do this – shop and cook and clean and look after his kids while he spent time with his mother at Elizabeth's, and afterwards, when Margaret could no longer be made comfortable there, in the hospice – she offered it herself. She made it clear she was doing it for Dig and Frankie, but he does not believe his children were the only reason why Moy stayed. – Because you wouldn't, would you? Delay your trip, give up your work, just for the sake of someone else's kids. However fond you were of them. You wouldn't, at their grandmother's funeral, sit next to their daddy in the *family pew*. To risk that, you'd have to have some deeper purpose, surely?

He visits his mother's grave. She lies beside his father, on a slope, in the overflow cemetery behind the parish churchyard. The slope – it's more like a hill – is rough cut and looks far from restful, gives the impression the dead are having to stand, or brace themselves. The headstones add to this effect. The ones that don't tip dangerously forwards (like his father's), lean far back, in a crazy attempt to ward off gravity.

Margaret doesn't have a headstone yet. It's too early – the earth hasn't settled – to put a headstone in that hilly ground, but it's in hand. A neighbour gave him the name of an excellent local stonemason, and it's in hand.

Another worry he has about his mother – was it a good death? It seemed peaceful, at the very end, to those, himself included, who witnessed it; the nurses said it was; but Margaret was the one doing it. The only one actually doing it. Was it okay for her?

Some good did come out of her death. Taking turns to hold their mother's hand, he and his sister Anna got to know one another. To like each other, he believes. Anna has promised to help him on the farm, first time her hospital allows her leave.

No deathbed bonding with his sister Elizabeth. She hasn't spoken to him for months. Because he owns the farm? Because of their mother's watch, which Elizabeth wanted, which Margaret left to Anna? Whatever, he's not bothered. He has worse problems, and better people, to think about.

Moy – all thoughts return to Moy. He talks to her on the phone. She misses him, she says, though she's not sure what the future holds for them; if they *have* a future together. She's still thinking about her life, she says, still considering her next career move. Though she is not quite done with stained glass.

A few weeks ago Moy met someone at a party, and he's commissioned her to finish the Doom window. This Californian venture capitalist plans to instal Moy's window in his LA offices – he has a sense of *humour*! Moy told Dexter, he wants devils *everywhere* – and when he comes to England in the fall will check up on work in progress; or, if she's finished the window by then, arrange shipment. I won't tell you how much he's paying me, Moy told Dexter on the phone – it's obscene.

293

Moy's flying home next Friday – dreading the flight – and has arranged to stay with Leila and Robert until she finds a place of her own to rent. She's promised to come to the farm some time – 'but just for a visit, Dexter, you must make sure the kids understand it's only a visit'. He did not argue with Moy, or try to persuade her to think of her visit as a more permanent thing. He has not once mentioned the word marriage to Moy in any of their transatlantic conversations, except in relation to Joe and Kirsten (who were married the week before Moy left for Seattle, Joe wearing a Russian fur hat on the hottest day of July. Reception in the courtyard of Joe's local, where Frankie got pissed, and disgraced himself. Since then, the newly-weds have both, but separately, spent time in hospital).

Dexter accepts now that his and Moy's union will not be solemnized the way he hoped, but absence has made his heart grow fonder, he wants her back on any terms. And not because he needs a farmhand. There's a hole in his life without Moy, a black hole, dark and depressing matter. Without Moy, he's decided, it's a honky tonk parade.

Moy does not know this, Dexter has not told her, but next Friday, when she and her luggage trolley emerge from customs, he will be at the barrier, his mother's old Peugeot waiting in the Heathrow short-stay car park.

Something else Moy does not know: he and the kids have cleared out the old dining room/junk room at the farm. The room now contains a workbench and a bar stool, plus a load of newly wired, intelligently sited, power points. There's excellent natural light from the french windows. The perfect workplace for a maker of stained glass.

Dexter has so many ideas, so many plans to tell Moy

when she gets home. He has not told her yet that a week ago he phoned Philip Cartwright with an idea he has for an occasional, or maybe regular column – *Scenes from Rural Life*, or some such – and that Philip had sounded interested. Said he'd give it proper thought and let Dexter know. Had sounded genuinely keen. And something else: Scott Marchant is still after him about that book, *The Snow Horses*, he's supposed to have written; is being so pushy and pursuant that last night in bed he decided to give it a go. You have to fill those long bucolic winter evenings somehow. And making money out of Marchant, if he can do that – and he ought to be able to, he bloody well ought to be able to – might be the most rewarding way of getting back at the bastard.

The rain is heavier than ever, driving straight into his face as he props his crook against the gate that separates the Upper Pasture from the Six Acre, wipes his mud-slicked hands on his oilskins, fumbles with the catch. It's a metal gate, as all the Bucknell farm gates have been for some time: easy-open, easy-swing, easy-shut, foolproof. Metal gates are compulsory these days, for certain crops or stock, at least; the inspector checks up on them, you can't get grants or subsidies without them. The gates can't be described as quaint or rustic – traditionalists disapprove – but Dexter finds them okay. They're lightweight and practical, nothing remotely heritage about them.

He can hear the ewe now, an exhausted panicky bleating further along the thorn hedge on his right. Can't see her yet. She's got herself stuck in the stock wire, poor old darling, or caught half in the wire, half in the thorn. He and Jessie, and his crook, are going to have a time getting her out.

'Good thing I know how to take the helicopter view.' He says it aloud, frowning, wiping the rain off his face, stopping because his boots are weighted with mud. 'Lucky for me I've always had a blue-skies attitude.'